Titles by Laura Childs

Tea Shop Mysteries

DEATH BY DARJEELING
GUNPOWDER GREEN
SHADES OF EARL GREY
THE ENGLISH BREAKFAST
MURDER
THE JASMINE MOON MURDER
CHAMOMILE MOURNING
BLOOD ORANGE BREWING
DRAGONWELL DEAD
THE SILVER NEEDLE MURDER
OOLONG DEAD

THE TEABERRY STRANGLER
SCONES & BONES
AGONY OF THE LEAVES
SWEET TEA REVENGE
STEEPED IN EVIL
MING TEA MURDER
DEVONSHIRE SCREAM
PEKOE MOST POISON
PLUM TEA CRAZY
BROKEN BONE CHINA

New Orleans Scrapbooking Mysteries

KEEPSAKE CRIMES
PHOTO FINISHED
BOUND FOR MURDER
MOTIF FOR MURDER
FRILL KILL
DEATH SWATCH
TRAGIC MAGIC
FIBER & BRIMSTONE

SKELETON LETTERS
POSTCARDS FROM THE DEAD
GILT TRIP
GOSSAMER GHOST
PARCHMENT AND OLD LACE
CREPE FACTOR
GLITTER BOMB
MUMBO GUMBO MURDER

Cackleberry Club Mysteries

EGGS IN PURGATORY
EGGS BENEDICT ARNOLD
BEDEVILED EGGS
STAKE & EGGS

EGGS IN A CASKET
SCORCHED EGGS
EGG DROP DEAD
EGGS ON ICE

Anthologies

DEATH BY DESIGN
TEA FOR THREE

Afton Tangler Thrillers writing as Gerry Schmitt

LITTLE GIRL GONE
SHADOW GIRL

W9-BLK-882

Praise for the New York Times *bestselling*
Tea Shop Mysteries

❦

**Featured Selection of the Mystery Book Club
"Highly recommended" by the Ladies' Tea Guild**

❦

"A love letter to Charleston, tea, and fine living."
—*Kirkus Reviews*

"Begins and ends with a bang. . . . Childs's trademark style is infusing her mysteries with atmosphere and ambiance and she doesn't disappoint in this latest installment."
—RT Book Reviews

"Another superbly crafted and inherently riveting novel in author Laura Childs's outstanding Tea Shop Mystery series."
—Midwest Book Review

"Laura Childs has definitely made her mark as one of the best authors of cozy mysteries. . . . Engaging and mysterious, the story moves at a fast pace, making it easy for me to devour this book in a single setting."
—Fresh Fiction

"Tea lovers, mystery lovers, [this] is for you. Just the right blend of cozy fun and clever plotting."
—Susan Wittig Albert, *New York Times* bestselling author of *The Last Chance Olive Ranch*

"Enjoyable. . . . Childs proves herself skilled at local color, serving up cunning portraits of Southern society and delectable descriptions of dishes."
—*Publishers Weekly*

"Along the way, the author provides enough scrumptious descriptions of teas and baked goods to throw anyone off the killer's scent."
—*Library Journal*

"Tasty suspense!"
—*St. Paul (MN) Sun-Sailor*

BROKEN BONE CHINA

Tea Shop Mystery #20

LAURA CHILDS

BERKLEY PRIME CRIME
New York

BERKLEY PRIME CRIME
Published by Berkley
An imprint of Penguin Random House LLC
penguinrandomhouse.com

Copyright © 2019 by Gerry Schmitt & Associates, Inc.
Excerpt from *Mumbo Gumbo Murder* by Laura Childs copyright © 2019 by Gerry Schmitt
Penguin Random House supports copyright. Copyright fuels creativity, encourages
diverse voices, promotes free speech, and creates a vibrant culture. Thank you for buying
an authorized edition of this book and for complying with copyright laws by not
reproducing, scanning, or distributing any part of it in any form without permission.
You are supporting writers and allowing Penguin Random House to continue to
publish books for every reader.

BERKLEY and the BERKLEY & B colophon are registered trademarks and BERKLEY
PRIME CRIME is a trademark of Penguin Random House LLC.

ISBN: 9780451489647

Berkley Prime Crime hardcover edition / March 2019
Berkley Prime Crime mass-market edition / January 2020

Printed in the United States of America
1   3   5   7   9   10   8   6   4   2

Cover art by Rene Milot

This is a work of fiction. Names, characters, places, and incidents either are the product
of the author's imagination or are used fictitiously, and any resemblance to actual persons,
living or dead, business establishments, events, or locales is entirely coincidental.

PUBLISHER'S NOTE: The recipes contained in this book are to be followed exactly
as written. The publisher is not responsible for your specific health or allergy needs that
may require medical supervision. The publisher is not responsible for any adverse
reactions to the recipes contained in this book.

If you purchased this book without a cover, you should be aware that this book is stolen
property. It was reported as "unsold and destroyed" to the publisher, and neither the author
nor the publisher has received any payment for this "stripped book."

ACKNOWLEDGMENTS

A special thank-you to Sam, Tom, Grace, Tara, Fareeda, Danielle, M.J., Bob, Jennie, and all the amazing people at Berkley Prime Crime and Penguin Random House who handle editing, design, publicity, copywriting, social media, bookstore sales, gift sales, production, and shipping. Heartfelt thanks as well to all the tea lovers, tea shop owners, book clubs, bookshop folks, librarians, reviewers, magazine editors and writers, websites, broadcasters, and bloggers who have enjoyed the Tea Shop Mysteries and helped spread the word. You make this all possible!

And I am forever (forever!) filled with gratitude for you, my dear readers, who have embraced Theodosia, Drayton, Haley, Earl Grey, and the rest of the tea shop gang as friends and family. Thank you so much and I promise you many more Tea Shop Mysteries!

1

Red and yellow flames belched from propane burners, inflating the hot-air balloon to heroic proportions and propelling it skyward. High above the grassy flats of Charleston's Hampton Park, the balloon joined a half dozen others as they bumped along on gentle currents, looking like a super-sized drift of colorful soap bubbles.

"This is amazing," Theodosia cried out to Drayton as the wind blew her auburn hair into long streamers. "Almost as good as sailing or jumping a horse." Her blue eyes sparkled with merriment, and a smile lit up her face as she reveled in her first-ever balloon ride.

With her fine complexion, natural endowment of hair, and pleasing features, Theodosia Browning was the apotheosis of what Lord Byron might have described as an English beauty in one of his novels. She was, however, modest to a fault and would have blushed at the very thought.

"Is this not the coolest thing you've ever done?" Theodosia asked as blips of exhilaration filled her heart.

"No, it's terrifying," Drayton Conneley responded.

He'd wedged himself into the corner of their wicker basket, teeth gritted, knuckles white, as he hung on for dear life. "When you talked me into serving afternoon tea for the Top Flight Balloon Club, I had no idea you'd twist my arm and make me go for an actual ride."

"It's good to live a little dangerously," Theodosia said. As the proprietor of the Indigo Tea Shop on Church Street, she was often tapped to host weekend tea parties. This one in Hampton Park, smack-dab in the middle of Charleston, South Carolina, was no different. Except that after pouring tea and serving her trademark cream scones and crab salad tea sandwiches, Theodosia had been offered a hot-air balloon ride. Gratis. And, really, who in their right mind would turn down a wild adventure like that! Certainly not Theodosia. To an outside eye, she might appear tea-shop-demure, but she possessed the bold soul of an adrenaline junkie.

"I'm afraid the weather's beginning to shift," Drayton said. "Perhaps we should cut our ride short?" The sky, which had been pigeon egg blue just twenty minutes ago, now had a few gray clouds scudding across it.

"Wind's kicking up, too," said Rafe Meyer, their FAA certified pilot. He opened the blast valve one more time, shooting a fiery tongue high into the balloon's interior. "This will keep us at altitude along with the other balloons. But we should probably think about landing in another fifteen minutes or so. Weather conditions do look like they might deteriorate."

"Five minutes would be better," Drayton said under his breath. As Theodosia's resident tea sommelier and self-appointed arbiter of taste, he was definitely not a devotee of adventure sports. Sixty-something, genteel, with a serious addiction to tweed jackets and bow ties, Drayton's idea of high adventure was sitting in a wing chair in front of his fireplace, sipping a glass of ruby port, and reading a Joseph Conrad novel.

"Take a look at that patchwork balloon over there. You see how it's descending ever so gently?" Theodosia said. "You don't have a thing to worry about. When we hit the ground you won't even feel a bump."

But Drayton was squinting over the side of their gondola at something else. "What on earth is that whirligig thing?" he asked.

Theodosia was still reveling in her bird's-eye view and the hypnotic whoosh from the propane burner, so she wasn't exactly giving Drayton her full attention.

"What? What are you talking about?" she finally asked.

"I'm puzzled about the small, silver object that appears to be flying in our direction."

Theodosia could barely pry her eyes away from the delicious banquet of scenery and greenery, history and antiquity, that spilled out below her. Crooked, narrow streets. Elegant grande dame homes lining the Battery. The azure sweep of Charleston Harbor. The dozens of churches that poked their steeples skyward. How lucky was she to live in this amazing city?

But as Theodosia turned, she, too, caught a flash of something bright and shiny buzzing its way toward them. Her first impression was that it looked like some kind of mechanized seagull. Something you might see in a stop-action cartoon. Only, instead of dipping and diving and surfing the wind, the object was zooming right at them.

"I think it's a drone. Someone must have put up a drone," Theodosia said. She watched with growing curiosity as it headed their way, coming closer and closer. The drone swooped upward and then dipped down, doing a fancy series of aerial maneuvers. Finally, it zoomed in and hovered alongside their basket for a long moment. Strangely, the drone appeared to be making up its mind about something. Then it peeled away.

"What's the drone for? Some kind of TV news thing?" Drayton asked. "You know, 'Film at eleven'?"

"I don't think it's a commercial drone. Probably someone who's filming the balloons for fun." Theodosia's attention slowly shifted to the weather as she scanned the sky to the east, in the direction of the Atlantic Ocean. A few more clouds had rolled in, turning the horizon into a dim blot. Hopefully, there wasn't a storm brewing.

"Such a strange, buzzing thing," Drayton said, unable to unkink the knot of worry that had formed in his head. His hands gripped the side of the wicker basket even tighter. "Like some kind of giant, nasty hornet. Just having it circle around like that gives me the heebie-jeebies."

"There's really nothing to worry . . ." Theodosia began. Then she practically choked back her words as she watched the little drone lift straight up like a miniature helicopter or Harrier jet. Up, up, up it rose until it was flying level with the red-and-white balloon that hovered just ahead of them but at a slightly higher altitude.

"Now the drone has edged precipitously close to that balloon," Drayton said as he continued to gaze upward. "That can't be good."

"No, it's not." Alarmed now, Theodosia tapped their pilot on the shoulder and, when he turned, she pointed wordlessly at the drone that now hovered some forty feet above them.

The pilot glanced up and frowned, his expression telling her all she needed to know. "That shouldn't be there," he said.

"It's strange. Almost as if the drone is checking out each of the balloons," Drayton said. "Peeking in the baskets to see who the passengers are."

"Because it has a camera," Theodosia said slowly. She glanced down toward terra firma, wondering who in the crowd below them might be manipulating the drone—and why were they doing so? Was it for fun or a joke or maybe some kind of daredevil promotional film? But the balloon she was riding in was flying way too high to make out anything meaningful.

"I think the object is flying away," Drayton said. "Good riddance."

But the drone didn't fly away.

Instead, it circled back around, hovered for a few moments, revved its engine to an almost supersonic speed, and flew directly into the red-and-white balloon.

RIP. ZSSST. WHOMP!

A burst of brilliant light, bright as an atomic bomb, lit the sky.

"No!" Drayton cried out.

Theodosia threw up an arm to shield her eyes and then watched in horror as the red-and-white balloon was ripped wide open, top to bottom, like a hapless fish being gutted.

Tongues of ugly red and purple flames roiled and twisted, practically drowning out the screams of the hapless passengers. Then the gigantic balloon exploded in a hellish conflagration, sizzling and popping and wobbling for a few long seconds. Finally, the whole thing began to slowly collapse inward as the fireball deflated.

"Dear Lord, it's the Hindenburg all over again," Drayton said in a hoarse whisper.

Against the darkening sky, the burning balloon and dangling basket looked like some sort of Hollywood special effect. Then, almost in slow motion, the entire rig tumbled from the sky like a faulty rocket dropping out of orbit.

Screams rent the air—maybe from the dying passengers, certainly from the horrified observers on the ground.

Hearts in their throats, eyes unable to resist this gruesome sight, Theodosia and Drayton continued to watch the sickening spectacle unfold.

"What a catastrophe!" Drayton cried out. "Will anyone survive?"

Theodosia whispered a quick prayer. She didn't think so.

The burning balloon roared and rumbled as it continued its downward plunge, unleashing a blizzard of blistered nylon, hot metal, and exploding propane. Ash and sparks fluttered everywhere; the sound was like a blast furnace. Then, in a final ghastly incendiary burst, the balloon and its seared basket smashed down on top of Theodosia's tea table. Tongues of flame spewed out as bone china teacups were crushed. A pink-and-green teapot exploded like a bomb.

And lives were surely lost.

2

Almost as a climactic final act, the heavens opened up and a fierce rain hammered down.

"Hang on, this is going to be a hard landing," the pilot yelled to Theodosia and Drayton.

Grim-faced and stunned, they dropped as fast as the pilot and the laws of physics would allow. Then, like an out-of-control elevator, they slammed into the earth with a bone-jouncing, filling-rattling thud.

Even before Theodosia hopped from their half-toppled basket, she was overwhelmed by the terrible scene that awaited them. Her tea table was an enormous pile of burning debris, panicked bystanders were screaming and crying, dozens of tables and chairs had been upended, and clouds of dark, acrid smoke were spreading everywhere. And bodies. Theodosia didn't see any at the moment, but she knew there had to be bodies. No one could survive this.

"This is just unbelievable," she said to Drayton.

"Senseless," Drayton said, shaking his head. "Tragic." Gazing around, he saw that several onlookers had also been injured by falling debris.

Anger and outrage bubbled inside Theodosia. She tilted her head back to hastily scan the skies overhead, searching for the drone. But the drone, the cause of all this misery, had seemingly disappeared. Like a supersonic fighter jet on a stealth bombing mission. Or had the drone crashed and burned somewhere as well?

And where was the drone's operator? Theodosia wondered. Who on earth had been manipulating the controls and caused this accident? But as the still-flaming debris sent up an acrid stink, a tendril of fear touched her heart. Or had it been deliberate?

To make matters worse, low hanging clouds had cut visibility to a minimum, and the storm's onslaught was whipping everything into a frenzy. Trees thrashed, lines for the hot-air balloons that were hastily descending were hopelessly tangled, and a couple of metal folding chairs had turned into nasty, flying missiles.

"How many people?" a uniformed police officer shouted to Theodosia as he ran toward her. He was heading for the crash site, a radio clutched in his hand. "Did you see it happen? How many people in the explosion?"

"Two, I think," Theodosia shouted. Her jaw felt leaden, like it was wired shut. "No, wait. Maybe three people, counting the pilot."

The officer skidded to a halt next to her, touched a hand to his cheek, and muttered, "Dear Lord." Then he was on his radio, his voice rising in panic as he called for first responders. Police, ambulances, firefighters, whatever help he could muster as fast as possible.

Unfortunately, WCSC-TV, Channel 8, arrived first. The white van emblazoned with the red TV8 logo and supporting a satellite dish on top careened across the grass at an ungodly speed, rocking to a stop directly in front of Theodosia and Drayton. Dale Dickerson, one of TV8's roving reporters, jumped out, looking perfectly attired and blow combed, even in the pouring rain. Dickerson nodded to himself when he recognized Theodosia and immediately stuck a microphone in her face.

"Tell us what you saw," Dickerson said.

"It was awful," Theodosia said. She could barely comprehend the magnitude of what had just happened.

"Tell us how you *felt* when you saw the hot-air balloon catch fire and come crashing down," Dickerson said.

Theodosia lifted a hand and pushed the microphone away. This wasn't right. People had been killed. "No," she said. "I'm not doing this. I can't."

"The station will want this footage for the five and six o'clock news," Dickerson said, as if he was offering a huge incentive.

Theodosia couldn't care less. "No. Go pester someone else."

Dickerson gave a hopeful glance in Drayton's direction, then caught the look of utter disdain on Drayton's face.

"Whatever," Dickerson said, rushing off.

Police cruisers, ambulances, and fire trucks arrived, adding to the mayhem. A young man, his face pale as a ghost, sprinted past them. He skidded to a stop a few feet away, both arms extended, and spun around full tilt on the soggy grass. Then he ran back toward them, clearly in a blind panic.

"Whoa." Theodosia reached out and snagged his jacket sleeve. "Slow down. Take it easy."

"Did you see it? Did you see Mr. Kingsley's balloon get hit?" the young man screamed at her.

"Is that who was in the balloon?" Theodosia asked. "A man named Kingsley?" She knew the police would need to know these names.

"Who else was with him?" Drayton asked.

"It was . . . it was . . ." The young man suddenly fell to his knees and dropped his head, as if he were bracing for a plane crash.

"Take a deep breath," Theodosia said. She leaned down and put a hand on the young man's shoulder. He was hyperventilating so badly she feared he might give himself a stroke.

"Yeah, okay," the young man said as he struggled to his feet. "But who's . . . who's going to tell Mrs. Kingsley?" he asked with a sorrowful moan.

Theodosia grabbed his shoulders and gave him a small shake to try to rouse him from his confused state. "Who are you?" she asked.

"I'm . . . I'm Charles Townsend."

"Do you work for Mr. Kingsley?" Drayton asked.

Townsend bobbed his head. "I'm Mr. Kingsley's private secretary."

"Oh dear," Drayton said.

"You need to pull yourself together and identify yourself to those police officers over there," Theodosia said. "Tell them who exactly was in the hot-air balloon that crashed."

But Townsend seemed rooted in place, his expression a mixture of sorrow and distress. "And what are we going to do about the flag?" he whispered.

"I don't think he's tracking all that well," Drayton said in a low voice.

"No, he's not," Theodosia said. "I think I'd better . . ." She spoke louder and more forcefully now. "You'd better come with me, Mr. Townsend." She took him gently by the arm. "We're going to get you some help."

Theodosia led Charles Townsend over to the nearest ambulance and tapped a blue-coated EMT on his shoulder. "Excuse me?"

The EMT, a young African-American man whose name tag read T. RUSSEL, turned around to face her. "Yes?"

"This young man was a witness to the crash," Theodosia said. "And he's right on the fine edge of hysteria. Could you give him some oxygen or even something stronger to help him calm down?"

"We'll take care of him," the EMT promised.

"Thank you," Theodosia said.

An officer standing nearby said, "You witnessed the crash?"

"My friend and I were up in one of the balloons. We saw the whole thing."

"We need to interview you folks then," the officer said. "Get a statement."

"Sure. Okay."

The officer's radio crackled with static. "Yeah," he responded. "We're working on that now." Then he turned to Theodosia and said, "Just hold on, will you?"

Theodosia walked over and joined Drayton, who had somehow scrounged a dilapidated umbrella. They stood there, huddled beneath it, trying to find temporary respite from the pouring rain, but the umbrella wasn't doing much good. Rain pelted down, then made a nasty side trip and dripped down the backs of their necks. They were cold, miserable, and wet. Worse, they were stunned and trying desperately to process the horrible explosion they'd just witnessed.

"We have to wait and give a statement," Theodosia said.

"At least we don't have anything to pack up," Drayton said.

Theodosia glanced at her ruined tea table and grimaced. Then she turned away and watched as the crime scene van arrived, along with a K-9 officer who had a German shepherd straining against his leash. Theodosia immediately thought of her own dog, Earl Grey, waiting for her at home, and hoped they wouldn't be held there in limbo for too long.

Finally, a motorcade came screeching in: three police cruisers, red-and-blue light bars flashing and sirens blaring, followed by a shiny, black Suburban with smoked windows.

"Who's that?" Theodosia asked.

"Must be the mayor or police chief," Drayton said. "The big cheese."

The rear passenger door flew open and Detective Burt Tidwell, head of the Charleston Police Department's Robbery and Homicide Division, stepped out, albeit a bit ungainly. He was a large man wearing a voluminous dark suit. His eyes, always twin pinpricks of intensity, immediately roved across the entire park, taking in the still-smoldering balloon, the ambulances, the injured, the scrambling first responders, and the basic confusion of people.

"Looks like he might have a driver now," Theodosia said.

They watched as Tidwell spoke with two officers, barked out new orders, and hastily inspected the wreckage. Finally, the officer Theodosia had talked with earlier gestured toward Theodosia and Drayton.

Tidwell glanced around again, then those beady, insightful eyes landed squarely on Theodosia. He huffed across the grass toward her, a big man moving at a surprisingly fast pace, the two uniformed officers following behind him, straining to keep up.

"Miss Browning," Tidwell said, giving a hurried, acknowledging nod. "I understand you're a somewhat integral part of this situation. This debacle." It was a statement, not a question.

"I'm afraid so," Theodosia said. "We were . . . that is Drayton and myself . . . were up in one of the hot-air balloons when the one next to us exploded. The red-and-white one that's . . . well, it's over there." She swallowed hard. "What's left of it."

"Yes, yes," Tidwell said, digesting her words and ready to brush past her. "We've already alerted the FAA and are bringing in investigators from the NTSB. In cases such as this, error is generally either human, machine, or environment. So we need to determine . . ."

"No." Theodosia shook her head. "I can tell you exactly what happened."

Tidwell pursed his lips, clearly annoyed by her interruption. Then he seemed to bite back his frustration. "Excuse me, didn't I just say we had to wait for an NTSB investigator?"

"It was a drone," Theodosia said.

"What?" Tidwell barked, as if he were suddenly hard of hearing. "What did you say?"

"We saw a drone buzz in and fly among all the hot-air balloons," Drayton said. "A good-sized, silver drone."

Tidwell was glaring at them as if he didn't believe their story. "Wait a minute. You're telling me you actually *saw* a drone and that it was responsible for this crash?"

"We witnessed the whole sorry mess," Drayton said.

"From one of the balloons," Theodosia said. She glanced over her shoulder, saw that their hot-air balloon was still half-inflated. "We were riding in that blue one right over there when we saw the drone come buzzing in like some kind of giant, mechanized bird. The drone flew around for a while, kind of checking out all the balloons. Then it zeroed in on the red-and-white balloon and flew directly into it. Caused a huge explosion."

"Let me get this straight," Tidwell said. "The drone flew into the hot-air balloon that crashed?"

"More like attacked it!" Drayton said.

"The balloon that crashed, yes!" Theodosia shouted, trying to underscore her words. Was Tidwell not hearing her? Was he not understanding her? But it turned out he was.

"Oh no," Tidwell said, his voice suddenly going dull and hoarse. "So you truly did witness the explosion."

"Yes," Theodosia said.

"As well as the crash."

Theodosia just nodded.

"Officer Anson!" Tidwell shouted out as he threw up a chubby hand.

Anson came running over to join them. "Sir?"

"We need to take witness statements from both Miss Browning and Mr. Conneley here," Tidwell barked. "Immediately. Find a dry spot where you can question them and perhaps get them a cup of coffee." He peered at Theodosia, who looked shaken and ashen faced, not quite her usual confident self. Then Tidwell's face gradually softened, as if he were gazing at a fragile Dresden figurine. "Better yet, find them a cup of tea."

3

Clouds of tea-infused steam hung in the air as brass kettles chirped and whistled. Malty Assam, smoky gunpowder green, and fragrant Darjeeling drifted in delightful currents, then merged in an aphrodisiac swirl. It was eight o'clock Monday morning at the Indigo Tea Shop and Theodosia and Drayton were sitting at a rustic wooden table, drinking cups of Assam tea and nibbling on fresh-baked strawberry scones. They were also bringing Haley, their young chef and baker, up to speed on yesterday's hot-air balloon crash. This of course had sent Haley scrambling to the front door to pick up their rain-soaked morning newspaper.

"So it says here on the front page of the *Charleston Post and Courier* that three people were killed," Haley said as she bounced on the balls of her feet next to the table where Theodosia and Drayton sat. "They're calling it the hot-air balloon massacre." She wrinkled her pert nose and shook back her shoulder-length, blond hair. Haley was in her early twenties, deeply sensitive, and took everything to heart. Balloon crashes, homeless kittens, and sad movies all had an equal effect on stirring her emotions.

"It was dreadful," Drayton said. "Like riding a zip line into hell." Along with a tweed jacket and yellow bow tie, he also wore a stoic face. But the crash, the senseless deaths, had affected him just as much as it had Haley.

"It also says here that the crash was probably deliberate," Haley said.

"May I see that article?" Theodosia asked, reaching out a hand.

Haley passed over the main news section and Theodosia quickly skimmed the article. She thought she'd recovered from the initial shock of the crash, but reading about it today made her feel sad—and a touch anxious—all over again.

"I mean, what do *you* guys think?" Haley asked. "You were there, after all. The newspaper even mentions you by name. Because you hosted the tea party thing."

"Oh no," Drayton said. "That kind of PR we don't need."

Theodosia's eyes searched for her name as one of the witnesses, skimmed a bit more of the article, and slumped back in her chair. "One of the crash victims *was* Don Kingsley, the CEO of SyncSoft. They seem to think—the reporters, not the police—that Kingsley might have been the prime target."

"So we're talking cold-blooded murder and not just a terrible accident," Haley said. She sounded interested. And a little scared.

Drayton set his pink Shelley teacup onto his saucer with a tiny clink. "What, pray tell, is SyncSoft?"

"It's a local technology company, actually one of over two hundred fifty that now call Charleston home," Theodosia said. "SyncSoft, as I recall, develops different types of software. One of their products was written up a few weeks ago in the business section, a software for designing algorithms."

Drayton held up a hand and made a whooshing motion past his head. "I have no idea what that means."

"Wait a minute. Doesn't Angie's boyfriend work for a software company?" Haley asked. She was referring to their friend, Angie Congdon, who owned the Featherbed House B and B a few blocks away.

"Does he really?" Drayton asked. "I thought what's his name—um, Harold—just puttered around the Featherbed House doing odd jobs for Angie and tending the garden."

"No, I'm pretty sure that Harold has an actual day job in marketing," Haley said.

"He does work for SyncSoft," Theodosia said. "Harold used to work at Data Metrics, now he's at SyncSoft. Angie was quite excited when Harold landed the job, it was a big step up for him."

Haley jabbed a silver teaspoon in her direction. "What else does that article say?"

"The reporter probably included a horribly vivid description of the crash," Drayton said. "Pandering to readers who love to salivate over every macabre detail."

"You mean like blood and bones sticking out and stuff?" Haley asked.

Drayton scowled. "No need to be so graphic."

"Actually, this article puts more of a focus on the victims than the actual crash," Theodosia said. "It says that Roger Bennet, a major client of SyncSoft, was also killed. Along with Curtis Dean, the balloon's pilot."

"Anything else we should know about?" Haley asked. Now she was peering over Theodosia's shoulder, squinting at the newspaper pages.

"Let's see, there's also a sidebar written by a different reporter, the *Post and Courier*'s financial reporter. Anyway, his piece is a little murky, but it alludes to missing corporate funds," Theodosia said.

"Missing funds from SyncSoft?" Haley asked.

"That's what it says," Theodosia said.

"Interesting," Drayton said. "Perhaps now we're getting to the heart of the matter."

Theodosia continued reading the sidebar. "Apparently, Don Kingsley was under fire from his board of directors for misplacing a great deal of money."

"Exactly how great is a great deal?" Haley asked.

"It says here five million dollars," Theodosia said.

Drayton's eyebrows shot up. "So it's possible the crash was connected to missing money?"

Theodosia gave a slow nod. "Maybe. Could be."

"Jeez, I hope Harold still has a job to go to," Haley said. "You always hear about companies that lose their key execs in a private plane crash or on some team-building trek in the Himalayas. Once the head guys are out of the picture, the whole company is basically kaput."

"I can't imagine that's going to happen in this case," Drayton said. "SyncSoft obviously has a board of directors. Along with vice presidents and such."

"That's good," Haley said. "I guess." She twirled a finger in her hair. "I'm just happy you guys were able to land safely."

"So am I," Theodosia said. In her mind she could still feel the heart-stopping, gut-wrenching jounce as their basket slammed into wet earth. Unnerved by the explosion and subsequent fireball, their balloon pilot had brought their craft down at an accelerated rate of speed.

"To make matters worse, we landed just as the big storm hit," Drayton said. He glanced out the front window where rain continued to spatter down, practically obliterating any view of traffic going by on Church Street. "The weather people, the meteorologists, are predicting that it's going to rain all week." He touched a finger to his bow tie. "That could be disastrous for business."

"Let's not worry about what *could* happen," Theodosia said, "and try to focus on the present. After all, we've got some lovely tea events planned and have probably sold enough tickets to guarantee fairly good-sized crowds."

The hot-air balloon disaster had left her feeling nervous and on edge. Now she knew it was time to try and put it behind her. After all, there was nothing she could do for those three poor souls who'd perished.

"I'm looking forward to our Nancy Drew Tea this Wednesday and especially to our Beaux Arts Tea on Saturday," Drayton said. He glanced at Haley. "Are you still working on those surprise centerpieces?"

"For the Nancy Drew Tea, yeah," Haley said.

"And FYI, I'll be leaving work a little early tomorrow. I've been tapped to judge the Floral Teacups Competition," Theodosia said.

"What's that all about anyway?" Haley asked.

"It's basically a fund-raiser for the Heartsong Kids Club," Theodosia said.

"The rec center that Miss Josette's nephew runs," Drayton said. "Of course." Miss Josette was the African-American artist who'd created the stellar sweetgrass baskets that hung on one wall of the tea shop. Baskets that were always in high demand.

Theodosia nodded. "Anyway, it's basically teacup art. I'll be judging and awarding prizes to the teacups that showcase the best miniature floral displays. You know, flowers, mosses, grasses, vines, perhaps even miniature trees."

"Like Drayton's bonsai," Haley said.

"From what I understand, there are supposed to be almost fifty entries," Theodosia said.

"Entries from whom?" Haley asked. "Not us."

"Garden clubs, floral shops, antiques shops, vintage jewelry shops—even a few companies have seriously gotten into it," Theodosia said. "Really anyone who aspires to be creative. I believe there are a few corporate sponsors, too."

"That's nice. For the rec center anyway," Drayton said.

Theodosia focused her gaze on Drayton and smiled. "It seems our Drayton also has a major event coming up later this week."

Drayton's shoulders rose and dropped in a long, drawn out sigh. "I suppose you're talking about the crew of photographers, lighting people, and stylists that will be invading my home," he said in a flat tone.

"That's gonna be so exciting," Haley enthused. "*Southern Interiors Magazine* is a really big deal. It's so cool that they selected your house to feature in an article. I mean, shots of your house will be in their magazine right along with photos of fancy celebrities' homes. And country and western stars. And homes owned by people who are so rich you don't even know their names!"

"I'm afraid I don't share your abundant enthusiasm. In fact, I view this as a bit of a distraction and inconvenience," Drayton responded.

"Whoa," Theodosia said, holding up a hand. "What changed? You were positively over the moon when *Southern Interiors Magazine* first called."

"Yes . . . well, in thinking about the disruption to my private life, my enthusiasm has since waned," Drayton said.

"But it's fabulous publicity," Haley said.

"Publicity." Drayton spat out the word as if he were referring to llama dung. "Who wants publicity? Who would go so far as to *court* it?"

"You?" Haley asked in a squeaky voice.

Drayton let loose a shudder. "Never."

Five minutes later, the Indigo Tea Shop turned into a hub of activity. Haley scurried back to her kitchen to finish baking her scones, muffins, and quick breads, and begin prepping for lunch.

Drayton slipped behind the front counter where he reigned supreme over his prized floor-to-ceiling shelves of tea. This private domain featured the finest in loose-leaf teas and included first-flush Goomtee Garden Darjeeling from India, Neluwa Garden BOP from Ceylon, and Hao Ya 'A' black tea from China. Of course, there were hundreds of other varieties, along with his custom house blends.

Theodosia, on the other hand, focused all her efforts into turning her cozy little enterprise into a sparkling jewel box of a tea room. She smoothed white linen table-cloths over wooden tables and folded linen napkins just so—today she managed a tricky bishop's cap fold. Then there were the table settings to consider. Theodosia pulled out a set of Spode china in the Golden Valley pattern, and decided the gold trim and purple-and-green peaches and pears would be the perfect antidote to such a rainy, gloomy day.

Silverware was added along with sugar bowls, cream-ers, and tea light candles in small glass jars.

When the tables were finished and gleaming with perfection, Theodosia stepped back to admire her handiwork—actually her life's work. Several years ago, she'd left a hustle-bustle, 24-7 job in marketing to take the plunge and open the Indigo Tea Shop. She'd borrowed money, drawn up plans, worked like crazy, and eventually converted a former stable and blacksmith shop into a cozy, welcoming enterprise. Now the tea shop featured wood plank floors, a stone fireplace, gabled ceiling, and small windows with wavy antique glass—the perfect spot to offer elegant cream teas, luncheon teas, and high teas.

Drayton as tea master had also been a rare find and a true complement to her shop. Haley, her chef and baker, had been a lucky strike. Now, after almost a half dozen years together, they operated as a well-oiled machine.

"Theo?"

Theodosia's tea shop reverie burst like a soap bubble. "Yes, Haley?" she said.

"I've got today's menu for you to look at." Haley dodged two tables and a wayward captain's chair to hand Theodo-sia an index card filled with her left-canted printing.

"Strawberry scones and lemon scones," Theodosia

read out loud. "And for lunch, Cheddar and pimento tea sandwiches, another sandwich to be determined, citrus salad, three-cheese quiche, and beef barley soup."

"We can combo a cup of soup and half sandwich if you'd like," Haley said.

"Good idea. Hot soup is always appealing on a cold day."

"You got it." Haley disappeared as quickly as she'd appeared. She was an autocrat in the kitchen and ruled her domain with an iron fist in a quilted oven mitt. No greengrocer would dare stick Haley with wilted butter lettuce or slightly over-the-hill tomatoes. If they did, the full wrath of Haley Parker would descend upon their shoulders and they'd be cut out from her carefully cultivated list of providers.

"What's on the docket for today?" Drayton asked Theodosia. "Anything I can do a tricky match with?" He was balancing a tin of Taiwanese oolong in one hand and a tin of Plum Deluxe's Candlelight Blend in the other hand, deciding which tea would be the most apropos for a morning brew.

Theodosia read Haley's menu to Drayton.

Drayton smiled. "I've also got an itch to brew a few pots of Chinese gunpowder green tea, which I think will be the perfect accompaniment to Haley's lemon scones."

"Go for it."

"And I've been wondering about . . ."

Drayton's words were cut short by an earsplitting crash at the front door. What could it be? Had a hit and run accident on Church Street sent a car skidding onto the sidewalk? Did one of the horse-drawn jitneys throw a wheel?

Then the door flew open and whapped hard against the wall, ushering in a nasty onslaught of rain and cold air. From out of the fog and dampness, a distraught-looking man careened toward them.

The man stared at Theodosia and Drayton for all of one second and then cried, "I need some help!" He slammed the door behind him and stomped his feet.

Drayton was instantly on alert. "Are you injured? Were you in an auto accident? I'm sure the driving out there is *terrible*. Do you want me to dial 911? Or call a tow truck?"

The man vigorously shook his head "no" while he flapped his arms about his body like a flightless bird.

Drayton relaxed some. Not an accident. Just someone caught in the storm. "Perhaps we could offer you a cup of hot tea on an emergency basis?"

Looking more desperate than ever, the man gazed about with wild eyes. "No," he barked out. "What I need . . . what I have to talk to someone about . . . is yesterday's hot-air balloon crash!"

4

❧

"*Who are you?*" Theodosia asked. She'd crept forward to intercept this stranger, this interloper, before he advanced any farther into her tea shop. Yes, she was territorial and proud of it.

"Forgive me," the man said. A modicum of courtesy had returned to his voice. He touched a hand to the front of his beige rain-spattered trench coat. "I should introduce myself. I'm Tod Slawson."

"The antiques dealer," Drayton said immediately.

Slawson nodded. "That's right." He was tall, at least six feet two, with slicked back, dark blond hair, a slightly hawk nose, and soft amber eyes that darted to and fro.

Theodosia thought he looked like an Englishman who'd inherited a minor title and a dilapidated manor home. Someone who raised sheep, read poetry, and was slightly long in the tooth but short in the jaw.

But Drayton clearly knew who Slawson was. "You specialize in Chinese antiques," Drayton said.

"Not anymore I don't," Slawson said. He brushed at the front of his coat. "Now you can't *give* away Ming and Qing pieces. After the market in Chinese antiquities was flooded with thousands—maybe millions—of fakes and forgeries, it dropped like a brick. No, no, now I've completely moved into Americana. That's where the up-and-coming market is. Early American furniture, paintings, and decorative pieces." He waved a hand in the air, as if to erase his words. "But enough about me, I need to know what the two of you saw yesterday. At the crash site."

"Why exactly are you asking?" Theodosia said.

"Because it's critical. Practically a life and death matter," Slawson said.

"I'm afraid, Mr. Slawson, that I don't know you from Adam," Theodosia said. *And how do you know that Drayton and I were at the hot-air balloon rally yesterday?* Then she thought, *Oh, the newspaper.*

Slawson looked supremely injured. Then, deciding he ought to come up with a more suitable angle for this conversation, said, "What is it you want to know about me?"

"Probably a tad more than you've already told us," Theodosia said. She was polite but firm.

Slawson frowned. He clearly wasn't used to being stuck on the hot seat. "For one thing, I own Marquis Antiques over on King Street. We're one of the premier antiques dealers in Charleston and my clients include some of our fair city's finest families. The Ravenels, the Calhouns, the . . ."

"Oh," Theodosia said, interrupting him and looking slightly startled. "I do know who you are."

Deep in the recess of Theodosia's brain, she remembered her friend Delaine Dish rhapsodizing about a new boyfriend who was elegant, sweet-natured, and didn't mind accompanying her on the occasional shopping trip. A man named Tod Slawson. Clearly, this had to be the same Tod Slawson.

"I believe you're dating a friend of mine," Theodosia said. "Delaine Dish."

"Yes. Delaine," Slawson said. He gave a perfunctory

smile and said, "Now that we're all one big happy family, perhaps we can skip my curriculum vitae and you can help me out, answer a couple of questions. You see, I need to know *exactly* what you saw yesterday. Every single detail about the hot-air balloon crash that took the lives of those three people."

"Why do I have a feeling you're interested in *one* of those people in particular?" Theodosia asked.

Slawson's hands flew up and he turned his palms toward her, as if in capitulation. "You're right. I am," he said.

"Let me guess," Theodosia said. "Donald Kingsley."

Slawson pointed a finger at her. "Yes. Because I'm convinced that poor Don Kingsley was murdered. That the drone showing up wasn't random at all. That it was a carefully planned and choreographed attack."

"When you use the word 'attack,'" Drayton said, "you make it sound as if terrorists were at work."

"Maybe not full-blown, radical, suicide-vest terrorists, but I'm positive that hot-air balloon explosion wasn't an accident," Slawson said.

Theodosia pretty much agreed with him, but instead of saying so, said to Slawson, "Have you shared your suspicions with the Charleston police?"

Slawson nodded. "First thing this morning. I talked to a big guy . . . Well, he was a bigwig, too, I guess. A detective named Tidwell."

"Burt Tidwell. Yes, we know him," Theodosia said. *Do we ever.*

"Tidwell was the one who mentioned you were at the hot-air balloon rally. And then I read it in this morning's paper, too." Slawson looked pointedly at Theodosia and then at Drayton. "Tidwell said the two of you witnessed the drone flying directly into Kingsley's hot-air balloon."

"Why would Tidwell talk to you about this?" Drayton murmured.

"Because I asked him," Slawson said. "Because this whole thing—this crash—is too preposterous for words.

And the crazy thing is, *I* was supposed to be riding in the balloon with them!"

A tiny alert pinged in the back of Theodosia's brain. "Why weren't you riding with them?" she asked.

"Hmm?" Slawson fixed her with a slightly cockeyed gaze.

"Why didn't *you* go up in the balloon with the others?" she asked again.

"Um, a family matter came up," Slawson said. He held the back of his hand against his forehead as if his brains were about to explode. "But Don Kingsley and the other two getting killed. It's just unbelievable!"

Theodosia's curiosity was more than tickled. *Who wanted Don Kingsley and his client dead?* She wondered. *Who would send up a drone to purposely take down a hot-air balloon? And was the drone attack intended to kill Kingsley the CEO, or was his client, Roger Bennet, the target? Maybe Kingsley was merely collateral damage.*

"Are you familiar with drones?" Theodosia asked Slawson. "Do you know anything about them?"

"Only what I've seen on TV. Like, in a few years they're supposed to be delivering all sorts of things direct to our homes. Books, groceries, wine, whatever."

"As if that's ever going to happen," Drayton muttered. He was a confirmed Luddite who eschewed cell phones, cable TV, satellite radio, online banking, and the Internet. Drayton's idea of current technology was a vinyl record—preferably classical—played on his thirty-year-old RCA turntable.

"If you're so sure this drone attack was planned, that it was cold-blooded murder, you surely must have a perpetrator in mind," Theodosia said. She was keenly interested in hearing Slawson's answer.

"If anyone's capable of murder it's Earl Bullitt," Slawson said immediately.

"Another antiques dealer," Drayton said.

"Why on earth would you say that?" Theodosia asked.

It felt as if Slawson had randomly plucked a rival antiques dealer's name out of thin air. "And more importantly, why would an antiques dealer murder a software CEO? I'm afraid I don't see the connection."

"There's a huge connection. We were all vying to purchase the exact same item," Slawson said.

"Excuse me. You mean like a bidding war?" Drayton asked.

"Something like that," Slawson said.

"What were you bidding on?" Theodosia asked. *Antiques? This doesn't sound like business. Like anything SyncSoft would be involved in.*

"So there was some type of private auction?" Drayton asked.

"What exactly were you bidding on?" Theodosia asked again. She kept her tone courteous but direct.

"If you must know, it was a flag," Slawson said.

"A flag," Theodosia repeated. She recalled that when Charles Townsend had been running around yesterday, he'd been babbling about a flag.

"It was . . . well . . ." Slawson looked unhappy. "I suppose the details are bound to come out one way or another."

"What's going to come out?" Theodosia asked. Slawson's double-talk was beginning to wear on her.

"Details concerning the flag," Slawson said. "You see, Don Kingsley was about to sell an original flag that dates all the way back to the American Revolution."

"No," Drayton said. But it was said in stunned surprise rather than as a negative comment.

"There were several of us . . . *are* several of us," Slawson said. "All interested parties that were contacted by Kingsley."

"And . . ." Theodosia said. There had to be more.

"And now the flag is missing," Slawson said.

"Under what circumstances?" Drayton asked.

"Right after the crash—or possibly during—it simply

disappeared from Don Kingsley's home. Poof. Gone like a puff of smoke. Kingsley's secretary was the one who sent up the hue and cry that it was missing." Slawson massaged his forehead in disbelief. "I can't quite believe it."

"This missing flag," Theodosia said. "It's important? In a historical sense?"

Slawson screwed his face into an unflattering grimace. "It's an original Navy Jack flag."

Drayton was so startled he practically vaulted across the front counter. "Gracious me!" he said, in what was clearly a stunned tone of voice.

Theodosia knew something important had just been revealed. Feeling that her knowledge of early American history was somewhat challenged, she focused on Drayton, who possessed a much keener grasp of historical data. "Translation, please?" she asked him.

"Mr. Slawson is referring to the 'Don't Tread on Me' flag," Drayton said in a hushed, almost reverent tone.

"The *what*?" Theodosia was rocked back on her heels. She'd seen the DON'T TREAD ON ME flag depicted in various history books and on posters. It was a Navy Jack flag with a red and yellow snake wriggling against a background of red and white stripes.

"Amazing," Drayton breathed.

Theodosia opened her mouth to speak, then closed it. She let Slawson's words sink in for a moment. Then, like a Roman candle streaking across the night sky, she was struck with the realization that a flag such as that, if it proved to be genuine, would surely be . . . priceless.

5

Could Don Kingsley really have been in possession of an original Navy Jack flag?" Theodosia asked Drayton once Tod Slawson had left. "Where would he get something like that? More importantly, could a more than two-hundred-year-old flag have withstood the ravages of time? After these many years, wouldn't a flag of that vintage be in tatters and remnants? Or simply reduced to dust?"

But Drayton thought differently. "If the flag was properly cared for, stored correctly, and by that I mean temperature and humidity controlled, it might still be in fairly decent shape."

"That would be amazing."

Drayton scratched his cheek absently, as if deep in thought. "As I recall, there was a Continental Light Dragoons flag that went up for auction at Sotheby's a few years ago."

"Do you remember what it sold for?"

"It went for a pretty penny. Almost eighteen million dollars."

The number was so vast, it took Theodosia's breath away. She cleared her throat self-consciously. "So this 'Don't Tread on Me' flag might be worth even more?"

"I would guess . . . yes," Drayton said. "A *lot* more." He dropped his voice to a reverent tone. "Realize, please, these antique flags are sacred objects. People *died* defending them. Not just those serving in the Continental army and navy, but ordinary men and women who stood alongside them in the American Revolution and believed implicitly in the principles these flags stood for."

"Dear Lord," Theo said. "I'm shocked there's a flag of that vintage available. I would have thought most old, historic flags were enshrined in museums and history centers."

"I'm no expert, but I believe there are only thirty or so genuine Revolutionary War flags still in existence," Drayton said.

"Then I can certainly understand a collector's fervor. A Navy Jack flag is . . . well, it's incredibly inspirational," Theodosia said. "It would be akin to a holy relic."

"Exactly so."

"Where would Don Kingsley obtain a flag like that? And why would he want to sell it if he was a collector himself?"

"Hard to say. Maybe he inherited the flag, or maybe he picked it out of a junk store bin. Many pieces of fine art have been discovered that way," Drayton said.

"An occasional Jackson Pollock painting that turns up on Long Island maybe. But a Revolutionary War flag?"

"You never know."

"Who could tell us about this type of flag? Are there any flag experts in Charleston that could offer an opinion?"

"Possibly someone in the Americana Club."

"What is that? Some historical group? I've never heard you mention them before."

"And I'm sure the members would prefer to keep it that

way," Drayton said. He cleared his throat, as if he were about to impart a deep, dark secret. "The Americana Club is a small group of wealthy men who collect rare pieces of American history. Old documents, flags, medals, militaria, you name it."

"Civil War pieces, too?"

"Of course."

Theodosia felt her heart blip with interest. "And you say this group is local?"

"Most of them live right here in Charleston. They reside in the Historic District, of course. And own homes along the Battery and Tradd Street."

"So really a hop, skip, and a jump away from us."

"Correct."

"Does this Americana Club have its own private museum?"

Drayton chuckled. "No, but all the members probably have a secret room in their home."

"Sounds like they fly under the radar."

"You know, Theo, I don't think you should get all wound up about this purported Union Jack. Now that I think about it, there's a good chance the flag isn't genuine."

"But what if it is?"

"Well, what if it is?" Drayton said. "What's the problem?"

"For one thing, the flag's owner was just murdered along with two other innocent people. So it wasn't just an indiscriminate killing. I mean, there was a *reason* behind it. Somebody must have wanted something from Kingsley. And when they didn't get it . . . BOOM!"

"I suppose you do have a point."

"And now there seems to be a mad scramble going on."

"A treasure hunt to see who can possess that flag," Drayton said slowly.

"Or steal it," Theodosia said. *Missing money and a missing flag. How very . . . curious.*

* * *

The rain didn't keep customers away this morning and, five minutes later, the tea shop was busy. The door flew open constantly as merchants from up and down Church Street came in to grab their morning cuppa and a take-out scone. Tourists came in to seek refuge and get a bite to eat, their faces aglow when they saw what a lovely tea shop they'd discovered.

Theodosia took orders and ran them back to Haley. Drayton brewed pots of tea. Theodosia ran Haley's finished orders back to their guests, picking up the steeping pots on the way.

And all the while Theodosia's mind was in a whirl. Thinking about the deadly explosion yesterday, wondering about this missing flag. When there was a lull in the action she said to Drayton, "Do you mind if I skip out for five minutes and run next store to the bookshop?"

Drayton cocked an eye at her. "Looking to do a little research?"

"Couldn't hurt."

Theodosia grabbed an umbrella and ducked out into the storm. The rain had let up some, but the wind was whooshing down the street. It caught her hair and made the auburn tendrils stream out like ribbons on a maypole.

Theodosia gritted her teeth. When her hair got wet—or slightly damp—it took on a life of its own. Not exactly frizzing, but expanding in size until it became an abundant halo around her head.

Luckily, the Antiquarian Bookshop was only three doors down from the Indigo Tea Shop. It was housed in a tall, redbrick building and had a classic storefront, with gold, curlicue letters painted on the window. Theodosia ran in, shaking rain from her umbrella, and breathed a sigh of relief. Inside the bookshop it smelled like old paper, ink, and leather book covers. Tall, wooden bookcases were crammed full of used books as well as new books written by local authors. Antique library tables held interesting displays and vintage leather club chairs were scattered about so you could sit a spell and do some reading.

Lois Chamberlain, the owner and a former librarian, was at her usual place, hunched over the front desk. She was a compact woman, late fifties, wearing a purple shawl and bright-red half-glasses. Her long gray hair was plaited in a single braid that extended halfway down her back. With her sharp eyes and crinkly smile, she reminded Theodosia of one of the traditional low-country wise women who knew just when and where to gather healing herbs and tender roots in the forest.

Lois looked up and smiled as Theodosia approached her desk.

"Rainy out there," Lois said. "Bad for business. Keeps the tourists indoors."

"Hopefully this weather won't last all week."

"It will because this Thursday I'm supposed to have a booth at an outdoor bookfair over in Columbia." Lois rapped her knuckles against the front desk and said, "What can I do for you?"

"What do you know about flags?" Theodosia asked.

"Not much, but we probably have several books about them."

"From the Revolutionary War era?"

Lois's chair creaked as she stood up. "That could be tricky, but let's go take a look."

Theodosia was in luck. Lois found two separate books about Revolutionary War uniforms, battle dress, and flags.

"I need to purchase these books," Theodosia said.

"You're welcome to borrow them."

"No, I want to buy them. It's important."

"Well, let me at least wrap them in plastic. Since it's raining cats and dogs out there."

* * *

"Hurry up, we're really getting busy," Drayton called to Theodosia the minute she stepped through the front door.

Theodosia glanced around the tea shop. Only four tables were occupied and none of the guests looked particularly anxious or irritable. They nibbled scones and sipped cups of tea, seemingly enjoying their respite from the inclement weather.

Theodosia held up an index finger. "Give me one more minute."

She disappeared behind the celadon velvet curtains that separated the tea room proper from the kitchen and her own small office. She tossed her purse on her messy desk and dumped the two books alongside it. She turned, ready to get back to work, and then stopped and glanced back at the books.

Just one quick peek. What could it hurt?

Theodosia flipped through the book entitled *Emblems of the American Revolution*. When she got to the chapter on flags, she scanned the illustrations and photos and carefully read the captions. The fact that all the flags were homespun and hand-sewn gave them a resolute do-or-die feel. And the more Theodosia studied the flags, the more she had the sense that she was looking at something remarkable, something that carried a great deal of spiritual significance.

Yes, it took only a few pages and Theodosia was hooked.

6

The tea sandwich you mentioned that was sort of up in the air," Theodosia said. "Have you settled on a particular filling?" She stood in the doorway, looking in at their postage-stamp kitchen. It was remarkable that Haley functioned so well in there. Theodosia was well aware of the space constraints and figured the heat from the oven and dishwasher would drive her bonkers. But Haley loved it. Wouldn't have it any other way. Didn't want to remodel.

"I'm just finishing that now," Haley said. She stirred a cream cheese mixture in a silver bowl, tossed in a cup of chopped almonds, and stirred some more.

"So what is the filling exactly? I don't want to keep our luncheon guests guessing."

"Just my basic cream cheese, green olive, and almond mixture," Haley said. She gave it a couple more quick stirs and then tapped her spoon against the rim of the bowl. "There. Done."

"And you're spreading it on . . . ?"

"White sandwich bread. But you know I always keep my bread frozen so I get a nice clean cut." Haley grabbed a loaf of bread from the freezer and dealt the slices out onto the counter. "I spread my mixture on the bread while it's still frozen, pop on a top piece, and trim the crusts. The mixture stays cool while the bread thaws out nicely in about four or five minutes." Haley explained her technique as she worked. "See how crisp the cut is?" she said as she sliced the sandwich into four triangles. "I use frozen bread when I do double stackers, too."

"Are you doing a double stacker tea sandwich today?"

"I could. Maybe do three slices of bread with cheese spread between the top two slices and ham on the bottom."

"I love it," Theodosia said.

Just then the oven bell dinged loudly.

Haley peered in. "Lemon scones are done."

Out in the tea room Theodosia seated a few more customers and took their orders for tea.

"Table six is asking for Japanese green tea," Theodosia told Drayton.

"Good. I've been itching for a chance to brew a pot of Gyokuro."

Like Haley, his hands worked efficiently as he talked. "A measured scoop and a pinch for the pot. Then we steep for about two minutes."

"Have you gotten over your nervousness about your home being photographed?"

"Not a bit. In fact, I'm working myself into a mad panic over it," Drayton said in a pleasant voice.

"When the idea was first presented, you were so pleased. We all were. Aunt Libby even wanted to come and watch the photo shoot."

Drayton bobbled his head back and forth. "I know. I was bubbling over with unbridled enthusiasm as well when *Southern Interiors Magazine* first called. But now, the idea of opening up my home to strangers—and magazine readers—simply paralyzes me."

"Then don't do it."

"I *have* to do it, Theo," Drayton said with intensity. "I made a *commitment*. You know as well as I do that a gentleman never goes back on his word."

"Then I must not know any gentlemen," Haley said. She hurried toward them, carrying a silver tray heaped with a dozen fresh-baked lemon scones, each one dripping with creamy white frosting. "Because the guys I know are forever going back on their word."

"Then they are not gentlemen," Drayton said.

Haley smiled sweetly at him. "Well . . . duh."

The take-out orders kept coming. Customers and inn-keepers alike—mostly from local hotels and B and Bs—called in droves to order lunches. Haley made tea sandwiches and wrapped scones like crazy while Drayton poured to-go tea orders into indigo-blue paper cups and snapped on the tops. Needless to say, there was a steady stream of pickups at the front counter.

At one o'clock, Burt Tidwell came shuffling in. He wore a strange-looking raincoat that could have been cut from oilcloth or sailcloth and then coated with wax. Whatever it was, water had beaded up on it to keep him relatively dry.

"Taking time out from your investigation?" Theodosia asked him.

Tidwell gave a noncommittal grunt.

"Interested in a spot of lunch then?" Theodosia led him to the small table near the stone fireplace and waited while he got seated. "I'll have to run and grab whatever from the kitchen. We've been doing take-out orders like mad so I can't make any promises about what Haley has left."

"No problem," Tidwell said.

Theodosia went into the kitchen, placed two ham and cheese tea sandwiches on a plate, and then added a lemon scone and a small glass bowl of Devonshire cream. She stopped at the front counter and grabbed a pot of Yunnan tea. The flavor of the tea was slightly peppery, much like Tidwell's general disposition.

Setting everything down on his table, Theodosia watched him dig in. Since this luncheon was gratis— Tidwell never paid for anything, never *offered* to pay— she decided it wouldn't be too forward to ask him a few questions.

"It's been almost twenty-four hours since the crash," Theodosia said. "Have you dug up any evidence?"

"There's not a lot to go on. The explosion pretty much took care of any fingerprints or trace evidence."

"Then do you have any suspects, anyone under suspicion?"

Tidwell nodded as he pushed the remains of his first sandwich into his mouth. "A few, yes. But what I really need is for you to give me a few more details concerning the crash."

"I don't know what to tell you," Theodosia said.

"That's never stopped you before."

Touché.

"Okay . . ." Theodosia thought for a few moments. "The whole incident had an almost dreamlike quality about it. I mean, there we were in this gently swaying basket, rising slowly up toward the clouds, almost no sound at all, and suddenly this horrible buzzing thing came out of no-where."

"No," Tidwell said. "It came out of somewhere. Which way were you facing when you first became aware of the drone?"

"I remember seeing the dog park, so I must have been facing . . . what? North?"

"So perhaps the drone came from south of the park?"

"What would be back there?" Theodosia asked.

"Parking lot set behind a row of trees."

"So you're thinking that the drone operator wasn't

someone who was part of the hot-air balloon rally. Not a spectator."

"Not a friendly participant anyway," Tidwell said.

"Anybody could have been back there," Theodosia said. "It's a one-in-a-million shot."

"I'm sure Charleston PD can narrow our suspect list down to a more manageable number than that." Tidwell picked up his second sandwich and took an enormous bite.

"Tell me about possible suspects," Theodosia said.

"There were a few people at odds with the victim."

"Victims," Theodosia said. "Three people were killed."

"Yes, but only one victim has garnered our attention so far," Tidwell said.

"Don Kingsley," Theodosia said. She decided Kingsley had to be the main target since Tod Slawson was so rabid about the missing flag. "So who are you looking at? Disgruntled coworkers? Business rivals?"

"Interesting you should ask. I just spent an hour asking Tawney Kingsley those same pertinent questions about her deceased husband."

"The wife?" There had been a small mention of Tawney in this morning's paper and now her name was starting to ring a bell. "Does she have something to do with a brand-new bed-and-breakfast?"

"Tawney Kingsley has recently purchased the Graham-Royce Mansion over on Tradd Street," Tidwell said.

"Fancy neighborhood." Then, fishing for a few more details, Theodosia said, "I imagine she's in serious mourning?"

"More like bright and cheery as a morning glory," Tidwell replied. "The newly minted Widow Kingsley did not appear to be shedding a great deal of tears."

"That's . . . interesting." *Especially since her husband was just killed.*

"As for the newly purchased mansion, it would appear

that Mrs. Kingsley is giving it a much needed spit and polish," Tidwell said.

"I think the place was in pretty tough shape," Theodosia said.

"Not anymore it's not. She's renovating her new white elephant from top to bottom."

"I'd guess that mansion is about a block away from the Featherbed House," Theodosia said.

Tidwell took a sip of tea and puckered his lips. "About that."

Theodosia couldn't help but make a rather strange, convoluted connection. *The wife of a murdered man, a man who had in his possession a priceless flag, is opening a fancy B and B near the Featherbed House. And the owner of the Featherbed House is the girlfriend of a man who works at SyncSoft. Why does that seem strange to me? A little too close for comfort?*

Theodosia decided to tuck this information away for now and ask Tidwell about the flag.

"What can you tell me about this valuable Navy Jack that Mr. Kingsley had in his possession?"

Tidwell's brows pinched together. "How do you know about the missing flag?"

"For one thing, a young man was running around last night like a chicken on crack cocaine crying about a flag. Then Tod Slawson came storming in here this morning, wanting to squeeze Drayton and me on details of the crash. When we weren't exactly forthcoming, he mentioned the Navy flag, the Navy Jack."

"Alright, yes. The first inkling I had that the flag was missing was when I followed up with that foppish fellow Charles Townsend. He was . . . is, apparently, Don Kingsley's private assistant and possibly his curator."

"Don Kingsley has a museum?" Theodosia asked.

"More like a dedicated series of rooms in his home. All filled with paintings and documents and such."

"And this Revolutionary War flag, if that's what it really is, is truly missing?"

"It would appear so," Tidwell said. He nibbled a bite of scone then topped it with an extra pouf of Devonshire cream.

"Do you think someone killed Donald Kingsley over the flag?"

"That was my initial gut feeling. The flag is apparently worth a great deal of money. We're talking in the millions."

"Then you don't just have a triple homicide on your hands," Theodosia said. "If Don Kingsley possessed this flag, was intending to auction it off to the highest bidder, and now it's gone missing, you're looking at a robbery, too."

"Aren't you the astute amateur detective," Tidwell said.

Theodosia smiled at him. "Aren't I just?"

7

Did Tidwell pay for his luncheon?" Haley asked. She'd just emerged from the kitchen and was wiping her hands on a blue tea towel. Her outfit consisted of a white chef's jacket over black leggings. Her feet were shod in Keds high-tops that she claimed helped maintain her superior cooking mojo.

"He did not pay," Theodosia said. "It turned out to be a sort of quid pro quo."

"Meaning you actually pried some information out of him?" Drayton asked.

There were still two tables of guests left, so Theodosia dropped her voice to a lower pitch. "A few details, yes."

Theodosia and Haley crowded up against the counter so they could confer with Drayton.

"Tidwell had a talk with Tawney Kingsley, the widow," Theodosia told them.

"They were divorced?" Haley asked.

"Not yet," Theodosia said.

Drayton inhaled sharply. "Then she stands to inherit."

"Maybe she does," Theodosia said.

"Which makes her a serious suspect," Haley said. She grinned and slapped her hand down hard against the counter. "Man, I love this crazy stuff."

Drayton's right eyebrow rose in a questioning quiver. It was one of his unique talents. "You mean you *enjoy* murder?"

Haley tried to backpedal fast. "Well, no. More like the investigating part."

"We're not investigating," Drayton said, shooting a warning look in Theodosia's direction.

"Not yet," Haley muttered under her breath.

"Haley," Theodosia said, suddenly eager to change the subject until she'd had time to ruminate on whether to get involved or not. "What have you come up with for our Nancy Drew Tea?"

"I was thinking ginger scones . . ." Haley began.

"Perfect," Drayton said. "We can also serve cardamom tea."

"Along with what else?" Theodosia asked.

"The middle part of the menu is still a little iffy—it depends on what kind of fresh crabmeat or lobster I can source—but I was thinking dark chocolate cake pops for dessert."

"At least we're halfway there," Drayton said. "The sugary part anyway."

"I've got most of the decorations handled," Theodosia said. "And Haley is working on our centerpieces."

"Yes, I've been wondering about those. What exactly are they?" Drayton asked.

"It's a secret," Haley said.

"You'll have to ask our psychic," Theodosia said to Drayton.

Haley gave a little shiver. "Ooh, I'm really intrigued by this psychic we've got coming in."

"Madame Poporov," Theodosia said. Instead of relying on ESP or mental telepathy, she'd found the psychic the old-fashioned way—through the woman's website.

"I understand Madame Poporov claims to be a displaced Lithuanian royal," Haley said.

"But of course she is," Drayton said with a wry smile.

"Even if she's not of royal blood, do you think she's a genuine psychic?" Haley asked.

"There's no such thing as psychics," Drayton said. "It's all hocus-pocus and slick chicanery."

"Me, I'm reserving judgment," Haley said.

"You must want to ask her something." Drayton's eyes twinkled.

"Maybe."

"Romance-wise?"

"Hey, buster, that's between me and the psychic."

When it got to be the tail end of afternoon tea, Theodosia strolled into the kitchen. "How many scones do we have left?" she asked.

Haley glanced around. "Um, six lemon scones and two—no, just one because I ate it—strawberry scone."

"But enough for a nice basket."

"Maybe if you stick in a jar of jam to round things out."

Theodosia packed the remaining scones into a clear plastic bag, placed it in a wicker basket, and added a jar of jam and a jar of honey. She'd decided to take a gift basket over to the Graham-Royce Mansion and introduce herself to Tawney Kingsley. For some reason, Tidwell's description of the woman had intrigued her. There was also the chance she could scrounge up a little more information.

It was still damp and cold when Theodosia hit the streets. She was bundled up in her raincoat and had found a red paisley scarf that she'd tied babushka-style around her head. With her wicker basket, she figured she looked like Little Red Riding Hood's crazy aunt out for an afternoon jaunt.

When Theodosia was a half block away from the Graham-Royce Mansion, she noticed a woman exit the very same mansion she was heading toward. The woman had a swirl of dark hair, looked fairly young, and appeared to have an excellent figure, though she had a pink shawl wrapped around her shoulders and upper body. Her head was bent forward, probably because she was being buffeted so hard by the wind, and she looked perplexed. Maybe even a little upset.

Interesting. I wonder who she is?

Theodosia climbed the steps of the mansion and stood on the wide veranda, watching the woman disappear down the block. Then she focused on the mansion itself. It was built in the Classical Revival style, meaning a little bit Grecian and a little bit Roman, with large heavy columns and a fair amount of ornamental statuary.

When Theodosia reached out and rang the buzzer, she heard faint music coming from inside. Classical music, light and sweet. Debussy perhaps?

Seconds later, Tawney Kingsley flung open the door with a surprised look on her face. "Hello," she said, as if she hadn't expected to see another caller quite so soon. Tawney was thin, slightly bug-eyed, and looked to be on the fine edge of hyper. She also had the shortest, blondest hair Theodosia had ever seen. It was so short it reminded Theodosia of the skinned, almost shaved heads that the French Resistance had bestowed upon the women who'd collaborated with the Nazis during World War II.

When Theodosia introduced herself, Tawney gave a knowing nod.

"I do know who you are. You own that charming little tea shop over on Church Street. The Indigo Tea Shop."

"Yes and I've come to offer my condolences," Theodosia said. "I was one of the witnesses yesterday. I saw the whole thing happen." She held the basket out. "This is a small offering and certainly can't make up for your sadness, but I've brought you some scones."

"Thank you so much," Tawney said as she accepted the basket. "Won't you come in?"

I'd love to.

Theodosia followed Tawney inside.

"It's terribly sad about Donald," Tawney said as she led Theodosia down a hallway and into a small room that was half-furnished. "But the truth of the matter is, we were in the process of dissolving our marriage. We hadn't really been . . . what you'd call *together* . . . for a number of months."

"I'm sorry to hear that." Theodosia seated herself on a blue velvet sofa, and Tawney draped herself in an easy chair across from her.

"Don't be. We were both getting along okay. I have my mansion to renovate and Donald had his company." Tawney stopped as a perplexed expression crossed her face. "Now I suppose the company will have to go on without him."

"I understand there might be a problem with the company," Theodosia said. *I may as well dive right in.*

Tawney stared at her with huge eyes. "Why would you say that?"

"There was a sidebar article in this morning's paper . . ."

"I haven't paid much attention to the media. What did it say?"

"The article mentioned that some of SyncSoft's money seems to have disappeared."

"Money," Tawney said slowly, letting the word roll off her tongue as if this was a completely new concept to her.

"Yes, they're missing a rather tidy pool of investor funds. Or maybe it was working capital. I'm not exactly sure. Maybe you'd know better?"

"I don't know a single thing about their corporate finances. But . . ." Tawney narrowed her eyes in a critical, almost analytical manner. "I wouldn't put it past Donald to siphon off money for his own foolish pursuits. And to keep me from getting my fair share in a divorce settlement." She shrugged. "But now Donald is dead. And, as the old maxim goes, you can't take it with you."

"So now he's left it all behind," Theodosia said. *For you?*

"Not my problem, not my doing."

Isn't it? Theodosia wondered. *Or is it possible you could have masterminded that drone attack all by yourself?* Tawney struck her as being fairly clever with the potential to be manipulative—a far cry from the little girl attitude she tried to project.

"Besides offering my condolences, I wanted to ask you about the missing flag," Theodosia said.

"That's so interesting. The woman who was here just before you wanted to know about the flag as well."

"I saw someone on your front walk . . ." Theodosia said in an encouraging tone. Maybe Tawney would fill in the blanks?

"That was Dr. Brooklyn Vance," Tawney said. "She represents a museum that also wanted to bid on the flag."

"I'm guessing she was upset when you told her that it's disappeared?" *Because she sure looked upset. Or maybe just befuddled.*

"Oh, Dr. Vance already knew it was missing. Mostly she just wanted to ask a few polite questions."

"About the flag?" Theodosia said.

"About what will happen if the flag should turn up."

"Like, will it still be for sale?" Theodosia said. "And who will be in charge of selling it or auctioning it off?"

"Those questions came up, yes. But in an easygoing manner. Dr. Vance struck me as being smart and highly cultured. Quite dedicated to her job at the museum."

"Which museum is she affiliated with?"

"It's in North Carolina." Tawney looked around with a helpless glance. "I put her card somewhere."

"Getting back to the flag. You really don't know what happened to it?" Theodosia asked. "Perhaps your husband removed it from his home and placed it in a lockbox for safekeeping. Maybe it's not really missing at all."

Tawney's eyes grew larger. "I already pointed the police in the direction of First Security where Donald did his private banking. They checked his lockbox and the flag isn't there. It's not at his country house, either. In fact, no one seems to know where the flag disappeared to."

"Do you believe it was stolen from your husband's home yesterday?" Theodosia wondered if the flag had gone missing before or after the balloon crash. Or during. If it happened during the balloon flight, maybe two people were involved. A stone-cold killer *and* a master thief.

"Stolen from his home, yes. That's what Donald's assistant, Charles Townsend, claims. That's what I've been told by the police."

"So you have no idea at all about the flag's possible whereabouts?"

Tawney shook her head. "I've never even laid eyes on it."

The doorbell rang, a loud *briiiing* that reverberated throughout the entire downstairs.

Tawney popped up from her chair. "Excuse me."

Two minutes later she was back with a deliveryman who wheeled in an enormous package wrapped in brown paper. It looked like it might be an oil painting or large mirror.

Tawney signed for it, thanked the deliveryman, and then gave a little giggle. "I'm so excited it finally arrived. Want to take a peek?" she asked Theodosia.

"Why not?"

Tawney proceeded to rip the paper away from the painting or whatever it was. When the wrapping was half off, she grinned and beckoned with her fingers. "Come closer and take a look."

It was a stained glass window—an enormous stained glass window that must have cost a small fortune to create.

"It's gorgeous," Theodosia said. And it was. The window depicted birds and trees in the foreground and a small French village in the background. The colors were predominantly gold, yellow, and amber.

"Custom made to grace my main salon."

"You sure are pulling out all the stops here."

"You have no idea," Tawney said. She grabbed a thick roll of wallpaper off a sofa table and unfurled it. "Look at this. Hand-painted wallpaper from France."

"That's amazing," Theodosia said as she studied hand-dabbed swirls on a background of . . . was that silk? Yes, it was.

"And I've ordered eiderdown beds from Switzerland, genuine Art Nouveau lamps from Paris, and Pratesi sheets and towels."

"You're a veritable United Nations of décor. Visitors to Charleston will be beating a path to your door," Theodosia said.

"They will because I'm going to create Charleston's first-ever six-star B and B. There won't be any other hotel, guest house, or B and B that can touch it for first-class service and luxury."

"When do you intend to open for business?"

Tawney made a face. "Unfortunately, not until September. There's a ton of work still to be done in the upstairs bedrooms. Plumbing for the spa tubs, heated towel racks, skylights, more stained glass, all the little niceties."

Theodosia wondered exactly how Tawney was going to pay for all of this. Was she wealthy in her own right? Or—and this would be the kicker—had the SyncSoft money somehow found its way into Tawney's pocket? Or was about to? And if Tawney was using SyncSoft money, it meant she could have had a hand in the death of her husband as well as his client and balloon pilot.

"What are you going to call this place?" Theodosia asked as she looked around. "Will you be keeping the name Graham-Royce Mansion or . . . ?" Her eyes landed on Tawney's shoes. Purple suede uppers, bright-red soles. Christian Louboutin. Known simply, by ladies-who-lunch, as Louboutins.

"I'm calling it Château Roubine after my favorite wine château in Provence," Tawney said. "I feel that particular name conveys class, elegance, and luxury. After all, I desire only the best."

Theodosia nodded. "I can see that."

"Not a single guest amenity will be spared."

"Does that mean you'll have dog-friendly rooms, like several of the other B and Bs?"

Tawney frowned. "Dog-friendly? Absolutely not."

Back on the sidewalk, Theodosia decided to give Drayton a call at the tea shop. She struggled to dial the number with one hand as she fought pounding gusts of wind and rain that threatened to rip her umbrella right out of her hand.

When Drayton answered, she said, "How would you like to come to my house for dinner tonight?"

Drayton was instantly on alert. "What's wrong?"

"Nothing's wrong. I just want to talk. Tell you about my meeting with Tawney Kingsley and get your take on a couple of things."

"Alright then, that does sound lovely. What time do you want me to darken your doorstep?"

"Seven?"

"I look forward to it."

8

❧

Hoppin' John was a sort of Southern chowder-soup-stew that everyone and his brother-in-law had a favorite family recipe for. Well, Theodosia had her own recipe as well, handed down from her Aunt Libby. And she figured it was the perfect antidote to the cool, rainy weather that had swooshed in, stalled out, and seemed determined to hunker over Charleston for a while. So she'd chopped celery, onions, a bell pepper, and garlic, and sautéed it with some thick-cut bacon in a pan.

Now, as her black-eyed peas and Carolina Gold rice bubbled in the mixture and offered up a tantalizing aroma, she buzzed about her kitchen, finishing up the salad. As she worked, Theodosia heard the rain beating down and could almost feel her little house utter the occasional creak and groan.

"I'll bet Mrs. Barry didn't take you for a very long walk today, did she?" Theodosia said to Earl Grey. Mrs. Barry was a retired school teacher and the neighborhood dog walker. Earl Grey was Theodosia's dog, but really her roommate, constant companion, and jogging partner. He was basically a Heinz 57 dog, but Theodosia had decided Earl Grey was a nice medley of dalmatian and Labrador. So . . . a "Dalbrador."

"Did you wear your plaid coat?" Theodosia asked. Then she spotted his coat folded across the back of one of the kitchen chairs. Along with a note from Mrs. Barry.

Theodosia smiled as she read it: *Short walk today, Earl Grey unhappy about paws getting wet. Be back tomorrow. Mrs. B.*

The phone rang while Theodosia was fixing dinner.

Is Drayton calling to cancel?

No, it was Pete Riley, her "amour du jour" and one of Tidwell's assistant detectives, calling from Minneapolis.

"Theo," he said.

"Riley," she said, sounding pleased. That was how they addressed each other. He called her Theo and she called him Riley. *Hey, Riley, pick up a bottle of wine, will you? Want to go to a jazz concert this Saturday, Riley?* It suited him. Actually, it suited both of them.

"I didn't think you were going to call until tomorrow night," Theodosia said. He'd only been gone two days, but she was secretly pleased that she was talking to him now.

"Would you believe I miss you?" Riley asked. He sounded as intense as he looked. Tall, with an aristocratic nose and cheekbones, cobalt blue eyes. Quite a hunk.

"I certainly hope you do." Theodosia felt a little thrill just hearing the sound of his voice. "How's your seminar going?"

"It's interesting," Riley said. But he actually sounded so disinterested he was practically stifling a yawn.

"That bad?"

"Ah, it's just repetitive. Nothing I don't already know or couldn't get from reading a book."

"Or from practical experience?" Theodosia said.

"Well, I did attend a two-hour-long seminar today on mitochondrial DNA."

"How was that?"

"As exciting as the previous lecture on mass spectrometry. Which means I didn't understand a single word."

"That's what you've got the lab rats for," Theodosia said. "Let the crime scene guys do the tricky analysis once you find some evidence and catch the bad guys."

"Say now, I heard via the grapevine that you were involved in some major excitement yesterday."

"The hot-air balloon crash. You know about that?" Theodosia asked.

"I know *you* were there."

He'd caught her off guard. "But I . . ."

"Don't try to deny it, since the rumor mill has already been cranking away."

"I was there alright, but luckily not in the balloon that was shot down."

"Is that what happened?" Pete asked. "I thought it was a drone hit and run."

"Same thing," Theodosia said.

When Theodosia finally said goodbye to Pete Riley, she realized that time was starting to slip away from her. So she ran around her kitchen like a madwoman, grabbing plates, bowls, silverware, and wineglasses. She set it all out on her dining room table, added a pair of tall white candles, touched a match to them, and heaved a sigh of relief.

Theodosia's dining room, which was basically a nice-sized passageway between the living room and the kitchen, was accented with a glass-front cabinet that contained some of her treasures—teapots from her extensive collection, a few silver hotel water pitchers, Chinese vases, and a classic English mantle clock.

But it was her living room that was really her pride and joy. Wood-burning fireplace, beveled cypress walls, beamed ceiling, and a polished wood floor. To cozy up this picture-perfect room even more, she'd added damask- and chintz-covered furniture, a blue-and-gold Aubusson carpet, and a few oil paintings hung on the walls for a finishing touch.

The house itself was small and compact, built in a classic Tudor style with arched doors, cross gables, and a small turret. Rough cedar roof tiles gave it a thatched look, much like a traditional Hansel and Gretel cottage.

BANG, BANG, BANG.

As Earl Grey let out a long woof, Theodosia said, "Drayton."

She hurried to the front door and let him in.

"You made it," Theodosia said as Drayton, wearing a Burberry cap and long black raincoat, stepped inside. Earl Grey gave him a quick sniff, his doggy once-over, and then walked away. He'd met Drayton lots of times. If Drayton hadn't stashed treats in his coat pocket or brought along his dog, Honey Bee, then Earl Grey wasn't much interested.

"I made it by the skin of my teeth. The rain's coming down harder than ever now." Drayton slipped out of his raincoat and hung it on a brass coatrack. He held up his collapsed umbrella, which looked like a bedraggled black bat, and said, "This is going to drip everywhere."

"Don't worry about it," Theodosia said. The floor in her small foyer was paved with antique bricks, so no harm there.

"And I would have stopped to buy a sponge cake, but it probably would have sopped up all this rain. I tell you, this storm seems to be getting progressively worse," Drayton said as he wandered into the living room and breathed a sigh of relief. "Early hurricane warnings and all that. Going to be with us for at least a few days." He stopped, lifted his nose like a hungry coyote, and said, "Please tell me what smells so delightful?"

"I made hoppin' John."

"Be still my heart. You really did?"

"I labored over a hot stove just for you. Are you hungry? Do you want to eat right away?"

"Are you serious? I'm famished."

In the kitchen, Theodosia picked up a wooden spoon, gave her hoppin' John a final stir, and took a taste. Good. Actually better than good. "This is definitely ready to serve," she told Drayton. "Shall we open a bottle of wine to go with it?"

"Perhaps a cabernet?" Drayton said.

Theodosia grabbed two bottles from her wine rack. "I've got a côtes du rhône red and a nice cabernet from Caymus Vineyards in California. Your choice."

"Mmm, the côtes du rhône please." Drayton grabbed it and was already working the wine opener into the cork. "I believe *Wine Spectator* gave this something like ninety-seven points."

They sat down at the dining room table to a mixed green salad with blue cheese and golden beets, bowls of steaming hot hoppin' John, and glasses of red wine.

"Delicious," Drayton proclaimed.

"The wine, the salad, or the hoppin' John?" Theodosia asked.

"Everything! You are a secret gourmet cook."

"Shh, don't tell Haley."

As they enjoyed their dinner, Theodosia told Drayton all about her earlier visit with Tawney Kingsley. She described the huge mansion and the fantastic renovations the woman had planned.

"I tell you, Drayton, Tawney's got hand-painted wallpaper from France, a stained glass window, Swiss beds, Pratesi linens, and she's even ordered heated towel racks. Talk about glam!"

"More like expensive first-class taste. It sounds as if

Tawney wants to recreate the Doge's Palace or Versailles. Tell me, can she really afford this over-the-top décor?"

"That's the interesting thing," Theodosia said. "I figure Tawney is either enormously wealthy in her own right or she must have siphoned off some serious money from SyncSoft."

Drayton stopped, his spoon in midair. "You think Tawney *stole* money from her husband's company and then murdered him when she was found out?"

"I don't know. It's a theory, albeit a shaky one."

"Maybe you could run a Dun & Bradstreet to check on the free-spending Mrs. Kingsley. It might give you a more accurate picture of her finances."

"That's not a bad idea. Oh, and there was another woman, a Dr. somebody Vance, who was also there inquiring about the flag," Theodosia said.

"You talked to this woman, too?"

"Afraid not. She was rushing down the sidewalk just as I showed up. I only caught a quick glimpse of her."

"Was this woman another buyer? Or bidder?"

"Tawney said yes. Of course Tawney also denied any knowledge about her husband's flag. Claimed she's never laid eyes on it."

Drayton took a sip of wine. "Did you believe her?"

"I kind of did. Tawney's got this wide-eyed, childlike quality about her. She makes you want to believe."

"Except you think she could have also stolen money from SyncSoft," Drayton said.

"Well. There is that."

"Money and flag aside, is there any chance Tawney could have been the one who brought down the balloon?"

Theodosia shuddered. "I thought about that—and I was suspicious of her at first. But now I've pretty much discarded that idea. It would mean Tawney Kingsley is a cold, calculating woman with ice water running through her veins."

"There *are* female killers," Drayton said. "Though

most of them become so by dint of killing a husband or boyfriend." The corners of his mouth twisted up in a semi-smile. "They keep it in the family."

"And I'm so glad you mentioned that."

Drayton picked up the bottle of wine, ready to pour Theodosia another glass. "A refill for you?"

Theodosia held up her hand. "None for me, thanks."

Drayton refreshed his own glass, then said, "Do you think a fancy new B and B so close to the Featherbed House will have an impact on Angie's business?"

"I'm not sure," Theodosia said. "The newness of Tawney's B and B might pull customers away initially, but over the long haul I think it will be fine. There are quite a few B and Bs and guest houses in the Historic District already. They compete with one another, but they also seem to get along quite well, given there's enough business for everyone. Sometimes the B and Bs get together and advertise."

"Definitely good camaraderie," Drayton said.

They talked awhile longer, mostly about the tea events they had coming up later that week. When they were finished, they cleared away the dishes and carried them into the kitchen.

"If you want to fix us a pot of tea, I'll go start a fire," Theodosia said.

"Perhaps a dessert tea?"

"There's a tin of Grand Keemun in the cupboard."

"Perfect," Drayton said.

Theodosia was on her hands and knees in front of the fireplace, arranging a pile of kindling when the doorbell did its ding-ding. Drayton was still in the kitchen fixing a pot of tea.

"Somebody's here," Theodosia yelled loud enough for Drayton to hear. Her kindling was starting to burn nicely so she placed two small logs on top of it.

"Who could possibly be roaming around outside in

BROKEN BONE CHINA   59

this dreadful weather?" Drayton called back to her from the kitchen. He let loose a strange chortle. "Besides me."

Now Earl Grey started barking his head off. "ARK, ARK, ARK!"

"Shh, that's enough," Theodosia said as she hurried to the front door and pressed her nose against the lead-paned window to look out. "My goodness, it's Angie Congdon!" Angie was the proprietor of the Featherbed House, the B and B they'd just been talking about. Her showing up at this time of night, and in this horrific weather, was a huge surprise.

Pulling the door wide open, Theodosia said, "Angie, you must be soaked to the bone from being out in this rain. Come on in."

Angie Congdon stepped across the threshold into the small entryway. Her strawberry-blond hair was plastered against her head, and her slim figure was camouflaged by a bulky tan raincoat.

Standing there, ready to take Angie's coat, Theodosia was suddenly aware of the look of consternation on Angie's face. "Angie, what's wrong?"

"Everything," Angie said, her voice quavering. "I . . . I think I might need your help." Now Angie clutched anxiously at Theodosia's hand. "Or at least your good advice."

"What's happened?"

"It's about the hot-air balloon that crashed yesterday," Angie stammered. "I read in the newspaper that you were there. Serving tea. And that you witnessed the crash."

"Drayton and I were both there," Theodosia said. "We had the unfortunate luck of seeing the drone dive directly into the hot-air balloon and then getting rocked, literally rocked, by the explosion."

"That's why I'm here," Angie said. She stood there, dripping water on the brick floor, wringing her hands as if in utter anguish. "The police just took Harold in for questioning."

"Harold, your boyfriend?" Theodosia said, just as Drayton walked into the living room carrying a large silver tray laden with a teapot and three rattling teacups.

"Harold's my fiancé," Angie said. "We got engaged last week."

"Then congratulations are in order," Drayton said in a hearty voice. He set the tea tray down on a leather bolster and smiled broadly. He'd completely missed the part about Harold being hauled in for questioning.

"It's not exactly a congratulatory moment," Angie said to him as she slipped out of her coat and handed it to Theodosia.

"The police just took Harold in," Theodosia quickly explained.

"Why on earth would they do that?" Drayton asked.

"Come in and sit down," Theodosia said. "We'll warm you up with some nice hot tea and you can tell us all about it."

Angie collapsed into a wing chair while Theodosia and Drayton fussed with the tea. When everyone was seated and had a cup of tea on their lap, Theodosia said, "Okay, tell us why the police are questioning Harold."

Angie grimaced. "Two years ago Harold bought a drone. It was a spur-of-the-moment thing, a lark. They were starting to be all the rage and he just wanted to have fun with it. After a while, the newness wore off and he stashed the drone in my basement. I don't think he's even thought about it—or looked at it—in over a year. But after that terrible hot-air balloon crash yesterday, the police went through all the records of local companies that sold drones. Eventually, they hit on Harold's name and came calling."

"They're questioning *everyone* who bought a drone? That doesn't seem efficient," Drayton said. "There could be hundreds of buyers. Thousands."

"The problem is, Harold *works* at SyncSoft," Angie said. "So the police are a little more than fifty percent suspicious that it could have been Harold's drone that brought down the hot-air balloon."

"What!" Drayton cried. His teacup quivered in its saucer and he wasn't smiling anymore. Suddenly, he looked dead serious.

"You'd better tell us all about Harold and his drone," Theodosia said. "And his job at SyncSoft. Start from the beginning. And don't leave out a single thing."

9

❧

Tuesday morning and Theodosia and Drayton were standing at the front counter, still puzzling about Harold being taken in for questioning.

"Wait a minute," Haley said. She waved both hands in the air as if to interrupt them. "You're talking about Angie's boyfriend, Harold?"

"He's not her boyfriend anymore. He's her fiancé," Drayton said.

"They got engaged?" Haley asked.

"That's right," Theodosia said. "And now poor Harold's being questioned about the hot-air balloon crash because he happens to own a drone and works at SyncSoft."

"Harold *Affolter*?" Haley said.

"That's the Harold we've been talking about, yes," Drayton said. He sounded slightly annoyed with her.

"Harold is, like, your basic little lamb," Haley said. "I worked with him when we catered the Valentine's Day brunch at the Featherbed House. You know, when we did the chocolate scones and the chicken salad sandwiches? I don't think Harold is capable of hurting a fly."

"That's not what the police are saying," Theodosia said.

"Or the NTSB," Drayton added.

Haley put a hand to her mouth. "You're telling me that Harold's in serious trouble? But why?"

"Because of what looks like an amazing coincidence," Theodosia said. "Think about it. Harold owns a drone *and* he works at SyncSoft."

Haley nodded. "Something to do with marketing."

"Actually, he's an assistant product manager. And apparently very good at his job," Theodosia said. She glanced at Drayton and then continued. "But according to Angie, Harold spotted some sort of design glitch in a new software product just as it was about to go to market."

"That's good, huh?" Haley said. "To catch a problem like that?"

"You'd think so, but when Harold brought it up to his boss he was told to leave it alone," Theodosia said. "To let it go. Harold was so offended at being rebuffed, he took it all the way up the ladder and wrangled a meeting with Don Kingsley, the CEO. But Kingsley pooh-poohed Harold as well. It seems he wanted SyncSoft to be the first out with their new product."

"And that's why the police think Harold caused the crash?" Haley asked.

"That's one theory the police think is quite plausible," Theodosia said. "That Harold tried his best to be a whistle-blower but was ignored."

"The police just assumed that Harold was walking around with this gigantic chip on his shoulder? That he wanted to retaliate for being dissed?" Haley asked. "That's nutty."

"Even so, the police see a connection," Drayton said.

Haley pounded a fist against the table. "But the police are *wrong*."

"They probably are," Theodosia said. "But that doesn't change the facts. Harold is probably going to be questioned repeatedly by the police and may end up persona non grata at work."

"That's why Angie asked Theodosia for help," Drayton said. "Which, I'm afraid, is quite impossible." He gave a helpless shrug. "I mean, our Theo is bright but she's not exactly a criminal attorney or software engineer."

"But Harold's predicament isn't an insurmountable problem," Haley said. She turned toward Theodosia with an impassioned look on her young face. "All you have to do is get your cute little detective boyfriend on the case and have him straighten things out."

"Therein lies another problem," Theodosia said. "My cute little detective boyfriend is out of town right now."

"Out of town where?" Haley asked.

"He's in Minneapolis. There's some sort of big-time forensics conference for non-techs and Pete was selected to represent the Charleston PD."

Haley put her hands on her hips. "Well, you have to get him back here immediately."

"It's not that simple." Theodosia knew that Pete Riley wasn't about to blow off his conference. He was far too dedicated to his job.

"Then what are you going to do?" Haley asked.

"I honestly don't know," Theodosia said. "Angie did ask for my help but . . ."

"Angie's our friend," Haley said. "Which means we *have* to help her."

"Angie asked Theo for help. Not you, not us," Drayton said, but his voice was kind.

"But if Theodosia's involved, aren't we all involved?" Haley asked. "Aren't we a team?"

"I don't think . . ." Theodosia began.

But Drayton interrupted her. "I'm afraid Haley's got you there, Theo. On second thought, she's quite right. We *are* a team."

"And you've already done a little snooping," Haley prompted. "I know you took that basket of scones over to

Tawney Kingsley. So you must have asked her a bunch of questions. I mean, you did, didn't you?"

Drayton made a noise somewhere in the back of his throat. A tentative note of agreement.

Theodosia put an elbow on the table, rested her chin in her hand, and said, "Oh dear."

Theodosia wondered and worried as she readied the tea shop. She checked the highboy and straightened out the dozens of jars of jam, honey, and Devonshire cream that were on display and available for sale. There were also teacups, teapots, wooden honey dippers, tea cozies, and a few tea books.

She studied the wall where sweetgrass baskets, made by their favorite artisan Miss Josette, hung alongside homemade grapevine wreaths that she'd woven with gold gossamer ribbon and hung with teacups.

Looks almost . . . perfect.

But her brain was still in a whirl about helping Angie as she went into the kitchen, grabbed the luncheon menu from Haley, and brought it out to Drayton.

"Maple cream scones and almond muffins," Theodosia said, gazing at him across the counter. "Which tea would you like to pair them with?"

"Let's suggest a chai masala black tea to our guests," Drayton said. "Obviously, they can order anything they'd like, but I think this particular tea will go well with Haley's baked goods."

"I was also thinking of a nice Tippy Yunnan China black tea."

"That also makes an excellent pairing," Drayton said. "I say, you're getting as good at this as I am."

"Oh, I don't think so."

"Did you make up your mind about helping Angie?" Drayton asked.

"Still working on it."

* * *

As soon as Theodosia hung the OPEN sign on the front door, Delaine Dish careened in like a grand duchess driving an Indy car. Dressed to the nines in a nipped-in purple skirt suit with a matching purple fur boa, she bounced off the front counter, caromed off a nearby table, and ended up at a small table next to the window.

Theodosia approached Delaine's table with a friendly "Nice to see you, Delaine."

Delaine waved a hand in front of her face as if she didn't have time for pleasantries. "Isn't this weather *dreadful*! Couldn't you just *die* for all this nasty wind and rain? And the thunder. I tell you, it's driving my poor cats *insane*!" That's how Delaine talked. In italics and exclamation points.

"Has the storm hurt your business?" Delaine was the proprietor of Cotton Duck, one of Charleston's premier boutiques. If you were in the market for a silk blouse, leather slacks, a pashmina, sparkly jewelry, or a formal evening dress, Cotton Duck was the place to go.

Delaine gazed at Theodosia. "Business has been steady. But it's just about *impossible* to get around town. Do you know the storm sewers over on Bay Street actually backed up? And that my invitation to an outdoor luncheon at Linden Gardens was *canceled*!"

"Life's tough," Theodosia said.

"I'll say." Delaine pulled a compact out of her Fendi bag and carefully studied her heart-shaped face. She was dark-haired, dark-eyed, and had (Theodosia thought) the tiniest bits of Botox injected to smooth the lines in her forehead and plump up her lips. Delaine was also silly, frivolous, gossipy, and a tad indiscreet. She was the Scarlett O'Hara of her day.

"Are you meeting someone here for tea?" Theodosia asked.

"No, it's just little old me today, popping in to say how do," Delaine said as she dug into her voluminous bag, scratching around for a lipstick. "I've got Janine watching the store with strict instructions to call me if anything major occurs."

"You mean like a hurricane or a hot-air balloon crash?"

Delaine blinked. Now she was busy applying her Jezebel-red lipstick. "What did you say, dear?" She snapped the cap back on her lipstick with a hard click.

"Never mind. What can I get you?" Two more parties had just come into the tea shop so Theodosia decided she'd better hurry Delaine along.

"I'd love a pot of your delicious peaches and ginger blend along with a small snack. But nothing with carbs. You know me, I'm seriously into brothing so I try to avoid carbs at any cost."

"So no tea sandwiches? No scones?" Theodosia asked.

"Oh, I'll have a scone."

Theodosia waited on the other two tables and seated another group of four that had wandered in. She took orders, gave the tea requests to Drayton, and went into the kitchen to give Haley the food orders.

"Is there such a thing as a no-carb scone?" Theodosia asked.

Haley looked at her like she was crazy. "Are you asking me to mash up some chickpeas and carrots and bake them into scones?"

"It was just a question. Although chickpeas and carrots *are* carbohydrates, are they not?"

"This is about Delaine, isn't it?" Haley said. "She's sitting out there. Being her usual difficult self."

"Yup."

Haley just shook her head and went back to plating orders.

When Theodosia delivered Delaine's tea and scone (fully carbed) to her table, she decided to broach the subject of Tod Slawson.

"Delaine, are you aware that your antiques dealer friend Tod Slawson was angling to purchase a famous flag that just went missing?"

Delaine responded with a dazzling smile. "I don't know anything about a flag, but I'm thrilled that you know my sweet Toddy." She touched an index finger to her cheek. "I didn't think I'd introduced the two of you yet. I was saving that for a special occasion."

"Tod Slawson came stumbling in here yesterday, asking Drayton and I about the hot-air balloon crash where Donald Kingsley was killed."

Delaine wrinkled her nose. "Such a nasty business, that crash."

Theodosia decided to give it a second try and reframe her question. "Did Tod Slawson mention anything to you about trying to buy a Revolutionary War flag?"

Delaine broke off a piece of her scone and slathered on some strawberry jam. "He *might* have mentioned something about it. But I rarely pay attention to other people's business dealings."

Theodosia nearly choked to death. That's all Delaine did was poke her nose into other people's business! It was her main reason for living, her driving force.

Now Delaine had a dreamy look on her face. "Toddy is really quite a wonderful man . . . so kind and considerate. I know it's a little premature to say this, but . . . he might even be husband material."

"Delaine. Seriously?"

Theodosia was gobsmacked. The last time Delaine had gotten divorced, she'd sworn on a stack of designer bags that she'd never walk down a church aisle again. And, truth be told, Delaine didn't have the best track record when it came to choosing dateable men. If you lined up nine perfectly respectable gentlemen and stuck a single

heel-cad-stinker-rat-reprobate in among them, she'd un-
erringly pick the rotten egg.

"You know, a girl can't play the field all her life." Delaine giggled. "Tod Slawson is really quite dreamy. You
might say I'm head over heels."

All Theodosia could manage to stammer out was, "Lots
of luck with that, Delaine."

10

❧

They were smack-dab in the middle of a surprisingly busy lunch service. Thankfully, the rain had abated somewhat, allowing regulars and visitors to make their way to the Indigo Tea Shop. There was even a tour group of eight that had just completed a fascinating (though somewhat damp) ramble down Gateway Walk.

Theodosia was delivering a pot of Puerh black tea and a three-tiered tray filled with scones and tea sandwiches to their table when the front door flew open and Brooklyn Vance walked in.

Theodosia recognized Brooklyn immediately. This was definitely the same woman she'd seen leaving Tawney Kingsley's house yesterday afternoon.

Though Brooklyn had been hunched and huddled against the wind yesterday, Theodosia's impression today was that she moved like a cat. Quiet, contained, and graceful. Her second impression was that Brooklyn looked like a fairly smart cookie. And it wasn't just because she had a

PhD attached to her name. She carried herself well and projected an air of confidence.

Theodosia immediately headed over to greet her.

"Welcome to the Indigo Tea Shop," Theodosia said, and then added, in a friendly aside, "I think we might have passed each other yesterday morning, on the sidewalk outside Tawney Kingsley's place."

Brooklyn gave her a look of keen interest. "We could have. I was completely lost in thought and feeling somewhat upset, so if I was rude to you, I apologize."

"No need for that, we don't know each other and I thought you did look somewhat preoccupied."

"It's this awful hot-air balloon crash . . . and missing flag." Brooklyn made a distracted hand gesture.

"Yes, I spoke to Tawney about some of that right after your visit with her," Theodosia said.

"She's a lovely person. But . . ."

"Yes?" Theodosia said. Brooklyn was looking at her somewhat strangely.

"I'm afraid she wasn't much help." Brooklyn gave a nervous laugh. "That's why I came here today. I understand that you were an eyewitness."

When Theodosia hesitated for a moment, Brooklyn said, "I also spoke with the police and then contacted the Charleston Historical Society, where you came highly recommended by Timothy Neville, their executive director. As did your tea master, Drayton Conneley."

At the mention of Timothy's name, Theodosia gave a warm smile. "Timothy," she said. "He's a dear soul."

"Well, I didn't get *that* impression from him." Brooklyn laughed. "But Mr. Neville was quite polite and amenable to all my questions. And he did mention that you were . . . Let's see, how did he phrase it? The friendly neighborhood sleuth."

"Oh dear."

Tawney grinned. "His words, not mine."

"May I ask what your interest in this is?" Theodosia said, though she already knew. Tawney had mentioned that Brooklyn Vance represented a museum somewhere in North Carolina.

Brooklyn nodded. "I'm looking to purchase the Navy Jack flag, of course. Still hoping to track it down."

"The word on the street is it was stolen," Theodosia said. "During or right after the hot-air balloon crash."

"Yes, but there's stolen and then there's missing."

"That's an interesting way to look at it," Theodosia said.

"The thing is, I represent a private collector in Wilmington, North Carolina," Brooklyn said, handing Theodosia a crisp, creamy business card. "This collector is in the initial stages of opening the Keystone Museum and wants to add the Navy Jack flag to his collection."

"There's a lot of that going around. Wanting dibs on the flag, I mean."

"Of course there is, because the flag has such immense historical significance. But my client doesn't want it for his personal pleasure. He's working to build a museum collection, yes, but not one for public gazing. The Keystone Museum will be geared to serious scholars only. It will be a place where students, professors, and other museum and historical society educators can come to do research on the American Revolution as well as early American history in general."

"That does sound rather academic and worthwhile," Theodosia said.

"It's a longtime dream of my client."

"So you also reside in Wilmington?"

"I do now. But I'm originally from Bluffton. My father is Joshua Vance."

Drayton glanced up from behind the counter. "Colonel Joshua Vance?"

Brooklyn smiled warmly. "You know him?"

"Only by reputation," Drayton said. He looked at Theodosia and raised his eyebrows, a subtle signal that Vance was some kind of big deal VIP.

"I wish I could be of help," Theodosia said. "Unfortunately, Drayton and I only witnessed the drone fly into the hot-air balloon and cause it to explode. We've never seen the flag and actually don't know Don Kingsley except by reputation."

"Ah," Brooklyn said. She looked disappointed. "You were my last hope."

"I'm sorry we're such a dead end," Theodosia said.

Brooklyn waved a hand. "That's okay. I'm not about to give up."

"You say you've spoken with the police?"

"I have and they appear to be quite stumped," Brooklyn said. "Which surprises me."

Then, because Brooklyn seemed to be at loose ends, Theodosia said, "What did you do before you worked for this private museum?"

"After I got my PhD at NYU, I interned at the Gardner Museum in Boston."

"Where the Rembrandt and Vermeer were stolen."

"Yes, but not on my watch, thank goodness. After the Gardner, I worked as a sales agent for The Neufelt Gallery in Zurich, Switzerland, where I had a kind of hit list of international clients . . ." Brooklyn shrugged. "It was an awful lot of fun but I'm glad to be back home again."

"You've had an intriguing career so far," Theodosia said.

"I'm passionate about working in the art world. No matter what I'm dealing with—paintings, decorative arts, sculpture, photography, antiquities—they all nourish my soul." As she spoke, Brooklyn glanced about, taking in her surroundings, obviously charmed by the tea shop. "It looks as if you've found a rewarding career, too. I mean, this place is just too cute for words. And the aromas . . ." Brooklyn rolled her eyes. ". . . are basically to die for."

"Then you should probably sit down and enjoy a cup of tea and a scone," Theodosia said.

Brooklyn glanced at her watch. "Unfortunately, I only have time for takeout today. But I do want to come back later for a proper tea."

"Tomorrow," Drayton murmured.

Brooklyn turned toward him. "Excuse me?" she said.

"Drayton and I are hoping you can come back tomorrow," Theodosia said, jumping in to second his suggestion. "It might sound kind of funny to you, but we're having a Nancy Drew Tea, a special luncheon tea."

Brooklyn's face lit up like it was Christmas morning. "You're not serious," she gasped. "Nancy Drew was my *hero*. Those mysteries were some of the first books I fell in love with." She grinned and ducked her head. "Reading under the covers with a flashlight . . . *The Sign of the Twisted Candles, The Mystery of the Tolling Bell* . . . well, I could rhapsodize about those books forever."

"Better that you just come here tomorrow." Theodosia laughed. "And enjoy yourself. Indulge in a little Nancy Drew nostalgia."

"I will!" Brooklyn clapped her hands together. "This has to be kismet. Tell me, what shall I bring?"

"Just yourself and a love for Nancy Drew are all that's required."

"Thank you, Theodosia." She gave a little wave in Drayton's direction. "And thank you, Drayton!"

"You're quite welcome, dear lady," Drayton said. "And this is for you." He pushed a take-out cup across the counter to her. "Gratis."

"Thank you again." Brooklyn grinned. She picked up her tea and then turned and grasped Theodosia's hand. "I look forward to seeing you tomorrow. You, too, Drayton. And I'd be ever so grateful if you kept me in the loop."

"I'll do my best," Theodosia said. But her words felt slightly hollow. This whole murder and missing flag busi-

BROKEN BONE CHINA   75

ness was so confusing, Theodosia wondered if even *she* was in the loop.

"So tell me," Theodosia said to Drayton. "Who is Colonel Joshua Vance?"

"He's a West Point graduate who, for a while, served as a state representative."

"Is Colonel an honorary title or is he ex-military?"

"He's an ex-military man who became a bird colonel the hard way. He was in the Tet Offensive in the early days of the Vietnam War. Story is he rallied his men and held off a huge attacking force in Khe Sanh. Now Colonel Vance is retired and lives on his horse farm. Raises Morgans, I believe. Trotting horses. Shows them at events all around the country."

"So Brooklyn's from a good family," Theodosia said.

"In the South breeding always counts, be it horses, dogs, or people," Drayton said. He cocked his head and looked past Theodosia's shoulder. "Aren't you running a little behind schedule?"

Theodosia whirled about to find Miss Dimple, their twice-monthly bookkeeper and occasional server, hurrying toward them. Before the front door swung closed behind her, she was frantically pulling off a pink chiffon scarf and shucking off her raincoat.

"Apologies!" Miss Dimple cried. She flung her coat toward the coatrack, missed, and then had to try again. This time she made it. "The buses were running late and I couldn't get a cab."

"Probably because there aren't any cabs anymore," Drayton said. "Now everyone calls that Yuper thing."

"Uber," Theodosia said. Then to Miss Dimple, "You're here now, so no problem." Because it wasn't. Miss Dimple was an incredible sweetie and had a heart as big as all outdoors. Barely five feet one tall, pleasingly plump, and with a cap of silver-white curls, Miss Dimple had edged up into her early eighties but was still a capable little dynamo.

"But I was supposed to be here at eleven," Miss Dimple lamented. "I missed lunch service."

"No, it's okay," Theodosia assured her. "You can start now and work through afternoon tea."

Miss Dimple touched a hand to her ample chest, said, "Really? Oh goody." That was the way she really talked. Used quaint words and phrases like *goody goody gumdrop*, *kinfolk*, and *persnickety*, which endeared her to Theodosia even more.

"How are the cats?" Drayton asked. Miss Dimple was completely over the moon about her two cats, Sampson and Delilah.

"In this weather? They're permanently curled up on the sofa. Sleeping," Miss Dimple said.

"Which isn't a completely horrible idea," Drayton said.

"You're still going to help us with the Nancy Drew Tea tomorrow, aren't you?" Theodosia asked.

"Honey, I wouldn't miss it for the world," Miss Dimple said. "Even though I started out as a Trixie Belden fan, dear old Nancy eventually won my heart."

"Then you're going to love our décor," Theodosia said.

Miss Dimple's eyes sparkled. "Whatcha gonna do for decorations and centerpieces?"

"It's a surprise," Drayton said. "Or so I've been told by Theo and Haley."

"Come on, you can tell me," Miss Dimple said.

"Mum's the word," Theodosia said.

"You see?" Drayton said as the phone rang. "You'll just have to wait and see like the rest of us poor souls." He picked up the receiver. "Hello?" He listened for a hot moment and then passed it to Theodosia. "For you."

Theodosia grabbed the phone. "This is Theodosia."

"Miss Theodosia Browning?" said a friendly sounding woman on the other end.

"That's right."

"I understand your tea shop is hosting a Beaux Arts Tea this Saturday?"

"Yes, we are," Theodosia said. "Do you need a ticket? We still have some seats available."

"We've already purchased tickets," said the woman. "I'm just calling to give you a heads-up. *Tea Faire Magazine* is sending a secret sipper to your tea."

Theodosia's knuckles turned white on the phone. This was a big deal. *Tea Faire Magazine* was a big deal. "You're what?" She'd heard her, but she wanted to hear it again.

"If all goes well, there'll be a favorable review in our magazine sometime in the next three months."

"And if it doesn't go well?" Theodosia asked.

There was a warm chuckle. "The Indigo Tea Shop has an impeccable reputation. I can't imagine anything could go wrong."

Theodosia's mouth twitched into a wry smile. *But I can.*

11

Miss Dimple draped a black Parisian waiter's apron around her neck, grabbed two pots of tea, and bustled her way through the small maze of tables. As she poured refills she chatted amiably with their guests.

"She's a gem," Drayton said.

Theodosia was still feeling astounded. "That phone call I just took?" she said to Drayton. "It was from *Tea Faire Magazine*. They're sending a secret sipper to our Beaux Arts Tea this Saturday."

"Good gracious," Drayton said. "For real? A secret sipper? Is that anything like a secret shopper?"

"It must be."

"This changes everything, doesn't it? We'll have to make sure that every aspect of our event is pure perfection. Menu, tea selections, service, décor, the whole ball of wax."

"That's for sure," Theodosia said. She watched as Drayton picked a tin of orchid plum tea off the shelf.

"And I'll have to . . ." The phone rang again before Drayton was able to finish his sentence.

"Maybe that's *Tea Faire Magazine* calling to cancel," Theodosia said.

"Bite your tongue!" Drayton snatched up the phone, listened for a few moments, and passed it to Theodosia. "Someone else for you."

Theodosia took the phone with some trepidation. "Hello?"

It was Alicia Kellig, from WCSC-TV, Channel 8.

"You remember me?" Alicia asked. "I used to be a production associate, now I'm a producer."

"That's terrific, Alicia, congratulations on your promotion," Theodosia said.

"Thank you, I'm really having fun with it." Alicia cleared her throat, ready to get down to business. "As you know, we're right in the middle of our Action Auction where we raise funds for a select number of charities. And since the Indigo Tea Shop donated . . ."

"Some tea and teapots," Theodosia said.

"Yes," Alicia said. "Which got me to thinking— wouldn't it be fun if *you* were the one to talk about the tea and tea accoutrements and help us get the bidding started!"

"Was that a question?"

Alicia laughed. "Actually, it was. Would you do it? We'd need you for, like, five or ten minutes."

"When would this be?" Theodosia asked.

"This Friday afternoon?" Alicia said. "If you could be here around four o'clock, we'll just slide you in. I know this is last minute and I apologize. But does that give you enough time to prepare?"

Theodosia did a mental calculation. No special events on Friday, just business as usual, so . . . "That should work fine."

"Wonderful. You just saved my life," Alicia said. "We had the herbal lady cancel on us. Something about drowned marjoram."

"I'll be there," Theodosia said. Then she hesitated.

"Now, just to be clear, this is really about tea, right? Not the hot-air balloon crash?"

"Tea, that's right," Alicia said. "And you can mention the Indigo Tea Shop if you want to."

Theodosia was pleased. "I definitely want to."

At one thirty, just as lunch ended and afternoon tea was ramping up, Detective Burt Tidwell sauntered in. He was wearing the same weird raincoat he had on yesterday. Only this time he didn't bother hanging it up. He just stood there silently, dripping, shoulders drooped, waiting for Theodosia.

Deciding she wanted to talk to him in confidence, Theodosia led Tidwell to the small table next to the stone fireplace. Once he'd eased himself into a captain's chair—no small feat at his size—Theodosia said, "Well, is there anything new in the investigation?"

Tidwell gave a noncommittal shrug.

Oh, you're going to be like that, are you?

"Perhaps you need a cup of tea to warm you up." *And get you talking.*

Tidwell gave a brusque nod.

Theodosia brought him a pot of Darjeeling and two chocolate chip scones on a plate.

Tidwell's brows went into full beetle mode. "What are these?" he asked as he peered at the scones.

"Chocolate chip scones," Theodosia said.

"But you usually serve fruit scones. Apple, strawberry, blueberry."

"Haley baked something different today. Have a taste. I think you'll like them."

Tidwell still looked disconcerted. "Do I put jam and Devonshire cream on these?"

Theodosia sighed. "Whichever you prefer."

"Actually, I prefer *apple* scones."

"I know you do but Haley didn't bake those today. So. The investigation?"

Tidwell took a tiny bite of scone and chewed slowly. "It's proceeding. Not as quickly as I'd like, unfortunately. As you might guess, I'm anxious to get Detective Riley back in town."

So am I.

"Here, let me pour your tea." Theodosia picked up the Chinese blue-and-white teapot and poured him a cup. "This Darjeeling is from the Margaret's Hope Estate. Full-flavored and smooth with just a hint of crispness."

"Thank you." Tidwell had taken a bigger bite of his scone and seemed relatively content as he chewed. "Perhaps this tea could use a lump or two of sugar?"

"Perhaps." Theodosia knew the tea didn't really need sweetening. She also knew Tidwell was stalling and it was beginning to royally bug her. If he didn't want to share information, then why was he here? Yes, he was a sugar fanatic, never averse to stuffing his face. But you could find cake, brownies, muffins, and scones all over Charleston. All over Charleston County.

After several minutes of frustrating, one-sided conversation, Theodosia said, "I have an idea. Why don't we engage in a little quid pro quo?"

"Whatever do you mean?"

Cute. Now he's getting cute.

"I'm talking about a fair and equitable exchange of information."

Tidwell had been stirring sugar into his tea, his silver spoon hitting the edge of his Balleek teacup repeatedly. Incessantly. *Clink, clink, clink.* It was driving Theodosia crazy. Now Tidwell stopped and cocked his head like an interested magpie. "What information might you have?"

"You first."

"Alright." As Tidwell shifted his weight, his wooden chair let out a loud groan. He didn't seem to notice. "We are currently investigating all persons who have purchased drones in the last eighteen months."

"And what have you found? Besides receipts on drone sales."

"I think you know. Your friend at the Featherbed House . . ."

"Angie Congdon."

"Her paramour is apparently in possession of a drone. When we checked with Blue Sky Flying Machines, Mr. Affolter's name magically appeared on their customer list. The FAA is beginning to tighten up ownership on drones, you see, and sellers are required to keep careful records." Tidwell took a sip of tea. "But the connection I find most troubling is that Harold Affolter is an employee of SyncSoft."

"So you really are investigating Harold?" Theodosia had been holding out hope that Angie had misread the situation. Or that the police had talked to Harold and then discounted him.

"This is a murder investigation. Of course we're going to look at him. We *have* to look at him."

"It's a dead end. You're wasting your time. Harold didn't do it."

"That, Miss Browning, is your personal opinion. I base my conclusions on evidentiary findings."

"I can't believe you have any evidence at all," Theodosia said.

"Mr. Affolter was a disgruntled whistle-blower at SyncSoft."

"Not really whistle-blowing, more like acting as a friendly watchdog. I'm positive Harold thought he was doing the right thing for his company."

"That was obviously not the company's opinion." Tidwell's lips curled into the smile of a hungry wolverine. "Your turn."

"There's a group of local men who call themselves the Americana Club."

"What?"

She'd caught Tidwell off guard.

"There's a group of local men who . . ."

"No, I heard you just fine." He waved his hand. "Continue with your narration."

"These men are collectors . . . possibly underground collectors . . . of rare and antique Americana," Theodosia said.

"I've not heard of any such organization."

"Drayton tells me they're rather secretive."

"And based on what they collect, I'd imagine quite wealthy, too."

"That goes without saying," Theodosia said.

"Do you have a list? Does Drayton have a list?" Tidwell asked.

"No list, only rumors."

"That doesn't help much," Tidwell said.

"You didn't give me much of anything, either," Theodosia said.

"Are there . . . ?"

Theodosia leaned forward. "Yes?"

"Any more of those scones?"

Theodosia was feeling frustrated. Tawney Kingsley didn't know anything, Angie was frightened to death, Tod Slawson and Brooklyn Vance had been counting on her for help, and Tidwell wasn't exactly a fountain of knowledge.

"You look like you could use a pick-me-up," Drayton said. "Here, try this." He slid a cup of tea across the counter to her.

"What is it?"

"You tell me. Have a taste."

Theodosia took a sip. "Mmm, a black tea, maybe from India? But with a bit of mint?"

"Well done. I added peppermint, licorice, and anise to

give the black tea its velvety taste. Consider it one of my new house blends."

"The tea's delightful. Do you have a name for it?"

"Black Velvet," Drayton said. "Are you still nervous about the secret sipper?"

"More like concerned. This week has suddenly turned into a sticky hodgepodge of concerns."

"Some might call them problems," Drayton said.

Theodosia thought about the terrible crash she'd witnessed, the fear that Angie had expressed over Harold being arrested. She took another fortifying sip as a kernel of an idea began to form in her head. Was it a good idea? Maybe. All she could do was give it a shot and try to shake something loose.

"You know, since everyone keeps coming in here, asking about the hot-air balloon crash, it might be high time we pay Charles Townsend a visit," Theodosia said.

"You mean the associate professor or curator or whatever he is?" Drayton asked.

"Probably more like Donald Kingsley's personal assistant, also known in some companies as a gopher."

"Interviewing Townsend is an intriguing thought, but how are we going to pull it off?" Drayton's fingers nervously touched his polka dot bow tie. "We don't know Townsend. In fact, we only saw him flitting about in a blind panic that terrible afternoon."

"You're going to call Townsend and ask him for an appointment," Theodosia said.

Drayton reared back, stunned. "*Me*?"

"You're just as capable of spinning a fanciful story as I am. Besides, as a board member at the Heritage Society you've got impeccable credentials."

"To talk about what with Mr. Townsend?"

"About the flag," Theodosia said. "About its history. Whatever. Our ultimate goal is to get him talking and hope he divulges a few crucial details. Like when did he know the Navy Jack flag was missing? And was there an actual, physical break-in at Kingsley's home?"

"So you have decided to investigate," Drayton said.

"For Angie's sake."

"When would we want to meet with Townsend?"

Theodosia picked up the phone and handed it to Drayton. "How about right now? We can kill two birds with one stone. Talk to Charles Townsend and then pop over and take a second look at the Portman Mansion, which is just a few doors down from Kingsley's place. Haley's been bugging me about the Portman's kitchen facilities and we need to eyeball the dining room. Make sure we don't have to rent any additional tables and chairs."

"How many people do we need to accommodate for our Beaux Arts Tea this Saturday?"

"We have fifty-seven reservations so far with a secret sipper embedded in there somewhere. But I expect a few more guests will call at the last minute so I want to be ready."

"My goodness, aren't we just a rousing success," Drayton said.

"Trying to be." Theodosia smiled sweetly. "Make the call?"

Drayton called Townsend and immediately ran up against some strong opposition. He sputtered for a few moments and then lowered the phone to his chest and hissed, "Theo, *you* talk to him."

Theodosia squared her shoulders and took the phone. "Mr. Townsend," she said brightly. "I've been meaning to get in touch with you ever since our hasty meeting this past Sunday. I felt so bad that Mr. Kingsley was killed in such an unfortunate manner. It must have been a terrible shock to you . . . Well, it was to all of us, I assure you. And, of course, you and I only exchanged a few brief words that terrible day so I was unable to fully express to you my deepest sympathies."

Drayton raised his eyebrows as Theodosia rattled on for another few minutes. Sweet-talking young Mr. Townsend, working her Southern charm and magic on him until he couldn't help but agree to see them.

"That's it," Theodosia said, hanging up the phone. "We're in."

"When?" Drayton asked.

"Right now. Grab your raincoat and let's go."

"Where are we going?"

"Two twenty-one Lamboll Street," Theodosia said. "It's only a couple of blocks from here."

"Ah, the old Darrow Mansion," Drayton said, ever the historian.

12

Any walk in Charleston is a scenic, practically cinematic walk. There are block after block of elegant mansions, walled gardens, historical markers, old churches, fountains surrounded by riots of greenery, and narrow, cobblestone alleys. Theodosia and Drayton were taking a shortcut down one of those alleys right now—Price's Alley.

"Every time I stroll through here I feel like I'm on a treasure hunt," Theodosia said.

"Indeed you are because there's so much to see," Drayton said. He stopped and pointed to a metal plaque embedded in stone. It read PRICE'S ALLEY. "Amazing, isn't it? A narrow alley that can barely accommodate a single horse-drawn carriage, a wall of red bricks that were probably used as ballast in some old sailing frigate, and a peek into hidden gardens and the occasional undraped window."

"Like falling down the rabbit hole," Theodosia said. The slow drip-drip of falling raindrops and swirling tendrils of Atlantic fog gave the alley an ethereal feel.

"Look here," Drayton said, pointing. "Copper lanterns and hitching posts. It isn't often a city has the fortitude and strength of will to fight change for over three hundred years."

"Don't knock change," Theodosia said.

Drayton smiled. "Don't knock tradition."

"I'm always tempted to stand on tiptoes and peer over this brick wall," Theodosia said. "Drink in the beauty and lushness of these private gardens."

"Then let's do so."

They both stopped, curled fingers over the top of the brick wall, and pulled themselves up.

"Spectacular," Theodosia said. "A picture postcard waiting to happen." They gazed into a lush backyard garden that featured a long, narrow reflecting pool teeming with Japanese koi, and flower beds that were a riot of color.

When they finally emerged from the alley onto Lamboll Street, Drayton said, "There's a reason Charleston has been dubbed the 'Holy City.' How many church spires can you count just from here?"

"Um . . ." Theodosia spun around slowly. "Four . . . no, five."

"And we have another two dozen churches with spires all piercing the sky. I'd say it's a fine testament to the different faiths that make up our rich history. Of course, the churches do a fine job of showcasing our elegant eighteenth- and nineteenth-century architecture, too."

"Take a look at this particular bit of architecture," Theodosia said. They had walked halfway down the block and were standing in front of the enormous brick mansion that had served as Don Kingsley's home.

"Federal style," Drayton said. "Keenly influenced by Roman architecture and a kind of refinement of the Georgian style. You see those panels and friezes?"

Theodosia nodded as they went up the walkway and stepped onto the piazza that fronted the home.

"And the columns and moldings are narrower and less ostentatious. I'm curious about the interior . . ."

"We'll know soon enough," Theodosia said as she rang

a large brass doorbell, stepped back, and heard a hollow *boom* inside the enormous house.

When Charles Townsend met Theodosia and Drayton at the front door he was polite but formal. He ushered them into a lovely wood-paneled entry, took their coats, and then led them down a long center hallway that had a breathtaking, tea-stained (definitely on purpose) Oriental carpet. He stopped abruptly and gestured to his right. A signal that Theodosia and Drayton should precede him.

What they walked into was a suite of three connecting rooms that looked like the period rooms at the Gibbes Museum, or maybe Thomas Jefferson's house at Monticello.

At any rate, the three rooms were all furnished in early American furniture. Pine tables, Chippendale chairs, desks, sugar chests, and sideboards. But these were not pieces one could sit on or actually use; they were old and clearly museum quality. The walls were hung with framed documents, flags, and oil paintings. Pottery, pewter candlesticks, and crystal inkwells sat on shelves, and antique books were housed in glass-front cabinets.

Theodosia turned around to face Townsend. "This is all Don Kingsley's collection?"

"Most of it, anyway," Townsend said. "There are a few pieces in storage."

"Magnificent," Drayton said. "This is practically a museum."

"Mr. Kingsley always nurtured the dream of having his own museum separate from this house," Townsend said. "But now . . ." Townsend's face fell. "I'm afraid it's not to be."

"What a lovely silver coffeepot," Theodosia said, pointing to a tall, elegant pot.

"Sheffield," Townsend said. "One of our more recent acquisitions."

Drayton put on his tortoiseshell half-glasses and studied a framed flag that hung on the wall. "This flag is old?" he asked. It had thirteen stripes and thirty-three small stars clustered into one great star.

"From approximately 1860," Townsend said.

"And where was the Navy Jack flag stolen from?" Theodosia asked. She decided they'd had enough polite conversation. Now it was time to cut to the chase.

Townsend moved to an antique case and pointed to an empty spot. "It was here. Right here."

"You noticed that the flag was missing when you returned from the balloon accident last Sunday?" Theodosia asked.

"That's right," Townsend said.

"Why did you come here, instead of going to your own home?" Theodosia asked.

Townsend stared at her. "I . . . I don't know. I suppose I wasn't thinking too clearly at that point and this is where the police cruiser dropped me off."

"So you had a key."

"Of course."

"And you came in here to look around and that's when you discovered that the flag was missing?" Theodosia asked.

"No. I went directly to Mr. Kingsley's office and made some calls. Notification calls," Townsend said. "A difficult, gut-wrenching task, as you might imagine."

"And after that?"

"Then I came in here." He glanced around. "I thought these rooms would serve as a kind of touchstone . . . a calming . . . well, you know."

"And that's when you noticed the flag was missing."

"Exactly so," Townsend said. "At which point I immediately notified the police."

"Busy night for the police," Drayton said. He was standing there, arms crossed, listening intently to their conversation.

Townsend shook his head. "A sad night for all of us."

"Had any of the door locks been tampered with?" Theodosia asked.

"Not that I could see," Townsend said. "And the police checked all the doors, front and back."

"Windows?" Drayton asked.

Townsend shook his head. "Nothing looked disturbed."

"Ghosts," Drayton said.

"I hope not," Townsend said. "The lack of forced entry seemed . . . strange. That's why I told the police I thought it might be an inside job."

"An inside job . . . how?" Theodosia asked.

"Mr. Kingsley entertained many visitors here. Friends, antiques dealers . . ."

"People from the Americana Club?" Theodosia asked.

"A few, yes."

"Interesting," Theodosia said.

Townsend gazed at her. "Is it? Because the police haven't come up with anything yet."

"Will you be staying on here?" Theodosia asked. Since Townsend's employer had just been murdered, she figured there was probably some confusion as to his status as an employee.

"You mean . . . with the collection?"

"That's right." Theodosia decided that if Townsend talked a good game and put up a brave front, he might be enlisted to help find a new home for all these objects. Or, if Tawney was still in charge and had her way, to oversee their sale at Sotheby's.

"I would hope I'm staying here. That would be my first choice," Townsend said.

"Best of luck to you then," Drayton said. "If I had my druthers I'd want to remain among these precious objects, too."

Townsend took a step backward, edging for the door. "I take it you've seen everything that you wanted to see? That I've answered all of your questions?"

"Actually, we'd like to talk with you a little more," Theodosia said.

Townsend seemed taken aback. "Why is that?"

"Because you're the one who's smack-dab in the middle of this flag and drone furor," Drayton said.

"We're interested in your reaction, how you're making sense of all this," Theodosia said.

"Well, I'm not," Townsend said with as much earnestness as he could muster. "It's been just horrible."

"I'm sorry to hear that." Theodosia smiled at Townsend, who seemed to gather his wits about him and relax after a few moments. Then she dropped her bombshell.

"If you had to point the finger at someone, who would it be?" Theodosia asked.

Townsend made a choking sound in the back of his throat. He was either stalling for time or taken aback by the audacity of her question. Finally, he recovered enough to say, "You mean for crashing a drone into Mr. Kingsley's hot-air balloon or for stealing the flag?"

"How about both?" Theodosia said.

"Oh, well, I really couldn't say," Townsend said. "As I just mentioned, the police are completely stumped. And if they have stumbled onto something—or someone—they haven't shared their findings with me. They're playing it close to the vest."

Theodosia gave a tight nod, but was determined to hold Townsend's feet to the fire.

"But you must harbor some suspicions," she said.

"Well . . ." Townsend said, stalling.

"I'm sincerely interested in your opinion," Theodosia said. "And, after witnessing that horrific crash, you can see why Drayton and I also have a vested interest."

Townsend swallowed hard and then said, "Please don't tell anyone." His face puckered up, as if he'd just swallowed a sour pickle, and then he said, "But I do have— this would be pure speculation—some ideas, I guess."

"Mum's the word," Drayton said. He made a zipping motion across his mouth.

Theodosia gave an encouraging nod.

"I think it could have been Tawney Kingsley or possibly that horrible antiques dealer, Earl Bullitt," Townsend said.

"Why Tawney?" Theodosia probed. "Why suspect her?"

"Two reasons. One, I think she still might have a key to this place," Townsend said. "So she could have come in here anytime Sunday afternoon and grabbed the Navy Jack. She could have hidden it in that new albatross of a home of hers or at her condo on Johns Island."

"And reason number two. Why it could be Tawney?" Theodosia asked.

"The woman adores money more than life itself," Townsend said. "From what I've heard, her credit card bills were astronomical. I think that's why Mr. Kingsley wanted to divorce her. She was just too darned expensive to maintain. It was like owning a home in Monaco, a Lamborghini, and a stable of race horses—all at the same time."

"Amusing," Drayton said, though he didn't look particularly amused.

"Would Tawney have the wherewithal to steal the flag and then sell it?" Theodosia asked.

Townsend took a few moments to form his answer. "Tawney's shrewd and fairly well connected, so I think she could pull it off. She's constantly flying to New York or London on various shopping trips where she could easily connect with wealthy collectors or dealers."

"Just as easy as Earl Bullitt could?" Theodosia said, referring to Townsend's second choice of suspects. Of course, she was already familiar with Earl Bullitt. Tod Slawson had also named him as a possible thief. And Bullitt's reputation preceded him as a local antiques dealer who was a definite hustler. Slawson might sell the occa-

sional top-dollar, A-plus piece, but Bullitt *moved* his
inventory—the good, the bad, and the ugly.

"Earl Bullitt is a distinct possibility," Townsend said.

"How did you get involved with him?"

"I didn't, but Mr. Kingsley had some dealings with
him," Townsend said. "Bullitt tried to sell him an original
painting by Thomas Hicks but, upon closer inspection, it
turned out to be . . . not so original."

"So Bullitt is a crook," Theodosia said.

"Bullitt is as crooked as the day is long," Townsend
said. "He sells fakes and he's a schemer. I understand he
works with a whole network of other dealers in New York,
Miami, and Dallas, most of them just this side of the law."

Theodosia glanced at Drayton. "Do you know anything about Mr. Bullitt's nefarious dealings?"

"I don't like to speak ill of anyone, but I have heard
rumors," Drayton said.

But rumors were only rumors, Theodosia told herself.
They weren't the solid, hard-core evidence that Tidwell
craved, the evidence she needed to help pull Angie and
Harold out of this sticky mess.

"Mr. Townsend . . . Charles . . . we appreciate your being so open with us," Theodosia said.

"I don't know if I've been any help because I'm not
sure what you're looking for." Townsend's eyes took on a
curious gleam. "Are you investigating this on your own?"

"Just helping out a friend," Theodosia said.

"Harold Affolter?" Townsend said.

"You know about him?" Drayton asked.

Townsend shrugged. "I know that Mr. Kingsley was
quite unhappy with Mr. Affolter. The man called here
several times, pestering him about something."

"I think he was more likely sounding an alarm," Theodosia said.

Townsend turned glum. "If that's what it was, then he
was too late."

* * *

"*What do you* think?" Drayton asked as they walked down Lamboll Street. "Did we learn anything?"

"Townsend mostly just reinforced the suspect names we've already heard bandied about," Theodosia said.

"What about the young man himself?"

"You mean Townsend as a suspect? I think he's mostly a frightened fellow who's hoping to keep his job."

Miss Chatfield, the event coordinator at the Portman Mansion down the street, was eager to show them around. In her early sixties and petite, she wore a conservative black suit and sensible shoes. Her silver hair was rolled into a tidy bun and her eyeglasses dangled on a silver chain. She looked like someone's great aunt who worked as a docent in a museum.

"We've never hosted a tea party here before," Miss Chatfield said. "It will be a first for us."

"For us, too," Drayton said. "Since we usually host them in our tea room."

"Oh, I've visited the Indigo Tea Shop," Miss Chatfield said. "You have a delightful little place. Delicious food and killer scones."

"And tea," Theodosia added. "Don't forget about our tea."

"Are you kidding?" Miss Chatfield said. "Last time I stopped in with a couple of friends I brought home three tins."

"That's what we like to hear," Drayton said.

"So . . . a quick tour," Miss Chatfield said. She took a deep breath and continued, "The Portman Mansion was built by an early phosphate manufacturer for his family. Then it served as a single family home for almost ten decades. Eight years ago, a consortium of investors purchased this place, made some needed renovations, and turned it into an event center."

"This is lovely," Drayton said as they peered into a side parlor. "All this crown molding and hand-carved wood."

"Wait until you see the dining room," Miss Chatfield told them.

And what a fanciful dining room it was.

"Impressive," Drayton said, gazing around.

"Very Gilded Age," Theodosia said. "Perfect for our tea."

Though the storm was still raging outside, the dining room felt light and airy, thanks to a wall of twelve-foot-high windows with insets of Tiffany glass at the top. The floors were made of inlaid marble, an enormous crystal chandelier hung overhead, and a mirrored china case filled with wineglasses and champagne flutes reflected what felt like a million points of light.

"We have tables and chairs to accommodate up to eighty-five guests in here and another side parlor that can handle an additional twenty-five guests," Miss Chatfield said.

"I see ample room for us to set up some paintings on easels," Drayton said. It was an idea he and Theodosia had talked about to help lend authenticity to their Beaux Arts Tea.

"And we have facilities to set up a custom bar if you like, plus we offer valet parking, audiovisual, and Wi-Fi access. We're also happy to provide security if you need it," Miss Chatfield added.

Security, Theodosia thought. *That's what we could have used at the hot-air balloon rally.*

From the dining room they looked at the kitchen, which Drayton deemed to be absolutely perfect for Haley's purposes.

"If it wasn't raining, I'd open the French doors and show you our back courtyard," Miss Chatfield said.

"That's okay, I'm sure it's lovely," Theodosia said.

Miss Chatfield gave a little shiver. "I hope all this wind and rain isn't going to turn into a rip-roaring hurricane."

"I believe it's too early in the year for hurricane season," Drayton said.

Theodosia glanced out the window where trees were shaking and rain continued to slice down. "Tell that to the weather gods."

13

❧

The Tolliver Building was a large, yellow brick building, a former textile mill, that had been rehabbed through a grant from the State Arts Commission. Earmarked now as a home for nonprofit organizations, its major tenants included the Lebeau Theatre, Xenon Dance Troupe, and Ceramics Guild. There was also below-market-rate studio and gallery space for a dozen or so artists and potters, as well as the large meeting hall where Theodosia was now standing.

It was the night of judging for the Floral Teacups Competition, and Theodosia had never seen so many gorgeous antique teacups overflowing with amazing bouquets and creative arrangements.

Tea roses, herbal bouquets, wildflowers, miniature fairy gardens, nosegays of violets, and small green plants filled the teacups. One teacup held a green carpet of moss, sprigs of lady fern, and a strand of pearls. Another teacup held a miniature bonsai, what was known in Japan as *mame.* The room smelled like a luxurious mix of flowers, peat moss, and freshly cut grass.

Theodosia's heart jumped with wonder as she gazed across the dozen or so tables where the teacup arrangements were displayed. It was as if she was seeing some sort of magic carpet composed solely of greenery, bright colored flowers, and elegant bone china teacups.

"Theodosia?" said a woman at her elbow.

Theodosia turned. "Julie?" She recognized the tall blonde in the floral dress as the president of the French Quarter Garden Club and the show's organizer.

"Yes, it's me," Julie said. "Lovely to see you again. Our club is thrilled that you've agreed to help judge this show. Everyone speaks so highly of you and your tea shop."

"But for sheer impact it can't compete with this amazing display of color and creativity." Theodosia glanced around again, taking it all in. The room was starting to fill up with people. Those who'd come to wander through the maze of tables and enjoy the show, as well as private exhibitors and floral artists who were probably waiting for the results—her votes—with bated breath.

"I don't envy you your task of choosing our winners," Julie said.

"This isn't going to be an easy task," Theodosia said. "Perhaps you'd better give me your parameters for judging so I can do this strictly by the book. I take it you have several different categories?"

"We do," Julie said. "But let me pull in our other judge, too. Then I can explain the categories and judging protocol to both of you." Julie looked around and then threw up a hand and said, "Earl! Over here, please."

Theodosia watched as a stocky, pug-nosed man shouldered his way through the crowd. With his freckled scalp, nicotine-stained fingers, and ill-fitting sport coat, he didn't look like the sort of judge a garden club would enlist. On the other hand, who was she to judge?

"Theodosia," Julie said, "I'd like you to meet Earl Bullitt."

"Earl . . ." Theodosia faltered momentarily and then

quickly recovered. "You're the antiques dealer," she said, shaking his outstretched hand. "Lovely to meet you." *I hope it is, anyway.*

"Yeah, likewise," Bullitt said. He shook hands with barely a perfunctory glance.

"Mr. Bullitt is an orchid aficionado," Julie explained. "He specializes in tropical varieties."

"Sounds exotic," Theodosia said while Bullitt just shrugged.

"So here are your judge's name tags and clipboards," Julie said, handing over the materials. "As you can see by scanning your judging sheets, there are three distinct categories—Floral, Greenery, and Whimsy. In each of these categories you'll want to pick a first, second, and third place winner."

"So nine winners in all," Theodosia said. She studied her clipboard, while Bullitt seemed oblivious.

"Ten winners actually. You two will also have to put your heads together and choose a grand prize winner," Julie said. "We've got a big purple-and-gold ribbon for that honor."

"Great. Got it," Theodosia said. "When do we start?"

"Right now," Julie said. "I suggest you both wander among the tables first, to get a feeling for the entries, then start making a few preliminary selections."

Bullitt hitched up a shoulder. "Do we both have to agree on everything?" he asked.

Theodosia and Julie just looked at him.

"Yes, of course you do," Julie said finally.

Bullitt gave a terse nod. "Okay." And walked away.

"Interesting choice for a judge," Theodosia remarked. Bullitt seemed like he didn't want to be here. Like this was an enormous bother for him.

"One of our board members recommended him based on his skill with growing orchids." Julie's teeth nibbled at her lower lip. "I hope he's taking this seriously. I hope you can work with him."

"Not a problem," Theodosia said, hoping it wouldn't be. She tucked her clipboard under her arm and started off. She decided to do exactly what Julie had suggested. Wander through the show, try to get a feel for the various entries, and keep an open mind. Then she could start narrowing down the entries she thought were outstanding in their categories.

Theodosia was perusing her fourth table when Bill Glass walked up behind her and tapped her on the shoulder.

"Hey, tea lady," Glass said.

Theodosia whirled around. When she saw who it was, she let out a sigh. Bill Glass was the pushy, acerbic, somewhat shady publisher of *Shooting Star*, a tabloid-type newspaper that chronicled goings-on in and around Charleston. Glass viewed his tabloid through rose-colored glasses and fancied it as an upscale society paper. Among his readers it was generally agreed that *Shooting Star* was, at best, a gossip rag.

"What are you doing here?" Theodosia asked.

"Shooting pictures," Glass said. "Looking for the beautiful people." He aimed a lopsided grin at Theodosia. "What? You think I *like* flowers?" He lifted up a Nikon camera that was strung around his neck. "Hey, I hear you were tapped to do the judging tonight."

"Trying to anyway."

"Aw, don't be like that." Glass was wearing one of his beige photojournalist vests tonight, a saggy, baggy khaki thing that contrasted sharply with his skinny legs.

Theodosia studied him. "How come your face looks so tan?"

"Would you believe it if I told you I'd just returned from some war-ravaged country in the Middle East? On assignment for *National Geographic*?"

"No."

"Chronicling society babes in Palm Beach?"

"No again," Theodosia said.

"How about bikini babes in Cocoa Beach?"

"If you'll excuse me . . ."

"Hey, I also heard you were front and center at that hot-air balloon fiasco last Sunday," Glass said, shuffling after Theodosia. He was harder to get rid of than a hunk of chewing gum stuck to the bottom of your shoe.

"It was more than a fiasco," Theodosia said. "Three people were killed."

One of Glass's eyebrows crinkled up. "Got a line on who was responsible?"

"Of course not." Theodosia jotted down entry number one-forty-eight. It was a swirl of bog grass in a Limoges teacup accented with a tiny ceramic toadstool and a few stems of sweet William.

"Aw, you disappoint me, tea lady. I thought you'd be poking around like crazy by now, looking for suspects." Glass favored her with a horsey grin. "Man, I wish I could have been there. I'd have gotten some terrific crash shots." He grasped his camera and aimed it at her. "Flames and rubble, just like when that zeppelin thing crashed back in the day. You know, the Hindenburg!"

"Excuse me," Theodosia said. And this time she really did push her way past him.

Hoping (and praying!) for no more interruptions, Theodosia buckled down to business. The entries, all ensconced in elegant teacups, were absolutely incredible. Pink roses with baby's breath, bundles of crocus, shoots of fresh heather, succulents, and lots of small green plants. There were also entries with bird's nests, robin's eggs, and tiny silk butterflies tucked in. One teacup was completely covered in bright-green moss, and another teacup was tipped on its side with English ivy tumbling out of it.

Theodosia was jotting down a few notes when Delaine sidled up to her.

"So who's the big winner going to be?" Delaine purred in a soft voice. She was wearing a daffodil-yellow sweater, cream-colored pencil skirt, and floral high heels. She looked as fresh and perky as the entries.

"Hard to say. But I've already noted five excellent contenders," Theodosia said.

"You can tell me who's at the top of your list," Delaine said in a pouty voice.

"Of course she can't," came a woman's voice. "Theodosia has principles."

Theodosia and Delaine both looked up to find Brooklyn Vance smiling at them.

"What are you doing here?" Theodosia blurted out. Then realized her question sounded awfully rude.

But Brooklyn didn't take it that way at all. She shrugged and said, "Having fun? Killing time?"

Then, of course, Theodosia hastily introduced Delaine and Brooklyn to each other. And, wouldn't you know it, two minutes later the two of them were chatting away like old friends. Favorite fashion designers were mentioned and shrieked about, and then they moved on to comparing each other's gold charm bracelets.

Sensing a photo opportunity, Bill Glass moved in.

"Here now," Glass said with a cheesy smile. "Why don't you lovely ladies all squeeze together and let me take a few snaps. Put your picture on the cover of *Shooting Star.*" He chuckled. "I can title it 'The Three Graces.'"

"Please don't," Theodosia said. But Delaine was already mugging for the camera, doing her fashion model pose, and Brooklyn wasn't far behind her.

Oh, alright. Theodosia joined in and smiled for the camera.

"Are you going to keep me waiting forever?" Earl Bullitt called out loudly to Theodosia, interrupting their impromptu photo shoot.

Delaine turned toward Bullitt, her eyes narrowed like a predatory cat, obviously upset by his words. "Excuse me, but how rude are *you*?" she said.

Bullitt simply ignored her. He gazed at Theodosia with darkly hooded eyes and said, "Hurry up, will you? We need to put our heads together and decide on these winners. I haven't got all night."

"I'll be there in a moment, Mr. Bullitt," Theodosia said. She pulled away from Delaine and Brooklyn, not wanting to ruffle anyone's feathers or cause any unnecessary problems.

"Bullitt?" Brooklyn Vance suddenly cried out in a sharp, staccato tone. "*Earl* Bullitt?" Her eyes blazed and her complexion darkened as her emotions seemed to rise to the surface. "I know who you are. I know all about you!" Brooklyn's mood had downshifted and she was suddenly very upset.

"That's nice, lady, now kindly get out of my way," Bullitt said.

But Brooklyn stood her ground. "You were one of the bidders on the Navy Jack flag."

Delaine's brow crinkled as her mouth formed a perfect O. Quickly putting two and two together, she said, "Oh, Brooklyn, I guess *you* were trying to buy that same flag?"

"You're Brooklyn Vance?" Bullitt snorted. "Huh. You don't look like any kind of hot shot."

"That would be *Dr. Vance* to you," Delaine said.

"Delaine," Theodosia said in a warning tone. *Please don't get in the middle of this and cause any problems.*

But it was Brooklyn who had her claws out, ready to tangle.

"I've heard the gossip about you and your tacky little antiques shop," Brooklyn said. "You're a crook and a laughing stock."

"What do *you* know about antiques?" Bullitt fired at her. "You're a snotty, not-very-bright academic who sits in an ivory tower."

"That's better than being a repugnant little reptile who lives under a rock," Brooklyn flung back at him.

"Say now," Bill Glass said, aiming his camera at the snarling group. Or, as Theodosia saw it, a group that might now be categorized as Dante's third ring of hell.

"Please don't," Theodosia said to Glass.

But Glass's reporter's antennae were up and twitching like crazy. "Hot dog!" he cried. "I thought this teacup show would be a complete and total snooze, but suddenly it's gotten *verrry* interesting." He thrust his camera out and dove forward to capture the fight.

After all, a picture was worth a thousand words.

14

※

Wednesday morning and the rain still hadn't let up. The day looked about as dour as Theodosia's mood. She hated the fact that Brooklyn Vance and Earl Bullitt had gotten into a nasty sniping match last night. And though no blows had been struck and it was pretty much over in a heartbeat, that one sour note had sucked the joy out of the evening. Of course, Delaine had been no help whatsoever when she tried to butt in.

And if I hadn't introduced Brooklyn and Delaine, maybe none of this would have happened.

Or maybe, unbeknownst to her, Earl Bullitt and Brooklyn Vance had already been set on a collision course.

When Theodosia told Drayton about the almost-fisticuffs last night, he'd been surprisingly philosophical. He assured her that it wasn't her fault and that she'd done a good deed by judging the show. He said he was proud that she managed to work with the rather surly Earl Bullitt in selecting the prize winners.

In fact, what Drayton really wanted to know was—

who won? And what kind of rare and antique teacups had her keen eyes spotted?

Oh well. Better today.

Theodosia finished folding a stack of cream-colored linen napkins and placed them on the tables. She looked over to where Miss Dimple was fluttering about the highboy set against the far wall. Miss Dimple was sipping a cup of tea while she stocked shelves and hung some of the new teacup wreaths that Theodosia had created.

"Where'd you find this grapevine, honey?" Miss Dimple asked Theodosia when she noticed her watching.

"Pulled it off a few trees at my Aunt Libby's plantation," Theodosia said. "The stuff grows wild and crazy out there. Almost as bad as kudzu."

"I love how you make these freestyle, cloud-like structures out of grapevines." She held one up to study it. "Then you tie in all these dainty teacups and tuck in a bird's nest, too. You're so clever."

"Thank you, I needed that," Theodosia said. She walked over and looked at the replenished highboy. "Do we need to add a few more T-Bath products?" These were Theodosia's private label facial and bath products, formulated from gentle antioxidant teas.

"Haley said she'd bring some out."

"Good. And maybe a few jars of DuBose Bees Honey as well. And some of those wooden honey spoons."

"Got them right here," Haley said as she walked toward them, struggling to balance the enormous cardboard box she was carrying.

"Is that you back there?" Miss Dimple called out merrily. Then she reached out to grab the box and help Haley muscle it to the floor.

"Everything going okay in the kitchen?" Theodosia asked.

"Right as rain," Haley said. "Most of the food is already prepped. I'm just waiting for scones and such to come out of the oven, then I'll put the quiche in." She glanced around the tea room. "You want me to bring out the you-know-whats?"

"Maybe wait until I get the tables set up," Theodosia said. "Then we'll put them out."

"What exactly are the you-know-whats?" Miss Dimple asked.

"Have to wait and see, I guess," Haley said.

Miss Dimple practically stomped one of her chubby little feet. "How can you keep me in suspense like this?"

"It's a mystery tea," Theodosia said with a twinkle in her eye.

"Thank goodness we're only doing takeout this morning," Haley said. "Gives us time to get our ducks in a row for lunch."

"Drayton's the one who's been shouldering most of the load," Theodosia said. "Taking care of our pop-in customers."

They all glanced toward the front counter where Drayton had take-out cups and packaged scones precisely lined up and ready to go.

"He's doing a great job, too," Miss Dimple said.

Drayton glanced over at them. "Neatness counts," he said. "And, thankfully, I do have a penchant for order and organization."

"Some might call it OCD," Haley said.

Before Drayton had a chance to answer, the bell above the front door da-dinged once again and he had to ready himself for yet another influx of eager customers.

"I can't wait to see what you're baking," Miss Dimple said to Haley. "The aromas wafting out of your kitchen are making my nose twitch. You're such a talented baker."

"Thank you," Haley said, giving her a mock curtsy.

"Did you ever think about entering the Sugar Arts Competition that the Commodore Hotel sponsors every year?" Miss Dimple asked. "You're as good if not better than some of the artisans at our local bakeries and patisseries."

"I don't know about that," Haley said.

"I think you should enter," Theodosia said, jumping on the bandwagon. "After all, you won that Chocolatier Contest a couple of years ago."

"Yeah, but chocolate is easy," Haley said. "It's mostly melting and swirling and using molds. In those sugar arts contests you need to really wow the judges. Incorporate flakes of gold leaf, create lots of three-dimensional flowers, and do special effects. You know, like spun sugar birds and butterflies?"

"Haley, if anybody can master that, you can," Theodosia said.

Haley looked hopeful. "You think?"

"I know," Theodosia said.

Theodosia went back to primping her tables for the Nancy Drew Tea. First, she set out place mats that she'd made herself. These were color copies of classic Nancy Drew book covers that had been enlarged and laminated with clear plastic. Then she added teacups, saucers, and luncheon plates in Coalport's Academy pattern, as well as crystal water glasses.

Okay, now for some fun.

The tables were pretty, to be sure, but Theodosia was ready to funk it up. After all, this was a fun, nostalgia-inspired tea. So, in keeping with the book titles, she added vases of lilacs, pewter candleholders with twisted candles, a couple of old clocks (still ticking), and a few magnifying glasses that she'd borrowed from the Antiquarian Bookshop.

"I see where you're going with all this," Miss Dimple said as she twirled a finger. "But what about these mysterious centerpieces I keep hearing about?"

"Haley," Theodosia called out. "I think it's time."

Haley came bustling out from behind the curtains. "Ta da!" she exclaimed. With a flourish she held up a clutch of old-fashioned lunch boxes that she'd decoupaged with dozens of small images from Nancy Drew book covers.

"Oh my goodness," Miss Dimple exclaimed. "Aren't these just cute as a bug." She took one of the lunch boxes from Haley and turned it around to study it. "How many did you make?"

"Twelve," Haley said. "One for each table."

Now Drayton came over to lend his two cents. "So this is the big surprise," he said. "Highly creative and very well done, Haley."

"I just hope our guests like them," Haley said.

"They're going to love everything," Drayton assured her.

An hour later, the psychic came swooping in. She wore a red, swirling skirt, white peasant blouse, purple velvet cape, and a matching purple-and-gold turban with a jeweled pin. She was fiftyish and jovial-looking, with frizzy blond curls that stuck out from beneath her turban.

"Madame Poporov, I presume," Drayton said, meeting her at the door and inclining his head slightly as if she were visiting royalty.

Madame Poporov smiled warmly at Drayton. "You know who I am. Do you possess psychic powers as well?"

"No," Drayton said. "I am simply well prepared. And your turban did give me a gentle hint."

Madame Poporov put a hand up to touch it. "I keep forgetting I'm wearing this."

"It's really quite stunning," Drayton said.

"We have you sitting at your own table," Theodosia said, hurrying over to greet Madame Poporov. "I hope that's okay with you."

"Perfect," Madame Poporov said. "And you are Theodosia?"

"Yes, it's wonderful to finally meet you in person," Theodosia said. "I'm so glad you could make it on such a blustery day."

"I brought along my crystal ball as well as a deck of

tarot cards," Madame Poporov said. "Do you have a pref-
erence?"

"Whatever you feel like channeling. Or, really, whatever our guests are most comfortable with," Theodosia
said.

"Then we shall play it by ear," Madame Poporov said.

Now Haley came slinking out from the kitchen. She
gave a shy wave and said, "Hello."

"You must be the baker," Madame Poporov said.

Haley's eyes widened. "You're *good*. How did you
know that?"

"Perhaps it's the smidgeon of flour adhering to your
left cheek?" Drayton said.

"Oh." Haley hastened to wipe it off. Then, shyly asked,
"Are you really a Lithuanian royal?"

Madame Poporov smiled, revealing an actual gold
tooth. "Of course I am."

"I thought so," Haley said.

Madame Poporov got busy then, fluffing out her cape
and arranging her table.

Haley, on the other hand, was all whipped up as she
followed Theodosia and Drayton back to the counter.
"Let's ask her who committed the murder at the hot-air
balloon rally," she whispered.

Drayton plucked a tin of Pouchong tea from a shelf.
"Let's not," he said.

Haley's face fell. "Why on earth not?"

"Because Drayton prefers to do things the old-
fashioned way," Theodosia said. "Instead of relying on a
psychic, he'd rather investigate."

Drayton pursed his lips and shook his head. "*I* am not
investigating. *You* are."

The first guest to show up was Brooke Carter Crockett, the
owner of Hearts Desire Jewelers, just down the block.

"Leave it to you, Theo, to come up with such a fun

idea," Brooke said. She was a youthful fifty with a pixie cut of silver-gray hair and an aristocratic bone structure. Brooke was also a jewelry designer who specialized in working with silver. Her specialty was silver charms that incorporated the images of Charleston—palmetto trees, sea turtles, magnolia blossoms, church spires, sweetgrass baskets, tiny sailboats, and mansions.

"Oh, you like Nancy Drew?" Drayton asked Brooke playfully.

"Who doesn't?" Brooke cried as another dozen or so guests came pouring in behind her.

Theodosia greeted her guests, seated them at tables, and then ran back to the front door to greet a few more. Brooklyn Vance arrived, still chattering about last night's encounter with Earl Bullitt. Then Mindy Reinert from The Bag Lady purse and hat shop and Leigh Carroll, the owner of The Cabbage Patch Gift Shop, came in. Leigh was an African-American woman in her midthirties, fairly close in age to Theodosia, with beautifully burnished skin, sepia-colored hair, and almond eyes. Upon meeting her and hearing her honeyed voice, men often fell madly in love with her.

When the tea shop was almost full, when Theodosia didn't think they could accommodate one more dripping raincoat on their coatrack, a familiar face came bobbing through the front door.

"Gracious me!" Tawney Kingsley cried. She stopped dead in her tracks and touched a hand to the hollow of her neck. "I came here hoping for a simple lunch and it looks as if you're having some kind of marvelous tea event."

"It's our Nancy Drew Tea," Theodosia told her.

Tawney's face lit up with enthusiasm. "What a fabulous idea. Dare I ask . . . is it too late to get a reservation?"

"You know what?" Theodosia said, consulting her seating chart. "You're in luck. We happen to have two seats left."

"Fabulous!" Tawney cried. She flung off her coat to

reveal a pink Chanel suit and an armload of jangling gold jewelry.

"In fact, I think . . . yes. Since you already know Brooklyn Vance, I think I'll seat the two of you together," Theodosia said.

"That would be wonderful," Tawney said.

"The perfume you're wearing is quite intoxicating," Theodosia said as she led Tawney to her table. "May I ask what it is?"

Tawney fluttered her manicured fingers. "Just a fun fragrance I had custom blended at Le Fleur Parfumerie in Miami. Asian lotus and almond with a top note of bergamot."

"Mmm, bergamot. I thought I recognized that scent. It's the same oil that tea masters add to Earl Grey tea," Theodosia said.

Brooklyn Vance was thrilled to have Tawney sitting across from her. "Like old times," she said. "Even though we've only met once before."

"But it feels like more," Tawney said. "Like we really know each other."

"Indeed it does," said Brooklyn.

"I have to confess," Tawney said, leaning forward and whispering to Theodosia and Brooklyn, "I'm dying to learn as much about tea and tea etiquette as is humanly possible. That way I'll be able to serve afternoon tea to all my guests at my fabulous new B and B."

"I'm sure," Theodosia said to Tawney. "And I'll be right back with your pot of tea."

At the counter, Drayton leaned forward and said to Theodosia, "I think your friend Tawney wants to learn the drill so her *waitstaff* can serve tea to her guests. Just from a fast first impression, I doubt she'll be any kind of hands-on innkeeper."

"You never know," Theodosia said. On the other hand, if it turned out Tawney *had* killed her husband, she might be doing twenty to life at the Women's Correctional Center in Columbia where having just a single tea bag would be a luxury.

Theodosia and Miss Dimple each grabbed pots of tea to deliver. As Theodosia slipped a Brown Betty teapot onto the table that Brooklyn and Tawney were sharing, Tawney touched a hand to her arm.

"I'd like to invite you to my husband's memorial service tomorrow."

Brooklyn's eyebrows shot up. "They've released his body?"

"Just this morning," Tawney said. "Anyway, the service is going to be short and sweet, just the way Donald would have wanted it. We'll do a private cremation, then friends and colleagues will gather for a few graveside prayers in Magnolia Cemetery where his family has a small plot."

"That sounds lovely," Theodosia said.

Brooklyn bobbed her head. "Dignified."

Tawney's smile was sad as she gently squeezed Theodosia's arm again and said, "I feel like we've also become good friends. I hope you can make it tomorrow. Brooklyn, if you could come, too?"

Brooklyn nodded as Theodosia said, "Of course." Though Tawney featured on her suspect list, the poor woman had just lost her husband. And no matter what petty grievances the Kingsleys had harbored between each other, they *had* been husband and wife. So how could she not go and support Tawney? And, as a lucky strike, do a little more snooping. See if a killer turned up at the grave.

Haley's anxious face peered out from between the velvet curtains. "Are we ready to start yet?" she mouthed to Theodosia.

Theodosia gave an exaggerated nod. Yes, it was definitely time for her and Drayton to kick off the luncheon. Delaine was supposed to be here but hadn't shown up yet, even though she'd specifically reserved and paid for two seats. But they couldn't delay the luncheon one second longer. After all, crab quiche waits for no one.

Theodosia strode to the center of the room, smiled, and rang a tiny bell. The buzz of conversation died down immediately.

"Welcome, everyone, to our first-ever Nancy Drew Tea," Theodosia said.

Her words prompted a spatter of applause and a few rich chuckles.

"To celebrate our favorite girl detective we're going to lavish you with a wonderful luncheon today. We'll start out with Bess's ginger scones slathered with Devonshire cream. Our main course will be Hannah Gruen's crab quiche accompanied by a mixed green salad. And for dessert we have George's favorite chocolate cake pops along with apple tarts."

"Bravo!" came an excited voice, one of the guests who could hardly wait to get started.

Theodosia held up a finger. "And of course we have tea." She smiled at Drayton and said, "Drayton?"

He stepped forward into the middle of the room.

"The tea you're drinking now is Reading Nook Tea from the Plum Deluxe Tea Company. It's a Chinese black tea blended with rosebuds, lavender, and chamomile. Very apropos with scones. Our crab quiche will be accompanied by Harney & Sons Chinese Silver Needle tea. And for a dessert tea I'll be serving cardamom tea as well as Black Velvet, my private house blend."

"Our resident psychic, Madame Poporov, is also with us today," Theodosia said. "So whenever you're ready to cut the cards or gaze into her crystal ball for a peek at the future, just head over to her table and say hello."

"Tell them about the contest," Drayton said.

Theodosia continued. "On the tables are various clues that relate closely to Nancy Drew books."

There was an immediate, excited gasp from the guests

as they studied the tables more carefully. Then one woman said, "I see twisted candles." Another woman spotted a pot of lilacs. "Ooh, lilacs! Must be from *The Mystery at Lilac Inn*." A third woman said, "There's an old leather diary on my table. Is that from *The Clue in the Diary*?"

"I'll pass out pencils and paper," Theodosia said, "so you can write down all the clues along with the book titles."

"Map! I see a map!" another guest shrieked.

"Has to be from *The Quest of the Missing Map*," Brooke said.

Drayton nodded. "Bravo. It looks as if you all might score an A and win a prize."

Just as Theodosia and Miss Dimple were serving the crab quiche, Delaine burst through the front door. She had a crazed look on her face and was dragging Tod Slawson behind her.

"Apologies, I know we're frightfully late!" Delaine called out loudly, basically interrupting the tea to announce her delayed arrival to everyone. "I put the blame squarely on this fiendish weather."

Theodosia turned toward her, teapot in hand, and said, "That's . . ."

It was the only word she was able to get out of her mouth.

Upon seeing Tod Slawson, Tawney Kingsley stood up so fast her chair tipped over backward and crashed to the floor. Then Tawney was pointing an index finger iced with a bloodred-painted nail and shrieking like a crazed banshee caught in a leg trap. Her words were so shrill and babbled together that it was difficult to make sense of them.

"Youyoumurderer!" Tawney screeched in a high-pitched voice at Slawson. "Itwasyou. Wanthastupidflag. Doanythingtogetit!"

There was dead silence in the tea shop. Everyone

stopped eating; you could've heard a pin drop. Slawson's face turned Valentine red. Delaine let loose a strangled cry.

A split-second later, Tawney launched into "Act Two." Grabbing a silver butter knife off the table, she raised it high above her head. And with a murderous look on her face, she rushed directly for Tod Slawson!

15

❧

"No, no, no!" Theodosia cried as she and Drayton both
launched themselves like bottle rockets. Making a mad
sprint for Tawney, they batted wildly at her butter knife–
wielding arm, trying to stop her from jabbing a cowering
Tod Slawson in the eye.

"No, you don't!" Drayton shouted at Tawney as he got
a hand on her and wrenched her arm sideways.

"Drop it!" Theodosia ordered.

"That man's a killer!" Tawney shrieked as she flailed
away, still trying to stab Slawson.

"You *lunatic!*" Delaine yelped at Tawney. Then she
fought to get in a quick punch at the woman. "What do
you think you're *do*ing to my poor Toddy?"

Now Miss Dimple rushed to join the fray. "Do you
think I should call 911?" she quavered.

"No," Drayton panted. "I've got . . ." He was still wres-
tling with Tawney, trying to gain control of her right arm.
"Theo, grab her around . . ."

Theodosia grabbed Tawney around the waist and
squeezed her with a python's grip. Tawney gasped for air

and bent forward slightly. She wiggled clumsily as she clutched her knife tightly and levered it at Slawson's face.

Finally, with one explosive jerk, Drayton pried the butter knife out of Tawney's hand. "I've got it," he cried with a triumphant gasp as he held it high in the air.

"Don't think I'll hesitate to rip those cheap eyelash extensions off your face!" Delaine screeched at Tawney. "How *dare* you attack my beloved Toddy!" When push came to shove, Delaine could be as mean and scrappy as a junkyard dog.

"Delaine, no," Theodosia said. She'd lowered her voice in an effort to lower the temperature in the room.

Didn't work. Everyone was still in a red-hot frenzy. Delaine was muttering threats, looking like she was going to smack Tawney in the mouth. Tawney was still shrieking like a madwoman with steam pouring out of her ears. And the guests in the tea room were held utterly spellbound by the bizarre tableau. It was a train wreck of epic proportions.

"That man killed my husband," Tawney cried out. She wept copiously now, trying to catch her breath as she flailed away, still trying hard to batter at Slawson's head.

"Hush, you don't know that at all," Theodosia said, struggling to put herself between Tawney and the embarrassed, squirming Tod Slawson.

"Well, somebody did," Tawney cried, trying for one final punch. When her fist failed to connect again, her shoulders drooped and her arms dropped to her sides. Her eyes glazed over as if she'd just plum run out of steam. She tottered on her high heels and began to slowly collapse against the overburdened coatrack.

Theodosia juked sideways to keep the coatrack from crashing over, while Drayton grabbed Tawney, pulled her up by the shoulders, and spun her around like a top.

"Get a grip on yourself," Drayton said.

Tawney dropped her head forward and let her tears flow harder. "You don't know what it's like . . ."

"Get that crazy woman out of here before she tries to

attack Toddy again," Delaine yelped. "Before I beat her head into tomato paste."

As Tawney blubbered uncontrollably, Theodosia physically took her by the arm and dragged her down the hallway in front of the stunned luncheon audience. She pulled Tawney into her office, shut the door, and sat her down in the chair across from her desk. "Sit. Stay," she commanded, as if she were talking to Earl Grey.

Tawney obeyed.

Sighing deeply, Theodosia handed Tawney a box of Kleenex tissues. Tawney continued to weep for a few minutes, and then pulled out a couple of tissues. She wiped her eyes and blew her nose. Dabbed at her eye makeup, too, which had smeared horribly and caused two dark rivulets to run down each side of her face. She looked, Theodosia thought, like a sad French clown.

"Tawney," Theodosia said when Tawney's sobs had finally quieted down. "Why on earth do you think Tod Slawson killed your husband?"

Tawney gazed at her with questioning, red-rimmed eyes. "Because Slawson was negotiating so hard to buy the flag! He was absolutely desperate to get his hands on it, wanted it more than any of the other buyers." One of Tawney's false eyelashes had come unglued and now it flicked up and down like a small jumping spider.

Theodosia let Tawney's words sink in for a moment and then said, "Wait a minute, you *know* who the other buyers are? Your husband confided this to you?"

"Yes. Well, somewhat."

Still skeptical, Theodosia lifted an eyebrow. "Somewhat?"

"Donald and I still talked," Tawney said in a reluctant tone of voice. "It's not like we wanted to work things out between us, because we had *serious* relationship problems. Money issues, too. But we weren't exactly scratching each other's eyes out, either."

"So who were they? The buyers, I mean?"

Tawney emitted a series of sharp cries and hiccups as she choked out her words. "Tod Slawson, Earl Bullitt, and Brooklyn Vance were the main ones. But there were a couple of other people, too."

"Do you know who they are?"

"No, I don't," Tawney said. She gave a loud honk into her tissue.

"But you're positive Slawson was desperate enough to harm your husband?"

"I think so."

"That's not exactly positive," Theodosia said.

"What do you want from me?" Tawney shot back.

"I want you to be straight with me," Theodosia said, and then paused. "You really believe Tod Slawson was the one who sent a drone careening into that hot-air balloon?"

"That's what I *suspect*, yes."

"But you don't have any suspicions at all about Brooklyn Vance?"

Tawney shook her head. "It couldn't have been Brooklyn. She's the nicest, most sincere person you'd ever want to meet."

Theodosia wasn't completely sure about that, but let it go for now.

"What about Earl Bullitt?" Theodosia asked.

Tawney lifted a hand and seesawed it back and forth. "Maybe. I don't know, he's certainly nasty enough. And so crude. Definitely a sociopathic type."

"Okay, wild card question. Do you think Harold Affolter could have killed your husband?"

"I don't know," Tawney said. "I mean, I've never actually *met* the man, but the police told me he was a whistleblower at SyncSoft. That he was responsible for trying to stall a major product release. So . . . you know . . . he *could* have had a really big chip on his shoulder."

I hope not. I truly do.

"Do you feel well enough to go back out into the tea shop and finish your lunch?" Theodosia asked.

Tawney shrugged. "I guess."

"And you promise to remain calm? No more knives or assault with a blunt object? No shattering of teacups?"

"I promise," Tawney said.

Theodosia gave her an encouraging smile. "Okay then."

Theodosia led Tawney back to her seat, poured her a fresh cup of tea, and brought her a slice of quiche. Brooklyn, with sympathy on her face, reached across the table and patted Tawney's hand. She was clearly sensitive to the woman's emotional needs.

Delaine and Tod Slawson were seated on the far side of the room well away from Tawney. Neither party spoke to or acknowledged the other. They'd settled into what a political scientist would probably call a nonaggression pact. Never going to be friends, but they weren't about to kill each other, either. At least not here and now.

Thank goodness, the Tawney-Slawson fracas hadn't dampened any spirits at the tea luncheon. Guests conversed excitedly as Theodosia and Miss Dimple cleared plates, poured cups of dessert tea, and passed out supersized desserts, which were much appreciated.

After a while, guests began to flit about, conferring excitedly with Madame Poporov while Theodosia handed out samples of Drayton's Black Velvet tea to everyone as a sort of apology gift.

Two winners were announced for the Nancy Drew contest, enthusiastic cheering ensued, and prizes of vintage Nancy Drew books, teapots, and tea were awarded.

Delaine and Tod Slawson slipped out early while the rest of the guests hung around to savor their tea, visit with Madame Poporov, and shop the gift area. Nobody mentioned the fight.

When Tawney Kingsley finally departed and there were only a few stragglers remaining, Drayton blew out a long breath and said, "Wasn't that a laugh and a half."

"I've never seen anything like it," Theodosia said. She was still stunned that mayhem had intruded into her tea shop, normally such a sane and pleasant oasis. She prayed that nothing like it would ever happen again.

Even Madame Poporov expressed her shock. "I didn't see that fight coming at all," she said. "And I should have." She pursed her lips and shook her head mournfully. "I'm supposed to be *attuned* to disturbances and fractures in the fabric of the universe."

"It's the storm," Drayton said. "It's probably knocked everything off-kilter."

"That must be it." She nodded.

"Would you care for another cup of tea and a chocolate cake pop?" he asked her. "We have plenty of both."

Madame Poporov smiled. "How kind of you."

While Drayton was fixing her a small pot of tea, Haley crept up to the counter. Drayton saw Haley out of the corner of his eye. Theodosia, who didn't consider herself remotely psychic, also saw the inquisitive look on Haley's face and knew precisely what she was up to.

"What's going on?" Theodosia asked Haley.

"Oh . . . uh. Do you think *now* we could ask Madame Poporov about the murders? The triple homicide?"

"I don't think that would be appropriate," Drayton said immediately.

"Why not?" Haley asked.

"Because . . ." Drayton struggled to come up with a good answer but wasn't able to dredge one up.

Haley turned to Theodosia. "What do you think?"

Theodosia considered Haley's question. "I think . . . what can it hurt?"

Drayton lifted a single eyebrow. "Looks like we've struck a happy medium, so to speak."

So the three of them, Theodosia, Drayton, and Haley—with Miss Dimple looking on expectantly—gave Madame Poporov a sort of CliffsNotes version of the hot-air balloon crash, the missing flag, and all the various players.

The little frown lines between Madame Poporov's brows grew deeper and deeper the more she heard.

"So you're on the lookout for a desperate character," she said finally.

"Exactly," Haley said. "A stone-cold killer."

"And you saw what happened here today," Drayton said. "The victim's wife attacking the antiques dealer."

"With a few folks pointing their fingers at other contenders," Theodosia said.

"So what do you think?" Haley asked.

Madame Poporov's hands were poised delicately above her crystal ball. "I'd say the killer is close by."

"That's it?" Haley said. "That's what you see after just a quick flutter over your crystal ball?"

Miss Dimple leaned forward. "You don't want to read your tarot cards, too?"

Madame Poporov shook her head. "My advice to every one of you is to use the utmost caution."

"Because the killer is close at hand," Theodosia said.

"Extremely close," Madame Poporov said.

"You're quite positive of this?" Drayton asked. As a nonbeliever in spiritualists, he certainly was hanging on her every word.

Madame Poporov gave a little shiver. "I can actually *feel* a ghostly presence!"

16

❦

As Theodosia bused dishes and put away candlesticks, her mind was in turmoil. *Could Tawney have been right about Tod Slawson? Had Slawson cleverly engineered the drone attack? And then managed to steal the Navy Jack flag for himself?*

Or was Tawney the real killer and flag thief and she'd just been throwing up a hellacious smoke screen today? Garnering a bit of sympathy so she was sure to get a nice piece of SyncSoft as well as Don Kingsley's money, life insurance, and stock options.

And if Tod Slawson *was* the guilty party, would Delaine associate with a killer? Maybe. But only if she didn't know the real truth about him and instead thought that he was a terrific guy. Marriage material.

And what about Earl Bullitt? He'd been bidding on the flag, too. Plus, he was rude and boorish, the proverbial bull in a china shop. And not only was he sneaky, but there was no love lost between him and Brooklyn Vance. They'd pretty much demonstrated that last night at the Floral Teacups Competition.

Bullitt.

Even his name sounded dangerous. Just speaking it was like spitting out a hunk of gristle.

Theodosia set down her plastic tub full of dishes and reached for the phone.

It took her five minutes and the persistence of Job to get through to Detective Tidwell. But now she finally had him on the line.

"What? What do you want now?" Tidwell asked. He sounded gruff. Busy.

"I want to know what you have on Earl Bullitt so far," Theodosia said.

"Who is this again?"

"You know who this is. I'm wondering if you've turned up anything on Earl Bullitt."

"Even if I had," Tidwell said, "why would I share such pertinent information with you?"

"Because I have a vested interest in this case," Theodosia said.

"Not really."

"Of course I do. Listen, you weren't there. You didn't see that hot-air balloon suddenly explode into flames and crash to the ground. You didn't hear the victims' screams."

Tidwell was silent for a few moments.

"Are you still there?" Theodosia asked.

"I'm here and I despise the fact that you're poking around in this."

"I'm sorry."

"No, you're not," Tidwell said. "I don't think you have any idea how desperate this situation really is."

"Now you're worried about me?"

"I have concerns for everyone involved."

"Let's get back to Earl Bullitt," Theodosia said. "Do you consider him dangerous?"

"Yes, I do," Tidwell said.

"Like crazed, sociopathic dangerous?"

"Define 'crazed.'"

"Do you think Bullitt could be the killer?"

"Could be. However, I have no proof," Tidwell said.

Proof. There's that pesky little stumbling block again. How do I go about finding some proof?

As if reading her mind, Tidwell said, "Please don't go bumbling about, trying to investigate. Just leave Mr. Bullitt well enough alone."

"Thank you, I'll take that under advisement," Theodosia said. She hung up the phone and walked to the front counter where Drayton was swishing out his last teapot.

"Come on," Theodosia said. "Grab your coat. We need to go bumbling in somewhere where we've been warned not to go."

"We need to what?" Drayton said.

"We need to check somebody out. Ask a few probing questions."

Drayton's mouth twisted up at the corners. "Who exactly are we going to probe?"

"Earl Bullitt."

Earl Bullitt's shop, Bullitt's Antiques & Collectibles, was located on King Street, a fairly glitzy, high-traffic shopping area where dozens of galleries, restaurants, and antiques shops were located. Bullitt's shop was located in a traditional redbrick building with dapper white shutters. Gold letters, like an old-fashioned mercantile sign, arced to form the words BULLITT'S ANTIQUES & COLLECTIBLES. BUY AND SELL.

"Parking space," Drayton sang out because it wasn't always easy to find a spot in this neighborhood.

Theodosia slid her Jeep into a spot directly behind a black Porsche Carrera that was parked in front of Bullitt's shop. The car looked sleek and dangerous, like some kind of predatory animal.

"That's some exotic-looking car," Drayton remarked as they stepped out of the Jeep and onto the sidewalk. "You think it belongs to Bullitt?"

"Take a gander at the license plate," Theodosia said. The blue-and-peach-colored South Carolina plate with its signature palmetto tree read BULLITT.

"Ah, personalized," Drayton said. There was the slightest *tone* to his voice.

"Hard to keep a low profile driving around town with a plate like that," Theodosia said. Early on, she'd toyed with the notion of getting a TEA LADY license plate. Then she'd dropped the idea like a hot potato once Bill Glass had started calling her that. Theodosia had also reached the conclusion that she didn't need to announce herself wherever she went. Better to be subtle. Something Earl Bullitt clearly didn't have a handle on.

Earl Bullitt was on the phone when they walked through the front door of his antiques shop. Looking past a tasty array of items that included a silver soup tureen, cut glass cruet set, brass clock, and Wedgwood vase, Theodosia could see Bullitt in his back office. He was sitting behind his desk, phone held tight to his ear, talking in a loud hail-hearty voice. From the sound of it he was probably trying to woo a client or potential client.

"Yes, yes, of course I can get it," Bullitt said. "Don't worry, I'm going to come through for you." He glanced out into the shop and noticed Theodosia and Drayton wandering around. He dropped his voice to a hoarse whisper. "Remember the Drews painting? I managed to snag that, didn't I?"

Theodosia glanced at Drayton and raised her eyebrows. This guy Bullitt was some kind of operator.

"Mr. Bullitt seems like a lovely man to do business with," Drayton responded in a quietly facetious voice.

"Remember what Tod Slawson said when he first came crashing into the tea shop? He said Bullitt was a crook."

"Maybe so, but he has some first-class pieces here. Take a look at this music box. Made by Bremond of Geneva, Switzerland, one of the best." Drayton lifted the burnished wood music box up, wound it, and then opened the top to let tinkling music flow out. "You see how it replicates the effect of a mandolin?"

"Bullitt also has some lovely antique jewelry," Theodosia said. She'd spotted a Burmese ruby ring, a Verdura cuff, and a spectacular South Seas pearl necklace whose price tag made her gasp. *One hundred twenty-eight thousand dollars? Yow.*

A few minutes later, Earl Bullitt emerged from his office with a snarky grin pasted across his face. "Well, well, we meet again, Miss Browning. Tell me, are you unhappy about how I cast my votes last night?"

"I think, all in all, we did a fine job," Theodosia said.

"Good." Bullitt seemed satisfied with her response. "I do, too. So."

Drayton stuck out his hand. "And I'm—"

"I know who you are," Bullitt said. "You work with her." He rocked back on his heels, obviously a lot more relaxed now. "How may I help you folks? Are you looking for a particular item?"

"I'm always interested in antique teaware," Drayton said.

Bullitt squinted at him. "Oh yeah? I do have a rather nice Victorian bachelor teapot." He reached into a glass case and pulled it out. "Sterling silver, manufactured around 1865. You see, there's a hand-embossed scene of the foxhunt on the side of the teapot and the hinged lid is crowned with a fox head finial."

"Quite nice," Drayton said. "I've not seen one like this. May I ask how much?"

"I've had it priced at two thousand. But there's a little wiggle room in that number. I'm sure we could work something out," Bullitt said.

"You come highly recommended as an antiques dealer," Theodosia said. She'd decided to use the honey versus vinegar ploy.

"Is that a fact?" Bullitt said. "Who recommended me?"

"Tod Slawson," Theodosia said. She wondered how Bullitt would react.

He didn't disappoint her.

Earl Bullitt curled his lip and practically chortled. "That crook? I hear the police are nipping at the heels of his fancy French loafers. They think *he* might have been responsible for that hot-air balloon explosion. That he might have stolen the Navy Jack flag, too."

Theodosia decided to take the gloves off—not that they were ever on.

"I understand you were also one of the bidders," she said.

"Where'd you hear that?" Bullitt growled.

Drayton folded his arms across his chest. "Basically all over town."

"But mostly from Tawney Kingsley," Theodosia said.

"Huh, that lady's a sneaky one," Bullitt said. "One day she professes to despise old Don, can't wait for their divorce to go through. And now that he's dead and buried . . . Wait, is he buried?"

"Tomorrow," Theodosia said.

"Anyway," Bullitt continued. "Now that Tawney stands to inherit every dang cent, she suddenly paints herself as the poor grieving widow." He flashed a smile that was all teeth and not a hint of warmth. "Nice job if you can get it."

"Maybe Tawney's the one who stole the flag," Theodosia said.

"If she's the culprit she'll get found out soon enough," Bullitt said. "Hard to sell something that important and keep it on the down low."

"What if you're dealing with a wealthy collector?" Theodosia asked. "One who values his privacy above all?"

"There *are* a number of those types around," Drayton said.

Bullitt gave an uninterested shrug. "Maybe."

"You were bidding on the flag," Theodosia said. "You must have an opinion about these rather strange coincidences."

"You mean do *I* know who crashed the hot-air balloon and stole the flag?" Bullitt said.

"Maybe it wasn't the same person," Theodosia said. "Culprit A could have killed Don Kingsley and the other two passengers, and culprit B, someone entirely different, could have stolen the flag."

"You pose an interesting theory," Bullitt said.

"But you don't care to wager a guess as to what might have happened?" Theodosia asked.

Bullitt shook his head. "Not me, I'm no investigator."

"Hmm," Theodosia said. She felt stumped, unsure of what to ask Bullitt next. Luckily, Drayton stepped in to fill the void.

"I was wondering if you ever handled any early American paintings," Drayton said.

Bullitt cocked his head. "Such as?"

"I'm always on the lookout for a nice William Ranney or Martin Johnson Heade," Drayton said.

"You're a high-end collector," Bullitt said, giving him a slightly more interested look.

"Well, the paintings would have to be priced at the lower end," Drayton said.

"I have a few oil paintings, but nothing of the caliber you're interested in," Bullitt said.

"Can we look at them anyway?" Theodosia asked. She'd spotted a door next to a lovely Chippendale highboy that was marked PRIVATE and wondered what was in there. "Are they in . . . What is this?" She stepped toward the door marked PRIVATE, ready to pull open the door. "A separate annex?"

"All the paintings I have are on the walls and that particular room is being used for storage at the moment," Bullitt said.

"For early American pieces?" Drayton asked. "Sounds interesting."

"It's nothing you'd be interested in," Bullitt hastened to say. He advanced a few steps closer to the door and maneuvered himself so that he was blocking it.

"You're sure we can't take a peek inside?" Theodosia asked.

"Quite sure," Bullitt said. "Maybe another time, once I get my merchandise appraised, priced, and straightened out." He made a big show of looking at his wristwatch. "Now. If there's nothing else I can help you with, I really have to get back to work."

Out on the sidewalk, Theodosia said, "He really didn't want us to look inside that room."

"Maybe it was full of junk," Drayton said. "Just like he said."

"Or maybe it's full of stolen goods."

"You mean like the Navy Jack flag?"

"That thought had crossed my mind," Theodosia said.

"Bullitt seems rather crafty," Drayton said. "But he doesn't strike me as being clever enough to pull off a drone attack and a major robbery all in one day."

"Maybe Earl Bullitt is simply opportunistic."

"What are you saying?" Drayton asked. "That Earl Bullitt *heard* about the hot-air balloon crash so he immediately rushed over to Don Kingsley's house to steal the flag?"

"It could have happened that way," Theodosia said.

"I don't see how that scenario could have played out. I mean, how would Earl Bullitt *know* that there'd been a terrible accident involving Don Kingsley?"

Theodosia was standing right next to Bullitt's car. She bent forward and peered inside. "Maybe because he's got a police scanner in his car?"

Drayton opened his mouth as if to say something, and then snapped it shut.

"I know," Theodosia said. "It's an odd coincidence and it does sound far-fetched but it *could* have happened that way."

The color drained from Drayton's face. "Dear Lord. I suppose it could have."

A soft chime echoed from deep inside Theodosia's handbag.

"Excuse me, I'd better get this," Theodosia said. "It might be Haley with a question about closing up the tea shop." She grabbed her phone and punched it on. "Hello?"

"Theodosia?" came a quavering voice.

"Angie?" *It's Angie Congdon. What could she want?*

"Can you come over here right now? I mean, to the Featherbed House?" Angie's voice veered from a nervous quaver to an almost-sob.

"Angie, what's wrong?"

"Everything!"

17

❧

There was a squad car along with an aging Crown Victoria parked in front of the Featherbed House when Theodosia and Drayton arrived. Theodosia immediately recognized the Crown Vic as belonging to Detective Tidwell. Ford didn't manufacture that particular model anymore, but Tidwell was hanging on tight to his old one. Clearly, Drayton wasn't the only person who was phobic about change.

Teddy Vickers, the longtime manager at the Featherbed House, met them in the lobby. He was dressed neatly, in a navy sweater and khaki slacks, his dark hair slicked back, but he looked upset. His eyes were unnaturally bright and his cheeks were blotches of pink.

"Where is she?" Theodosia asked.

"Angie? She called you?" Teddy Vickers asked. He seemed vastly relieved to see Theodosia and Drayton.

"Angie called and asked me to hurry over. She sounded upset."

"And rightly so. She's being questioned by a police detective. Harold, too," Vickers said.

"Is it Detective Tidwell?"

"I think that was his name, yes. And he brought along two of his flunkies," Vickers said.

"Where are they?" Drayton asked.

"In the dining room," Vickers said. "If you can do anything at all, anything to help Angie, that would be fantastic."

"We're going to try," Drayton said.

Vickers glanced at his wristwatch. "I don't know if this is a possibility, but if you could convince them to move into the breakfast room next door, that would be helpful. I'm supposed to be setting out wine and cheese for our guests right now. And all the glasses and things are stored in the dining room."

"You want to set up here in the lobby?"

"That's the plan," Vickers said.

Theodosia's eyes flicked around the elegant lobby of the Featherbed House. The walls were painted a pale yellow but had been shellacked or glazed so they fairly glistened in the light from a dozen flickering candles. A persimmon-red Oriental carpet covered the polished wood floor, and wing chairs and two sofas, all covered in yellow chintz, invited guests to come and sit a spell. Angie's trademark geese were all over the place, too. Needlepoint geese pillows on the plump sofas, hand-carved wooden geese decorating the fireplace mantle, bronze goose lamps, and an entire flock of ceramic geese.

Theodosia touched the door that led into the dining room. "I'll see if I can move things along."

Vickers nodded. "I'd appreciate it."

When Theodosia walked into the dining room, it felt like a scene right out of a B movie. Angie was sobbing quietly into a hanky while Harold Affolter, her fiancé, sputtered away indignantly. Detective Tidwell sat across the table from them looking like the judge on doomsday. His face wore a scowl that veered between angry and indignant. A young man sitting next to Tidwell just looked as if he were extremely interested in the proceedings. A uniformed officer sat next to him.

Theodosia cleared her throat. "Excuse me."

Tidwell glanced up at her. "Miss Browning," he said. He didn't seem surprised to see her. But he didn't give her a welcoming look, either.

Theodosia focused on the young man sitting beside Tidwell. "And who might you be?" she asked.

"I'm—" the young man started to say, but Tidwell cut him off immediately.

"This is Archibald Banks, a criminologist from our crime lab," Tidwell said.

"Archie," the man said. "Call me Archie."

"Crime lab?" Drayton said. "Has there been a crime committed here?"

"I'm asking the questions," Tidwell said, putting some grit in his voice. "And I don't appreciate the two of you barging in here."

"We didn't barge in, Angie invited us," Theodosia said. She stared directly at Tidwell. "I take it you've come to ask more questions about Harold's drone?"

"It is an ongoing investigation," Tidwell countered.

Theodosia looked at Angie. "Did you call a lawyer?"

Angie shook her head. "Not yet."

"Do you want me to call my uncle?" Theodosia asked.

Before Angie could answer, Tidwell said, "I don't see any need for legal interference. We're not here to arrest anyone, we merely want to take a look at Mr. Affolter's drone."

"You're here to look at Harold's drone," Theodosia repeated.

"That's correct," Tidwell said.

"Why do you want to inspect his drone?" Theodosia asked.

Anger flashed behind Tidwell's beady eyes for a split second, and then he turned a smile on her. But it was anything but warm. "Upon analyzing nylon shreds from the downed hot-air balloon, we discovered several small fragments of metal that were embedded—almost scorched—into it."

"If we can locate the drone, we can match the metal," Archie Banks said. "It's that simple." He sounded excited. Almost happy.

"Wait a minute. I thought the drone crash-landed," Theodosia said. Last she'd seen of the drone, it had dipped low and flown away as if trying to avoid the fiery explosion. She'd just assumed that the drone had spiraled down and ended up in a pile of metal not far from the hot-air balloon's crash site, and that the police had already confiscated the wrecked pieces.

"No such luck," Tidwell said. "The drone went rogue. Apparently buzzed off and made a clean getaway." Tidwell turned his gaze toward Harold. "Or maybe not so clean."

"So you just want to *look* at it?" Theodosia said.

"We're at the stage in our investigation where we need to physically examine a number of drones," Tidwell said.

"How many drones are you looking at?" Theodosia asked.

"Six, all told. Unfortunately . . . we're not getting the kind of cooperation we hoped for." Tidwell lifted a hand and pursed his lips as if to say, *What can you do?*

"This request doesn't seem unreasonable," Theodosia said to Angie and Harold. "Why don't you show Detective Tidwell your drone and then he can be on his way?"

"If you think it's okay . . ." Angie said.

"Where is the drone?" Theodosia asked.

"The last I recall, it was stashed in the basement," Harold said. "Right downstairs."

They all trooped out of the dining room and down a narrow hallway. The hallway led into the large kitchen, where two young chefs were prepping plates of cheese, fruit, and crackers. There were two doors against the far wall. One led to the outdoor patio, the other to the basement.

Harold led the way down a narrow wooden staircase. "Be careful," he warned. "These steps are somewhat rickety and difficult to negotiate."

Angie followed behind Harold, and Theodosia went down behind Tidwell, while Archie Banks and Drayton were last in line. Theodosia was aware of Tidwell's slightly wheezy breathing as he descended ahead of her, but was amazed that he appeared so light on his feet for such a large man. Like a dancer, she thought. One who's still got a few tricky moves left.

The first room they encountered was a storeroom. A string of overhead lights lit the place. Crates of oranges, cartons of coffee and other canned goods, extra dining room chairs, and extra umbrellas for the outdoor patio tables, were piled up against the walls. It looked exactly like what you'd expect in a busy B and B. Not precisely organized, but not a total mess, either.

The second room housed the wine cellar. At least three hundred bottles of wine were on display here, all resting on wooden wine racks. Theodosia spotted a Château Margaux and a Château Latour. Obviously, Angie had excellent taste. And so, probably, did a few of her guests.

"This is a big cellar," Archie Banks said as they walked through. Here the cement floor was uneven and patched. Spiderwebs hung everywhere.

Tidwell sneezed. "And quite dusty. I trust we have an actual destination. That we're making forward progress."

"It's just up ahead," Harold said, still leading the way.

They came to a room with hewn stone walls, the largest basement room yet. Though the light bulbs were yellow and it was considerably more dim in here, they could make out dozens of objects scattered around. Lawn chairs, four fat tire bicycles, a pair of sawhorses, tools, a pile of lumber, a Weedwacker, and bags of fertilizer. It was messy but not hoarder messy.

Harold scuttled ahead of the group. "It should be right . . ." He stopped abruptly in his tracks and peered down into a large cardboard box.

Everyone gathered around him and peered into the box, as if it held some wonderful, mystical answer.

Only problem was, the box was empty. There was no drone inside.

Harold lifted a hand and scrubbed hard at the side of his head. "Well, the drone *was* here." He looked puzzled. "I mean, it *should* be here."

"Unless your drone makes use of a Romulan cloaking device, I don't see it," Tidwell said.

"Neither do I," Theodosia said. She felt a surge of worry. Had Harold been involved in the hot-air balloon crash after all? No, she didn't think he had. Then again . . .

Harold Affolter was literally spinning in circles, tearing through the mishmash of stored junk. "It has to be here somewhere! I can't imagine where it went. A drone doesn't just disappear!"

Angie made a small sound in the back of her throat, like a startled rabbit. She looked terrified.

"Maybe during all our construction and rehabbing of the inn, the drone got packed up and moved somewhere," Harold said. "Out to one of the garages." He sounded both scared and hopeful. "Or maybe the workmen who were here thought it was a pile of junk that needed to be recycled."

"Let's look around again," Theodosia said. "Everybody spread out and take a careful look-see."

The search party of six combed through the entire basement, going from one room to another, looking behind old furniture, probing tarps and cloths, searching on overhead shelves. They found nothing.

"I can't believe it," Harold said. His voice had risen

two octaves to a shrill squawk. "It's completely up and disappeared."

"And we're sure we've looked everywhere?" Theodosia asked.

"This is a large building, so not quite everywhere," Tidwell said. "But a search warrant and some police reinforcements could easily fix that."

"Please, no," Angie said. "I beg you not to go poking around the premises. You've got to respect our guests."

This inn is her only livelihood, Theodosia thought.

Tidwell rocked back on the heels of his heavy cop shoes. "Clearly, the drone is no longer in your possession."

Harold was truly befuddled. "I honestly—*honestly*—don't know where it could have disappeared to."

"Don't you really?" Tidwell asked.

"No, and I don't like your tone of voice," Harold snapped back at him. "Or where this conversation seems to be going."

"I'm afraid," Tidwell warned, "that our conversation will remain *ongoing*. Until I lay my hands on that missing drone."

"How much access do your guests usually have to the kitchen?" Theodosia asked.

"Not too much," Angie said. "We serve breakfast in the dining room and wine and cheese in the lobby."

"What about in between?" Theodosia asked.

"We don't have lunch service, but we usually have cookies, fresh fruit, and bottles of water available all day in the breakfast room," Angie said. "So guests are invited to help themselves."

"And the breakfast room adjoins the kitchen," Theodosia said. "Which isn't exactly off-limits. So it's possible someone could have slipped in there and gone downstairs."

"I suppose it's possible," Angie said. "But . . ." She stopped and shook her head. She didn't have anything else to add.

* * *

Drayton led the way back upstairs, but Theodosia gestured to Tidwell to stay behind. She wanted to talk to him.

With only a modicum of politeness, Tidwell remained with her in the basement. "What?" he asked as he wiggled his nose, trying to contain another sneeze.

"Have you investigated any of the members of the Americana Club? Perhaps one of them . . ."

"There's nothing there," Tidwell said. "They are all solid, upstanding citizens."

"Are you sure about that?"

Tidwell sighed and started up the stairs. With his back to her, he said, "I'm quite positive."

Once Tidwell, Archie Banks, and the officer had left the Featherbed House, Angie pulled Theodosia out onto the front veranda. With the scent of magnolia blossoms perfuming the air around them and the sound of rain gurgling in the downspouts, Angie said, "Theo, I need to tell you something."

Theodosia nodded.

"I didn't want to say this in front of everyone, because Harold would be terribly embarrassed. But . . ." Angie took a hard swallow and waved a hand in front of her face as if to stave off more tears.

"Take your time," Theodosia urged.

Angie nodded. "It's just that . . . well, Harold lost his job."

"Oh no."

"He got a call from SyncSoft's director of HR this morning. It seems Harold's been summarily fired."

"Can they do that? Is that a legal move?" Theodosia asked.

"Well, they did it," Angie said. "They told Harold that

his entire department was being downsized and that he was entitled to two weeks of severance pay."

"So he has no recourse whatsoever?"

"He's still in shock and I'm not sure what to do about it. What I *can* do about it."

"Tell me," Theodosia said. "Has Harold ever said anything to you about the Americana Club?"

Angie thought for a minute. "Maybe."

"Maybe?"

"When we were doing some major renovations last year, I think Harold might have borrowed a couple books from one of their members."

"Books about flags?"

"No, architecture. Harold was concerned about preserving architectural integrity."

"But Harold never joined this club?" Theodosia asked.

Angie shook her head. "No. Never. Not to my knowledge anyway."

As Theodosia drove Drayton home, her fingers drummed an anxious beat against her steering wheel.

"Are you still worried?" Drayton asked.

"Aren't you? Tidwell's on a fishing expedition. Harold didn't crash his drone into that hot-air balloon."

"But what if he did?" Drayton said in a quiet, even tone.

Theodosia was so stunned she almost ran a red light. "Drayton, you can't be serious!" She glanced over at him, a quiet shadow in her passenger seat.

"How well do you know Harold? I mean, really?" Drayton asked. "How well does Angie know him?"

"I don't know." Theodosia lifted her foot off the gas pedal. She'd been cruising at forty in a twenty-five-mile-an-hour zone. Gotta watch out. She didn't want to hit a . . . tourist, or something. "Angie's been dating Harold for a while, I guess. Maybe a year and a half?"

"Harold could be one of those guys who keeps every-thing bottled up tight inside himself. Every anger, griev-ance, and imagined slight. Then one day, the cork blows sky-high and all those emotions come ripping out. Ker-pow!"

"Now you're really making me depressed."

"A sage piece of advice," Drayton said. "If you want to avoid a case of advanced clinical depression, then I sug-gest you *not* attend Don Kingsley's funeral tomorrow."

"I can hardly back out now. Not after I promised Taw-ney that I'd be there to support her. Besides, I told Tawney that you were coming with me."

"*Me*?" Drayton yelped.

"Drayton, we need to get to the bottom of this attack drone–disappearing flag business once and for all."

"By attending a funeral? By poking our nose in a mur-der investigation?" Drayton asked. "Do you think any of this is wise?"

Theodosia shook her head. "Probably not. But when has that ever stopped us before?"

18

❧

Earl Grey was wolfing down his kibble as Theodosia zipped up her blue nylon windbreaker. It was dark and still drizzling outside, but she felt jazzed and anxious and knew she needed a run. Even if it was a quick twice around the block, it always felt good to inhale a little extra oxygen and get the blood pumping. Running helped clear her head so she could think better. And tonight Theodosia had an awful lot to think about.

Earl Grey finished eating and moved to his water dish. *Slop, slop, slop.* He drank noisily and greedily, and then lifted his nose. Water streamed onto the floor making *that* a slippery wet mess.

Theodosia grabbed an old tea towel and gently wiped her dog's muzzle. "Are you sure you want to go with me tonight?" she asked him.

"Rrowr." *Yes.*

"Okay, but you could get splashed because there are going to be puddles. You know how much you hate getting your paws wet."

Earl Grey stared resolutely at her. His mind was made up. They were going for that walk.

"Okay. Don't say I didn't warn you."

Theodosia grabbed a flashlight, snapped the leash onto the dog's collar, and headed out the back door with him. They splashed past a tiny goldfish pond and ducked under a palmetto tree that was bent and heavy with rain. They walked single file down the narrow flagstone path that ran alongside Theodosia's cottage and led to the front of the house. Because the stones were wet and slippery, some with damp, velvety moss growing on top of them, they had to pick their way carefully.

Just as Theodosia and Earl Grey emerged onto the front sidewalk and were about to set out in the light mist, a shadow floated toward them from across the street.

Who . . . ?

"Hey!" A teenage boy raised a hand and hailed Theodosia with an enthusiastic wave. Then, with a goofy grin lighting his face, the boy dashed toward them. Theodosia recognized him immediately. It was Shep O'Neil, one of the neighbor kids. Though at almost six feet tall, Shep probably couldn't be classified as a kid anymore.

"Hey there, Shep," Theodosia said. "How's it going?"

"Miz Browning," Shep said in a friendly voice. "What up?" He wore a dark hoodie, jeans, and tennis shoes, just like every other young high school guy. He also looked a little damp and rain-spattered.

"What can I do for you?" Theodosia asked. Shep O'Neil was sixteen years old, string-bean thin, with large feet encased in the latest tennis shoes Nike had to offer. He had a permanently crooked smile and was favoring her with that smile right now.

"It's what I can do for you, Miz Browning," Shep said. He took a step back and made a vague gesture in the direction of her house. "It's your gutters, ma'am. With all the rain that's been pounding down lately, most folks' gutters are clogged up real bad."

"I suppose they are."

Shep held out his hand for Earl Grey to sniff. "I could clean 'em out for you if you want. I've been going around the neighborhood, cleaning out the muck and leaves and stuff for a lot of the neighbors. Well.. . ." His sales pitch faltered a bit as he shifted from one foot to the other. "I usually charge folks around twenty-five bucks."

Theodosia hesitated. Not because of the price—it was quite reasonable—but because Shep was not exactly known for finishing his odd jobs. Last summer she'd hired him to weed her back garden and, halfway through the job, he'd run off to play softball. When Theodosia checked with Shep's mom a few days later, Mrs. O'Neil told her that Shep had been packed off to sailing camp.

But Theodosia figured that, after all this pounding rain, most gutters and downspouts were clogged with great gobs of leaves and pine needles and Lord knows what else. Heck, if you listened carefully to all that gurgling, they actually *sounded* clogged.

"Okay, Shep, that would be fine. When do you suppose you can get to them?"

"We've got a deal then?" Shep seemed pleasantly surprised. "In the next couple of days for sure."

"You've got a ladder or do you need me to . . . ?"

"I got a ladder," Shep said.

"Okay, see you later then." Theodosia tightened up on Earl Grey's leash and they jogged off down the block.

The night was as dark as a coal bin, the streetlamps rimmed with faint yellow halos. There wasn't another soul on the street—nobody walking their dog or taking an evening constitutional. Theodosia heard the hiss of tires on wet streets from the occasional car, but that was blocks away over on Concord Street.

They jogged down East Bay and then turned into White Point Gardens, which was located at the exact tip of the peninsula. Wild gusts of wind swept in to thrash the trees. Streamers of fog drifted in and the salty smell of the Atlantic hung heavy in the air. When Theodosia and Earl Grey stepped onto the grass it was rain-soaked and squishy, so they wisely ran on the sidewalk that stretched along South Battery Street. They passed elegant mansions of all varieties—Victorian, Federal, Italianate, Gothic Revival, and Georgian. Like so many homes in the romantic city that was once christened "Charles Town," these grand old homes were painted in a soft French palette: dove gray, pale pink, eggshell white, cornflower blue.

Halfway down the length of the park, they came to a gravel path and veered onto it. They wound past antique Civil War cannons that stood like sentinels and an old bandstand where concerts and weddings were still held, ending up at the very tip of the point. Here, where the Ashley River flowed in to their right and the Cooper River did the same on their left, was where early settlers had first set foot on this land and rogue pirates had been hanged to death. Just across Charleston Harbor, a lighthouse beacon at Patriot's Point glowed warmly. Always a welcome and reassuring sight.

Rollers pounded the shell beach where, just last week, children had played in sunbeams and dabbled their toes in gentle flotsam. Now enormous waves surged in and white foam bubbled and hissed at the shoreline. In the morning, seabirds would flock there, pecking and probing, eagerly looking for tiny crustaceans that rough tides had swept in.

Feeling buoyed from the surge of oxygen that the waves had stirred up, Theodosia led Earl Grey down King Street. They jogged past enormous homes with tall, illuminated windows, and turned down a narrow alley. This was one of the supercool things about the Historic District—the narrow paths, alleys, and ancient carriage lanes that spread through it like a system of tiny capillaries.

But this one, the one that Theodosia had chosen tonight, wasn't one of the infamous Charleston alleys like Dueler's Alley or Philadelphia Alley. It was far more private. So narrow and hidden that most people didn't even know it existed. But it was one of Theodosia's favorites. Unlike the more traditional walled alleys, this one allowed an easy peek into fabulous backyards where fountains, fern gardens, reflecting ponds, and English rose gardens held sway.

This is how the other half lives, Theodosia thought. The homes were all large, luxe, and upper crust. Lovely but not exactly her cup of tea.

"We prefer a residence that's small and cozy, don't we?" Theodosia whispered to Earl Grey.

"Rrowr?"

As they walked down the narrow lane, Earl Grey lurched forward. Then, a split second later, he put on the brakes and skidded to a sudden halt. On guard and hyperalert, the dog stared into one of the backyards with absolute concentration. His ears pricked forward, the hackles on his back wrinkled up like a hedgehog that was anticipating . . . something.

"What is it, boy?" Theodosia asked. Then she realized her dog was staring into the darkness that surrounded Don Kingsley's house.

Don Kingsley's house. The murdered CEO. This is very weird.

A few lights burned behind heavy curtains, so maybe Charles Townsend was there, working late?

But Earl Grey wasn't looking at the lights. There was something in the dark backyard that had caught his attention and riled him up.

Earl Grey let loose a growl, deep and throaty, a canine warning.

Slowly, carefully, Theodosia lifted the latch on the wrought iron gate. She pushed it open gradually, trying not to make a sound as they stepped into the backyard.

What has got my dog so hot and bothered? What's wrong with this picture?

They padded along a stone path, weaving their way through a tumbled, unkempt garden. Though the path was lit by small accent lights snugged low to the ground, they were few and far between. And Theodosia's overall impression was of walking through a veritable tunnel of overgrown magnolias, palmettos, and crepe myrtles that closed tightly around them. It was intriguing but disturbing, too.

This was probably a bad idea. We shouldn't be in here.

"Come on," Theodosia whispered to Earl Grey. They continued through the dripping, damp tunnel of greenery and exited onto a small back patio. There, the house seemed to loom larger and far more imposing than when viewed from the street.

Theodosia tilted her head back and sniffed the wind, testing for danger, *looking* for danger. Nothing here? Something here? Earl Grey was holding himself rigid, his nostrils slightly flared.

Did he sense that something was amiss? Should she trust her dog? He wasn't any kind of hunting dog. Then again . . .

A car splashed by out front on Lamboll Street bringing Theodosia back to reality. It was time to get moving. There was nothing going on here. False alarm.

Theodosia tugged on Earl Grey's leash. If they hurried along the side of the house, they'd pop out on Lamboll, where they should've been walking in the first place. And nobody would be the wiser about their impromptu clandestine detour.

As Theodosia carefully led Earl Grey around a bow window, her foot struck something and she nearly tripped.

What the . . . ?

A root or maybe a coil of garden hose left out had caused her to stumble?

And then, as people so often do when they've been unexpectedly thrown off balance, Theodosia looked down at the reason for her misstep. And saw . . .

Is that a leg? Or an arm?

Theodosia gasped out loud and put her hand over her

mouth to stifle a scream. Just as she gathered herself together to make a mad dash out of there, she heard a dull groan, which caused her to do a complete double take. Because in the split second it took for her eyes to become accustomed to the utter incongruity of seeing human limbs on the ground, she realized a rather large body was attached to those limbs. Sprawled on the ground, half-hidden beneath a magnolia bush.

Hands shaking, Theodosia snapped on her flashlight and could hardly believe her eyes. It looked like . . . no, it was . . . Detective Tidwell!

19

❧

"*Detective Tidwell!*" *Theodosia* shouted. Stunned beyond belief, she dropped to her knees and touched a hand to his broad shoulder. "What happened? What are you doing here? Why are you sprawled on the ground like that?" Earl Grey nosed forward, also looking genuinely concerned.

"Huh?" Tidwell said. He gazed up at her but his eyes were unfocused and he seemed mentally confused. "What'd you say?"

Theodosia put an arm around Tidwell's shoulders and struggled to get him into a sitting position. "There. Is that better?"

"Better than what?" Tidwell said in a cranky, querulous tone. He blinked rapidly and stared at Theodosia as if seeing her for the first time. "Miss Browning?"

"Yes, it's me."

"What are you doing here?"

"A better question might be what are *you* doing here? Sprawled on the ground all crumpled up?"

Tidwell shook his head, still looking a little wonky. "If you must know, I was on an impromptu stakeout." He slurred his words, saying *wush* for *was* and *shtakeout* for *stakeout*. He sounded like he'd been drinking, but Theodosia knew better. He hadn't been drinking, he just got his bell rung.

"You were on a stakeout right here?" Theodosia asked. "At Don Kingsley's home?"

"Yes, *right here!*" Tidwell shouted as if she was hard of hearing. "Or more to the point, I was taking a casual look around the yard when some lunatic snuck up behind me and struck me on the head!"

"Who was it? Did you see?"

"If I knew who the miserable degenerate was I would have radioed for a police unit and had them arrested. Better yet, I would have *shot* them." Tidwell let loose a loud, shuddering wheeze. "Unfortunately, I stumbled and must have lost my balance."

"Must have lost consciousness, too."

"Um . . . perhaps," Tidwell said.

"That's not good at all. I think we'd better get you to a hospital."

Tidwell's hands flew up and he slashed wildly at the air. "No, absolutely not. I was only out for a minute or two."

"Still, there could be neurological damage . . ."

"No hospital, no damage," he barked.

"You don't know that," Theodosia said. *Dear Lord, this man is bullheaded.*

"Just let me . . . I have to catch my breath."

"Do you think Charles Townsend was the person who hit you?"

Tidwell touched a hand to his head and groaned. "I don't know. I don't think so. But he's in there alright, pussyfooting around like Hamlet's ghost."

"Townsend could have spotted you and hit the panic button," Theodosia said. "He might have thought you were a prowler. Or maybe he recognized you and got scared. It's not like you're . . . inconspicuous."

"Point taken," Tidwell said as he brushed bits of dirt

and leaves from his suit jacket. "Can you get that dog away from me?"

Theodosia pulled back on Earl Grey's leash. "Come on, fella." Then, "I don't know if I should be so nice to you after the way you treated Angie and Harold this afternoon."

"I was just doing my job."

"You were browbeating my friends."

"Oh, boo-hoo," Tidwell said. "Just let it go, will you? And help me get to my car."

"Are you sure you can walk?" Theodosia asked as Tidwell pulled himself up and took one lurching step. "No, you can't. I think we'd better ring the doorbell, go inside, and call for help."

But when they limped up to the back door, Theodosia noticed that it was open a crack.

"Somebody either came running in or out of here," Theodosia said. "And didn't stop to latch the door."

"Huh?" Tidwell said. He was up on his feet and walking but he still staggered like a drunken sailor.

"Charles!" Theodosia called out. "Mr. Townsend! Are you in there?" She rapped her knuckles hard against the partially open door.

Moments later, a shadow moved across the window, and then the door opened with a low moan. Townsend peered out. "Yes?"

"There's been an accident," Theodosia said. "A sort of mugging right here in your side yard."

When Townsend noticed that Theodosia was trying to prop up the listing-to-the-left Tidwell, he looked utterly stunned. "What happened?" he gasped.

"I found Tidwell lying under the shrubbery outside your house," Theodosia explained. "Somebody hit him on the head and he apparently lost consciousness for a few minutes."

"*Detective* Tidwell?" Townsend cried.

"Well, yes."

"You say he was outside . . . here?" Townsend stammered.

"Just doing a little impromptu investigating," Theodosia said. "Could we . . . ?"

"And someone hit him on the head?" Townsend asked.

"Hit me on the head," Tidwell muttered.

"You might have had a prowler on the property," Theodosia said.

When Townsend didn't respond immediately, Theodosia studied him carefully and said, "What's wrong, Charles? You look like you've just seen a ghost." Townsend's face was washed out, his hair looked like it had been electrostatically charged, and his hand shook as he held open the door.

"I . . . I'm fine." Townsend gulped. "Just a little surprised. You surprised me."

"You don't look fine," Theodosia said as Tidwell started to slump against her. "But here, why don't you help me get Detective Tidwell inside. I want to call the duty officer and get a squad car over here to pick him up. I hope you don't mind if my dog comes in, too."

"No, I . . . The police are coming *here*?" Townsend blurted out.

"Did something happen to you?" Theodosia asked. "Because your door was partially open and you're acting as if you're terrified."

"No, no, it's cool. The door was probably an oversight on my part," Townsend said in a shaky voice. "Here, let me give you guys a hand."

Together, Theodosia and Townsend walked the still-staggering Tidwell into the kitchen and sat him down in a chair. Earl Grey followed. Theodosia called the police station and hastily explained the situation. The dispatcher promised to send a squad car immediately, lights and sirens.

Tidwell cocked an eye open. "There's no need for this fuss. I feel perfectly fine."

"Everyone's fine," Theodosia said, looking from Tidwell to Townsend, and thinking to herself that people who claimed to be just fine under unusual circumstances, generally weren't fine at all. Often they were hiding something.

But Theodosia didn't have time to press Townsend on the subject because, two minutes later, a police cruiser pulled up in front and let loose a loud wail on the siren. Townsend ran out to meet the two officers and lead them back to the kitchen.

Though Tidwell had tried to reject Theodosia's help, he gratefully leaned on the arms of the two uniformed officers.

"Thank you," Theodosia said to Townsend as they all walked out onto the front veranda. "You've been very helpful."

Townsend fluttered a hand. "No problem."

"Are you sure everything's alright with you?" Theodosia asked him again. "You seem a little discombobulated."

"No, I'm fine and dandy," Townsend said. His voice sounded shaky, as if he were trying to keep up a brave front. "Good night. Take care."

The officers gingerly loaded Tidwell into the back seat of their cruiser. Tidwell got himself situated and then put down the window and gazed out at Theodosia and Earl Grey.

"Where are you going now?" Tidwell asked her.

"Home. You want to tag along? Maybe poke around and look for a discarded drone?" Theodosia's tone was slightly acerbic. She was still rankled that Tidwell had been so rude when he questioned Angie and Harold this afternoon.

"Hardly. Though if you have the offending object stashed somewhere I'll gladly take it off your hands."

"I wish." Theodosia leaned toward the car and dropped her voice. "Detective Tidwell, if you were here tonight, snooping around, you must be wondering the same thing I am."

"What am I wondering about?" Tidwell asked.

"What if the flag *wasn't* stolen by outside people at all? What if Charles Townsend took it himself and is biding his time? Maybe he stuck it in some deep, dark corner of that big house and he's sitting on top of it like a greedy little spider." She glanced at the Kingsley house. Townsend had shut off the lights on the front veranda. Now the house was couched in shadows. "You saw how he acted tonight. He was scared out of his mind. He's hiding something for sure."

Tidwell thought for a few moments. "There's no proof of his involvement."

"None whatsoever," Theodosia agreed. "On the other hand, Townsend worked for Kingsley and had complete and unfettered access to his collection and his home."

"So you have a hunch."

"Let's call it a spark of intuition," Theodosia said.

"I'm afraid female intuition is not the sort of evidence I can take to a prosecuting attorney."

"What do you need?"

"Proof positive, my dear Miss Browning. Always hard proof." Tidwell closed the window and banged the flat of his hand against the metal grate that separated the front of the police car from the back. "Go!" he shouted. "What are you waiting for!"

Theodosia and Earl Grey walked the few blocks home. It had started to rain a little harder and nobody, but nobody, was moving around on the streets.

Nobody but the person who conked Tidwell.

And maybe they were home by now, chuckling about it, warming themselves with a hot cup of coffee.

No. Better a cup of tea. At least for me, anyway.

Theodosia was just about to slip down the cobblestone path alongside her home, when a panel truck slid quietly to the curb. It was white, with a satellite dish on top and, though it was dark, Theodosia saw that the side of the van was emblazoned with the TV8 logo.

"You're out late," a voice called to her.

Theodosia and Earl Grey waited as Dale Dickerson jumped out of the passenger side and hurried over to join them.

"Not so late," she said.

Dickerson smiled broadly at her as he gave a shrug back and ran a hand through his roving reporter, finely coiffed hair.

Theodosia wondered how he could look so Pepsodent perfect when she felt like a drowned wren that had been fished out of a storm sewer. She guessed that roving reporters always had to look picture-perfect, as if they were carved out of cream cheese. They had to be ready to emote and sparkle for the camera.

"Have you had any more thoughts about the hot-air balloon massacre?" Dickerson asked her.

"Are you taping this? Are you wearing a lapel camera I should know about?"

Dickerson grinned to show off his set of perfect expensive teeth. "Of course not."

"It wouldn't matter," Theodosia said, crossing her fingers for the little white lie that was about to come. "Because I really haven't given it much thought."

"Truly?" Dickerson cocked his head, looking as if he didn't believe her. "Because word on the street is you're a pretty fair amateur detective."

Just fair?

Dickerson stared at her and bounced on his heels. "Where were you tonight? Did something happen?"

"Why on earth would you ask that?" Theodosia tried to keep her voice steady.

Dickerson tried to downplay his question. "I don't know. You look a little secretive. I can see it in your eyes.

They're smiley, but they're hiding something. Like maybe you're involved in . . . I don't know. What are you involved in?"

"Absolutely nothing," Theodosia said. "Look, it's been a long day. I want to go inside and warm up. Dry off my dog before he starts smelling like a wet dog."

"You're cute when you're trying to act all innocent, you know that?"

Theodosia gave a friendly wave as she turned away from him. "Good night. Take care."

Once they were inside, Theodosia rubbed Earl Grey with a soft, white towel and set the teakettle on to boil. Then she gifted Earl Grey with a chew bone (he'd certainly earned it), fixed herself a cup of chamomile tea (she'd earned it), and headed upstairs to her small suite of rooms.

As she sipped her tea, Theodosia wondered if Dickerson knew more than he was letting on. Or had this just been a fishing expedition? Maybe that's what roving reporters did. Wander around, try to stir up some trouble. And flirt. Yes, he had definitely been flirting with her.

Theodosia sighed. She was definitely not interested in returning *the flirt*. Certainly not now, not since she'd begun dating Pete Riley. Smiling about that, and about the fact that he'd be back home in a few days, Theodosia rummaged through her closet looking for something to wear to the funeral tomorrow. *Something warm. And probably black. Say now, how about this black skirt suit with a pair of black leather boots? Too severe? Way too Elvira, Mistress of the Dark?* No, she didn't care. That outfit would keep her warm and relatively dry.

Theodosia shuffled back to her tower room and curled up in an easy chair. Outside, the rain was coming down harder. Rain gurgled in the gutters and downspouts and sluiced off the edge of her roof, creating a burbling symphony. She decided it was a good thing Shep was going to clear out all the debris.

And as the wind picked up in intensity and whooshed through the crawl space above her, a branch scratched at the window, sounding like some kind of wild, clawed creature.

Still, Theodosia sipped tea as Earl Grey snoozed on his tufted dog bed. And she wondered what else she could do to help Tidwell. And, of course, Angie.

20

❧

Magnolia Cemetery had never been a particularly upbeat place. Today, with rain sluicing down, with thunder rumbling overhead like some kind of unholy bowling alley, the atmosphere was downright terrifying.

And then there were the tombs.

As Theodosia and Drayton drove through the wrought iron gates of this Victorian-era cemetery, their eyes were immediately drawn to the tablets, tombs, mausoleums, and enormous assemblage of marble statuary. There were angels with hollowed-out eyes, dogs that were perpetually on guard, and a marble monument to a dead infant that was carved in the shape of a baby stroller. Drive deeper into this eerie park-like setting with its winding dirt roads and you'd also find a pyramid-shaped crypt and a spooky-looking mausoleum that looked like it had been built for a French emperor.

"So many people buried here," Theodosia said, a kind of awe coloring her voice.

"From what you told me about the mishap last night, about Tidwell getting assaulted, it sounds like the population could have easily been increased by one more," Drayton said.

"He was hit hard, but not that hard."

"And so strange that it happened outside the Kingsley mansion. Right under Charles Townsend's nose."

"I grant you it's fishy, but we still can't prove anything."

"You think Townsend will be attending the funeral today?" Drayton asked.

"I don't think he'd miss it for the world."

"Probably trying hard to remain in Tawney Kingsley's good graces. So he can continue doing . . . whatever it is he does," Drayton said.

"Mmm." Theodosia frowned as she drove along. They were approaching a fork in the road. "Which way do you think to the graveside service?"

Drayton strained to see out the rain-spattered windshield. "There are a few cars parked over to our left."

Theodosia slowed as Spanish moss from giant oak trees whumped damply against her windshield. "Oh. I see them." She cranked her windshield wipers to high and headed up a steep hill.

"Huh," Drayton said. "I believe this is Green Hill."

"What's so special about Green Hill?"

"Supposed to be haunted." Drayton peered out the side window as if he were expecting an apparition to leap out at them. "There was a married couple interred here just two years apart. First the wife, then the husband. When they were finally reunited in death, a number of people claimed to see their spirits waltzing together among the tombstones."

"At night, I presume."

"Under cover of darkness, yes."

"But you don't believe in spirits or haunts," Theodosia said.

Drayton hunched his shoulders forward. "No, I don't."

"Except for the glowing orbs you once saw in St. Philip's Graveyard."

"Except for the glowing orbs," Drayton said.

Theodosia parked behind a long line of cars and said, "Better grab your umbrella. I'm afraid we're in for a bit of a hike." They turned up their collars to block the elements and climbed out of Theodosia's Jeep, reluctant to leave the warmth spewed out by the car's heater.

Drayton glanced at the sky where lightning strobed amidst a turmoil of dark clouds. "Besides this chill rain, all those lightning flashes are disturbing. If a lightning bolt should hit my umbrella I'm sure the current would travel right down the metal shaft and I'd be sizzled like a game bird on a spit."

"That's a colorful metaphor," Theodosia said.

"Do you want to hold the umbrella?"

"No."

Splinters of rain pelted down as Theodosia and Drayton walked gingerly across the cemetery lawn, shoes squishing loudly in the damp grass. They headed in the direction of a small black canopy stretched above a tiny patch of bright-green plastic funeral grass that was situated next to a small lagoon.

"There's already a sizeable crowd gathered," Drayton whispered. "We're never going to find a suitable seat under that shelter."

Theodosia patted his arm as she tried not to slip on the grass and twist an ankle. "We'll be fine."

But they weren't fine. They ended up being cold, miserable, and wet—the entire way through the service.

Tawney Kingsley sat in the front row, of course, well protected from the elements. Charles Townsend and Brooklyn Vance sat in the row directly behind her. And, interestingly, Earl Bullitt sat hunched in the back row, his eyes downcast. He was either freezing cold or bored out of his skull.

Theodosia didn't see a freshly dug grave anywhere and then decided it must be hidden under the ghastly bilious-green indoor-outdoor carpeting. For modesty purposes, no doubt. Or maybe because the grave was already half-full of water and the sight would be too much for everyone to bear.

The service was fairly standard as memorial services go. A somber welcome by a black-suited minister, a few songs that the mourners were urged to sing a cappella (which never worked out), and glowing eulogies by two executives from SyncSoft about their former CEO, Don Kingsley. Everyone listened politely but shivered in the chill air.

Some forty minutes later, when the service finally wound down, Tawney stood up and turned to address the gathering of mourners. She wore a snappy black hat, black slacks, and a black jacket with sequins on the lapels. She looked, Theodosia decided, like she was auditioning for the road company of *Cabaret*. In her hands Tawney clutched a silver urn that contained the ashes of her deceased and estranged husband.

"I'm not a big believer in final goodbyes," Tawney said in an almost too-bright voice. "Which is why I've chosen to place Donald's ashes inside a piece of custom-designed origami and float it out across the lagoon."

"Say what?" Drayton muttered.

Everyone watched spellbound as Tawney pried the top off the urn and poured a stream of gray ashes into a large paper origami crane. The crane was bright red and measured about ten inches high with a wingspan of maybe eighteen inches. Once the ashes were securely folded inside the paper crane, the minister beckoned for all the mourners to follow along.

So, once again, all the mourners squished across the grass to the soggy bank of the nearby lagoon.

"Feet feeling damp?" Theodosia whispered to Drayton.

"I'll have you know these are English shoes. From George Cleverley," Drayton said. "Not exactly your run-of-the-mill Hush Puppies."

"I guess that's a no," Theodosia said.

They stopped at the edge of the lagoon, where Tawney placed the crane gently in the water and gave it a farewell shove.

"Sad. So sad," Tawney said as the origami crane slowly floated away. She'd managed to conjure up a tear in one eye.

"Ashes to ashes, dust to dust," the minister intoned. Because everyone was still looking perplexed, he hastened to explain: "Since this lovely lagoon is tidal fed, Mr. Kingsley's ashes will be carried along where they will eventually migrate to the Cooper River."

"How weird," Theodosia said under her breath.

But there was still another event on tap.

"Thank you all for coming here today, to bid farewell to Donald," Tawney said in a chirpy voice. "I've arranged for a lovely post-funeral luncheon at the Veranda Bistro over on King Street, so I'd love you all to come."

"Do you want to go?" Theodosia whispered to Drayton.

"Maybe. At least it would give us a chance to dry off," Drayton said.

"We can do that at the tea shop."

"You're right. Perhaps we should skip the luncheon. What if Haley and Miss Dimple are horrifically busy?"

"Let's call them and find out," Theodosia said as the crowd around them dispersed quickly.

Haley answered on the first ring. "How was the funeral?"

"Sad," Theodosia said.

"Damp," Drayton said loudly into the phone.

"The thing is, Haley, we've been invited to a funeral luncheon. But we don't want to leave you and Miss Dimple shorthanded," Theodosia said.

"Go," Haley told her. "And don't stress about us. We're not one bit busy so Miss Dimple and I can easily take care of lunch. Only three tables are occupied right now and I don't know if any more customers will show up. I even whipped together a banana pudding cake and now it looks like Miss Dimple and I will have to eat the whole thing."

"Okay, Haley, thanks," Theodosia said. She turned to Drayton. "You catch that?" She checked her watch. "Do you have time? I know your photo shoot is scheduled for this afternoon."

Drayton nodded. "No problem. And I think we should attend the luncheon. At the very least it will give you a chance to snoop around some more and ask a few probing questions."

"You think that's what I do?"

"Yes. And you have it down to a fine science!"

Walking into the Veranda Bistro, Drayton said, "I'm surprised your detective friend wasn't shuffling around at the funeral, trying to look obscure but failing miserably."

"I'm guessing that Tidwell is still recovering from last night," Theodosia said. "He got whacked pretty hard."

"From what you told me, it sounded suspiciously like the one who did the whacking might have been Charles Townsend."

Theodosia shrugged. "Could have been him or somebody else. Lord knows, there are enough suspects."

"But you said Townsend acted nervous. As though he had something to hide."

"Yes, but Townsend always acts a little hinky," Theodosia said. She glanced around the interior of the restaurant. "This looks like a spot for ladies-who-lunch."

"What gave it away?" Drayton asked. "The pink floral wallpaper or the white wicker chairs?"

"Tawney's luncheon is in the back room, I guess. The party room."

"Funeral party room," Drayton said. They walked down a hallway lit with pink lights and hung with etchings of old Charleston scenes, and into a room that was actually called the Garden Room, probably because it seriously resembled a greenhouse. That is, glass windows formed two of the walls and afforded a nice view onto a small garden, while part of the ceiling was curved glass. Large potted plants were scattered everywhere and lacy ferns hung from the ceiling. There were a half dozen large circular tables and one long table where a buffet lunch was being served.

"I feel like I'm trapped inside a human terrarium," Drayton said.

"It is kind of weird to have rain pattering down on top of you," Theodosia said, glancing up at the partially glassed ceiling.

"But, I must say, the food smells delicious."

"What are we waiting for?" Theodosia said.

They ambled over to the buffet table, got in line, and grabbed their plates.

"Look at this," Theodosia said as she lifted the lid on a silver chafing dish. "Barbecued oysters."

"They knew we were coming," Drayton said. "Yum."

Theodosia took three oysters and moved on. "They're also serving ricotta-stuffed crepes with, hmm, I think huckleberry sauce."

"This is very well-done," Drayton said. "Tawney spent some money on this spread. Now I'm kind of hoping she's not the guilty party."

"Jasmine rice perloo and Parmesan crusted snapper down here," Theodosia said, moving along the line. She held no illusions either way about Tawney. The woman could be guilty or innocent. In fact, just coming here to spy on her today meant Theodosia was leaning slightly toward a guilty verdict.

Theodosia and Drayton grabbed glasses of wine and seated themselves at one of the round tables. Tawney sat at the front table, drinking what appeared to be a martini straight up and accepting condolences from several of the guests. Charles Townsend was at another table, conversing with an older, silver-haired woman that Theodosia recognized as a prominent socialite and denizen of the

Historic District. She went by the moniker Miss Callie, but Theodosia didn't know her last name.

Brooklyn Vance and Earl Bullitt had also showed up for the luncheon. They'd loaded up their plates and, now that more guests had arrived and seating was at a premium, circled each other like a couple of wary alley cats.

Theodosia nudged Drayton. "Look at Brooklyn Vance. She looks like she wants to claw Bullitt's eyes out."

Drayton nodded. "Maybe do us all a favor."

Theodosia had just headed back to the buffet table to grab another couple of oysters when the proverbial poop smashed into the fan.

The door to the Garden Room burst open and two uniformed police officers walked in. They were both tall and imposing, looking natty and official with their gold badges and neatly pressed blue shirts and slacks.

"Excuse me," one of the officers called out in a loud voice. "We're looking for Charles Townsend."

21

Conversation came to a screeching halt as every pair of eyeballs in the room roved about nervously and then landed squarely on Charles Townsend. For the police officers, it was as if a giant red arrow had been drawn and a target painted on Townsend's startled face.

The officers hurried over to Townsend. Theodosia caught the names on their ID tags as they went by. One said BEASLEY, the other said POWERS.

"Mr. Townsend," Officer Powers said. "If you would please come with us."

Blood drained from Townsend's face as he rose shakily from his seat. "What's this about?" he managed to squeak out.

"We'll explain it to you on the ride to the precinct station," Officer Beasley said.

"No! I want to know now!" Townsend cried. He looked terrified.

"We need to ask you a few questions," Powers said. His words were in no way harsh, but they weren't super friendly, either. Just the facts, ma'am.

"Am I under arrest?" Townsend's voice quavered then rose to hit a high note of hysteria.

Powers reached out and put a hand on Townsend's shoulder. "Please calm down, sir." Then, "We'll explain it all downtown."

"Help!" Townsend screeched at the top of his lungs. "Somebody help me!"

Nobody moved a muscle. With their mouths virtually hanging open, every guest simply stared at Townsend as if they were an audience watching some sort of experimental surrealistic play. What was happening onstage—the Sturm und Drang of it all—wasn't their business. They didn't want to get involved.

"Please won't someone *help* me?" Townsend yodeled again as Beasley gently took Townsend's other arm and the two officers eased him toward the exit.

"Do you think we should somehow intercede?" Drayton whispered to Theodosia. He was clearly uncomfortable with the situation.

"Why should we if Tawney isn't doing anything?"

They both craned their heads to get a look at her. Tawney's eyes were focused on her drink as she basically tried to ignore the fuss.

"Besides, what would we do?" Theodosia asked as Townsend continued his whimpering protestations. "Grab Townsend and try to make a getaway? We're not exactly the Lone Ranger and Tonto with horses saddled up, ready to gallop out of town."

Drayton's mouth twitched. "You paint an amusing image."

"Made only more ridiculous if Tidwell were the sheriff," Theodosia said. Then she added, "Which he kind of is."

Thirty seconds later, the incident with Charles Townsend was pretty much forgotten. Guests talked, chuckled, ate, and drank. They streamed back to the buffet table for seconds.

Theodosia, on the other hand, had turned her attention to Brooklyn Vance and Earl Bullitt. They'd ended up at the same table and now, through some bit of musical chairs, were seated next to each other. Not only that, they had their heads inclined toward each other and were talking in what looked like a conspiratorial manner.

"Look at Brooklyn and Bullitt," Theodosia whispered to Drayton.

Drayton glanced at them and said, "That's odd. Even though Bullitt has all the charm of a rattlesnake, they look positively friendly."

"Don't they?" Theodosia stood up and casually walked toward their table. She was hoping to catch some of their conversation. And, boy, did she get an earful!

"Now we're going to get some answers!" Bullitt was saying.

"I just knew it," Brooklyn responded. "I had a feeling Townsend killed the old man and stole the flag."

"He surely could have," Bullitt said. "I understand he was front and center at the hot-air balloon rally."

"Townsend could have ducked out, grabbed the drone from his car, and sent it skyward," Brooklyn said. "Then, once the damage was done, he could have ditched the controller and come running back to the scene. Nobody would have been the wiser."

"Nobody," Bullitt agreed.

Strange bedfellows. This was the one thought that spun wildly through Theodosia's brain. Now the two enemies were actually talking to each other? About the murder?

And, as Theodosia tried to make sense of this, she suddenly wondered if Brooklyn and Bullitt might not somehow be coconspirators. Had the open hostility she'd witnessed at the Floral Teacups Competition been a complete sham? Were they somehow working together?

Most frightening of all, were they the killers?

* * *

Theodosia and Drayton batted this idea back and forth as they drove to Drayton's house.

"You told me Brooklyn Vance and Earl Bullitt fought like cats and dogs at the Floral Teacups Competition," Drayton said.

"They did. But now I have to wonder if it was all for show."

"You mean they might have been throwing up a smoke screen?"

"There's a lot of that going around," Theodosia said. She pulled up to the curb in front of Drayton's house and said, "Good luck. I see the photographer's already here." A brown van that said WOODY HOVEL PHOTOGRAPHY was parked in front of Drayton's one-hundred-seventy-five-year-old home that had once belonged to a prominent Civil War doctor.

"And so it begins," Drayton said, looking unhappy. "I gave a key to Barbara Layton, the photo editor at *Southern Interiors Magazine*. She said she'd have the lighting and everything set up for the first shot by the time I got home."

Theodosia nodded toward Drayton's home. "Is Honey Bee at home?" Honey Bee was Drayton's Cavalier King Charles and the love of his life.

"She's staying with a neighbor today."

"Well, good luck with the shoot."

Drayton lingered, not getting out of the car. "Theo, if you're not too busy at the tea shop, maybe you could come over and help out?"

"You know I'm not exactly an art director. Or stylist."

"But you've honchoed photo shoots before," Drayton said. "So you understand the intricacies as well as how to, um, manage people."

"If you want my help, I'll check in with Haley and come back here as soon as I can."

"Thank you," Drayton said as he climbed out of her Jeep. "I knew I could count on you."

"Hey, look who's back," Haley called out as Theodosia came through the front door of the Indigo Tea Shop.

"Honey, you look kind of peaked," Miss Dimple said. "You must have been in the cold and damp all morning."

"Kind of," Theodosia said. *And then there was the police action at the luncheon.* But the aroma of fresh-brewed teas, the flickering candles, the fire crackling in the fireplace, were soothing and welcoming.

"You want me to fix you a cup of tea?" Miss Dimple asked. She wasn't happy unless she was mothering someone.

"Miss Dimple's been playing tea sommelier all morning," Haley said. "Getting pretty good at it, too."

"I wouldn't say no to a cup of oolong," Theodosia said.

"Coming right up," Miss Dimple said.

Theodosia glanced about the tea shop. Only two tables were occupied. "So it's been really quiet today, huh?"

"Like a tomb," Haley said. "Six tables at lunch and what you see here is the tail end of it. So this was the perfect day for you and Drayton to be AWOL." She hesitated. "Wait. Is Drayton coming back?"

"Doubtful. He pretty much has to be at the photo shoot all afternoon," Theodosia said. "You know how fussy he is about his house."

"Don't I know it."

"And I think the magazine asked him to pose in a couple of shots."

"He'll despise that," Haley said. "They'll want him to wear a tweed jacket and smoke a pipe or something. Try to look like an English lord of the manor."

"Drayton asked me to come back and help out. That's if we're not too busy here."

"Well, we're not. The only spark of life was a huge

take-out order from the Lady Goodwood Inn. I think they were having refrigeration issues."

"Here you go, dear." Miss Dimple slid a cup of tea across the counter to Theodosia.

Theodosia took a grateful sip. "Delicious. Thank you."

"Oh," Haley said. "Bill Glass dropped by. He left a few copies of *Shooting Star* for us."

"Such a nice man," Miss Dimple said.

"You know, he's really not," Theodosia told her.

Haley reached behind the counter and grabbed one of the copies. "Take a look. It's actually pretty interesting."

The first thing Theodosia saw on the front page was a hugely unflattering photo of Brooklyn Vance and Earl Bullitt. They'd obviously been caught mid-argument with their mouths gaping wide open, looking like a couple of T. rex dinosaurs about to rip each other to bits. Delaine was standing in the background. Not surprising, she looked great.

"This is weird," Theodosia said. She studied the photo a second time, again wondering if they could be working in collusion. Then she turned the tabloid facedown on the counter. "Is there anything else going on that I should know about?"

"Angie Congdon called," Haley said. "Said she needed to talk to you."

"Did she want me to call her back?" Theodosia asked.

"No, Angie said she had to run a couple of errands. She sounded pretty frazzled."

"I can't imagine why," Theodosia said. Poor Angie. Her first husband Mark had died a few years ago. Now, when she should be celebrating her engagement, her fiancé had been summarily fired from his job and she was desperately trying to untangle him from this drone attack mess. She'd had a tough string of bad luck.

Theodosia went into her office, kicked off her boots, and shoved her feet into a comfy pair of loafers that she kept there for emergency purposes. She speed-checked her e-mail and then paused to thumb through a tea magazine, noting a nice feature article on Yixing teapots.

She raised her head when she heard a knock at her door. Haley.

"Did you want something to eat?" Haley asked. "Because I have some clam chowder in the kitchen. Serve it with a cream scone, if you'd like. And add some cinnamon honey butter."

"That sounds great," Theodosia said. "But I ate too much at the luncheon as it was."

"Where was it held?"

"The Veranda Bistro."

"Good food?" Haley asked.

"Pretty good. Not as creative as your menus though," Theodosia said.

Haley flipped a hank of long blond hair over her shoulder and turned to leave. "Why am I not surprised."

Haley went back in the kitchen and Theodosia went back to her tea magazine. As she skimmed an article on tea spots in Paris, she heard voices out in the tea room. Slightly raised voices. *Uh-oh, some kind of trouble?*

Theodosia was about to get up and see what the fuss was about when Angie Congdon suddenly appeared at her office door. Her face looked drawn and tense and her hair was slightly unkempt. But that could have been from the rain.

"You went to Don Kingsley's funeral?" Angie asked Theodosia. She was cranked and in full-blown need-to-know mode. No *Nice to see you*, no *Hi how are you.*

"I just got back," Theodosia said.

Angie walked a few paces into Theodosia's office. "And I just got done putting the Featherbed House up as collateral for bail money."

"What?" Theodosia stood up so fast her chair almost flipped over backward. "Because Harold's been arrested?"

"No, but it's only a matter of time. I can feel the noose starting to tighten." Angie staggered another step and collapsed in the tufted chair across from Theodosia. Tears sparkled in her eyes, and her voice shook with fear. "I'm afraid I'll lose *everything* if Harold is arrested and this murder isn't solved!"

"Angie, no," Theodosia hastened to say. She came around her desk and sat down next to Angie, put her arms around her. "That's not going to happen. You don't know about this, but right after the funeral, at the funeral luncheon, two police officers came in and took Charles Townsend away for questioning."

"What!" Angie pulled back, her expressive eyes wide with surprise. "What are you saying, Theo?"

"Maybe . . . I don't know, I probably shouldn't read too much into it, but I got the distinct feeling that perhaps they were going to charge him."

"You mean charge Townsend with murder?"

"I'm taking a wild guess, but *possibly* they might do that." Theodosia knew she was hedging her words like crazy, but she desperately wanted to make Angie feel better.

"Really? That's what you think will happen?" Angie asked.

"The police are dealing with a messy triple homicide," Theodosia said. "Which puts them under tremendous pressure. And I know for a fact that they're itching to close the book on this. As quickly as possible."

Angie clapped a hand to her chest. "Praise the Lord. That means Harold is off the hook!"

As Theodosia gave Angie an encouraging nod, her common sense kicked in to warn her, to tell her to slow down. *Maybe Harold is off the hook. Then again, maybe he's not.*

22

❧

Drayton's home was a hive of activity when Theodosia arrived. Everyone, including Barbara Layton, the photo editor
from *Southern Interiors Magazine*, Woody Hovel, the photographer, Woody's two assistants, a stylist, two lighting
guys, and two interns, was working like crazy. This photo
shoot not only *looked* like a big deal, it pretty much was.

Theodosia spotted Drayton wringing his hands and
looking generally miserable as he stood in the dining room
with his back up against a barrister bookcase. As she walked
toward him, strategically dodging lights and stepping over
black cables that snaked across his blue-and-persimmon
Persian carpet, his expression brightened somewhat.

"How's the shoot going?" Theodosia asked.

Drayton turned soulful eyes on her. "Basically, I'm *en-
during* it. You know what a private person I am, Theo, so
this is baptism by fire for me. Everyone shouting ideas
and moving my precious furniture around. It's almost too
much to bear."

Theodosia glanced around the dining room. Drayton's
Chippendale table held an eight-piece setting of his prized

Limoges china, plus Baccarat stemware and Talisman Rose silverware. Two silver candelabras and an enormous bouquet of red roses and hot-pink freesia served as centerpieces. His favored oil painting of Charles Grey, the 2nd Earl Grey and former British Prime Minister (who served from 1830 to 1834), hung on the far wall.

"As far as I can see, everything looks terrific. I can understand why *Southern Interiors Magazine* was so eager to photograph it," Theodosia said.

"They're not just doing a photographic spread," Drayton said. He was poised on the verge of panic. "They're asking for actual *text* to accompany some of the photos."

"I'm sure they are. The magazine appeals to *readers*, after all."

"The editor wanted to know all about the history of my house. And what kind of restorations I did."

"Because it's interesting. And all those details will serve as inspiration to people who are trying to update their own homes while remaining historically accurate."

Drayton looked nonplussed. "You think that's it?"

"Yes, and it's all going to work out wonderfully," Theodosia said, infusing her voice with unbridled pep, hoping it might be contagious. "What'd they photograph first?"

"My kitchen."

"Which is drop-dead gorgeous. Especially with your copper sink and all those lovely cupboards that house your teapot collection."

"I put my Chinese famille rose teapot front and center," Drayton said with some pride.

"Good for you. That one's a beauty."

"And from the Qianlong Dynasty at that."

Barbara Layton came over to join them and introduce herself to Theodosia. She was midforties, wearing a black turtleneck, slim black slacks, and black flats. She looked like the epitome of a working editor with her honey-blond hair pulled back in a tiny ponytail and a pencil tucked behind one ear.

Once they'd exchanged pleasantries, Barbara said, "The shoot is coming along beautifully."

"I'm sure the photos will be gorgeous," Theodosia enthused. "They'll do Drayton's house proud."

"We've got good stuff to work with," Barbara said. "You can tell that every room has been lovingly restored. And this heart pine flooring is to die for." She flashed a dazzling smile at Drayton.

Drayton looked like a deer caught in the headlights until Theodosia bumped him with her elbow.

"Thank you," Drayton said to Barbara.

They watched the goings-on for a few more minutes and then Woody, the photographer, called out, "That's it, we're good. Let's move all the equipment into the next room." He came over to join them and Theodosia was introduced once more. Woody was tall and lanky, wearing a retro Stone Temple Pilots T-shirt and faded blue jeans. He had intense glacier-blue eyes and wore his sandy blond hair pulled into a tight man bun, almost like an ancient samurai.

"Are you finished?" Drayton asked Woody, a hopeful note creeping into his voice.

"Oh no, no, no," Woody said. "We've still got the most important room to do. Your living room."

"How long will that take?" Drayton asked.

"As long as they need," Theodosia said.

"Yeah." Woody looked thoughtful. "We gotta move our equipment and I want to fire off a few test shots." He cocked an eye at Drayton. "You're going to pose for a couple of the shots, am I correct?"

"That's right," Barbara said. "We definitely want Drayton in a shot or two. Our readers will be interested." She raised a hand and waved to her two interns. "Tabitha? Tonya? Could one of you grab my shot list?"

The identical-looking interns nodded and scrambled off to find Barbara's shot list.

"We should go pick out a couple of jackets for you," Theodosia said to Drayton.

"That'd be great," Woody said. "You've got time, too. Our stylist is going to experiment with a few different decorative pieces for your mantle."

Drayton went upstairs, dug through his closet, and brought four jackets down for Theodosia to look at.

"These are all pretty much the same," she said. They had the jackets spread out in Drayton's small library and every one of them was a tweed.

"Not exactly," Drayton said. "This one is a Harris Tweed." He fingered another one of the jackets. "While this is a Donegal Tweed. And this other one . . ."

"Is also a tweed," Theodosia said.

"Yes, but it's done in a Prince of Wales check."

"I love it."

"You're not just saying that? Humoring me?"

"No, it's really quite splendid," Theodosia said, fighting to keep a straight face.

Drayton paired his jacket with a white shirt and a dark brown silk bow tie by Drake's.

Theodosia picked a tiny piece of lint off his shoulder, adjusted Drayton's bow tie, spun him around, and shoved him out into the living room.

Drayton's living room was small but elegant. A white marble French fireplace, tufted leather sofa, Georgian mahogany coffee table, and two French provincial side chairs. Plush draperies swagged the beveled glass lattice windows and a celadon-and-gold Chinese rug covered the floor.

It was also busy as all get-out.

Woody and his assistants had almost finished setting up the lights and camera. The interns were running around, handing out cups of coffee while pausing to gape at the screen on an open MacBook Pro computer. The stylist was trying out an assortment of props on the mantle.

"No, too big," Woody said, looking through his lens. He straightened up and said, "We need something smaller. Colorful but smaller."

"Candlesticks?" said one of the interns. Either Tabitha or Tonya.

"More colorful," Woody said.

"Where's that antiques dealer we contacted?" Barbara asked. "He should've been here by now."

"What about a Chinese blue-and-white vase?" Theodosia suggested.

"That's okay, dear," Barbara said. "We've engaged an antiques expert who'll take care of that. Tonya, could you . . . ?"

"I'm Tabitha."

". . . be a dear and call our antiques fellow, will you? Make sure he's on his merry way."

"They're bringing in outside props," Drayton fussed to Theodosia. "What's wrong with *my* pieces?"

"Listen," Theodosia told him. "The magazine people haven't made many changes so far, so why not let them try their own accent pieces? If the mantle ends up looking junky and horrible, then we'll lodge a protest."

"I suppose."

"That's the spirit." Theodosia patted his arm.

But two minutes later, Theodosia was more than ready to lodge a formal protest. Because who should suddenly appear but Earl Bullitt!

"There you are," Barbara said, sounding relieved. "What tasty little pieces did you bring for us?"

"No," Drayton seethed under his breath as Earl Bullitt set a box of bubble-wrapped objects on the coffee table. "Not *him*."

"Easy, easy," Theodosia warned, though she would have loved to grab Bullitt by one of his flat little ears and drag him out the back door.

Bullitt gently unwrapped a Ming vase, a brass and glass clock, and a pair of antique Staffordshire dogs. Barbara exclaimed over each piece as Bullitt schmoozed her outrageously. Finally, when Theodosia and Drayton couldn't take it anymore, they pushed forward to find out exactly what was going on.

But Barbara had pulled Woody into the conversation with Bullitt, and now he was smiling as well.

"Perfection," Barbara said. She held up one of the Staffordshire dogs for everyone to see. "Isn't this little guy adorable? And we have a pair."

"I knew you'd love those," Bullitt said. He grinned at Barbara and then turned his attention on Theodosia and Drayton. "Well, hello there," he said, his voice fawning and smarmy.

"Staffordshire dogs," Drayton said between clenched teeth.

"Fine porcelain from the Victorian era. Three thousand, five hundred dollars for the pair," Bullitt said. He seemed to relish the fact that he'd been invited into Drayton's house. "They should help punch things up a notch."

"Pricey little pooches," Woody said.

"Then we'd better not drop them," Theodosia said.

"If they're even genuine," Drayton muttered.

It took forever to achieve the lighting that Woody was looking for. But finally, with the help of various scrims and key lights, they were ready. And then Woody clicked and clicked and clicked. He photographed all aspects of the room from every angle.

"Do you think we have it?" Barbara asked. It was six o'clock at night and she was starting to look pooped. The interns had gone home. Even Earl Bullitt had gotten bored and left, with an admonishment to the crew to be sure to return his Staffordshire dogs.

"Just a couple more setups," Woody said. He straightened up, glanced at Drayton, and said, "Mr. Conneley? I'd like to get one of you standing in front of your fireplace."

"Now?" Drayton asked.

Woody nodded. "Last but not least."

Drayton was still reluctant. Until Theodosia stepped in.

"You look elegant," she whispered to him. "And remember, this is your home, this is your big moment. So get over there and strike a pose like the dashing Southern gent that you are!"

Drayton walked over to the fireplace, threw back his shoulders, and positioned himself directly in front of the Staffordshire dogs so they were no longer visible.

Theodosia gave him a thumbs-up.

"Perfect," Woody said. "Now tilt your chin up and hold perfectly still . . . good. I like that. See? You're a natural."

The more shots Woody took, the more comfortable Drayton became. Finally, with arms folded across his chest, looking directly into the camera, Drayton hit the perfect pose.

"That's it," Woody said. "That's the money shot."

"And that's a wrap," Barbara said, sounding happy but exhausted. Lights were suddenly dimmed and everyone scurried to pack up the equipment.

Theodosia was especially pleased. Drayton had been so reticent and nervous. But in the end he'd turned out to be a real trooper.

"You looked great," she told him. "Natural, but with a lot of camera presence."

"I gave it my best," Drayton said. "The only thing that bothers me is the fact that it's digital photography. I hate the idea of not using actual film. That the photos will exist only on that cumulonimbus thing."

Theodosia had to chuckle, she couldn't help herself. "You mean the cloud?"

"Is that the technical term?"

"I don't think you should be so hasty in your judgment of digital photography. There are a few upsides as well."

Drayton put on a pair of tortoiseshell half-glasses and peered at her. "Name one."

"Well, you can see every shot immediately. Right there on Woody's computer. Didn't you notice how he checked to make sure his angles and lighting were spot-on?"

"Wait a minute, we can actually *see* the photos?" Drayton asked. "When could we do that?"

"Right now if you want."

"The photos are ready?"

"Sure," Theodosia said. "Come on, I'll show you."

They edged their way over to the computer that was sitting on a side table, still booted up.

"Oh my," Drayton said. "These are . . . not bad at all."

"Are you kidding me?" Theodosia touched the mouse and clicked through a few of the shots. "These are fantastic."

"You like them?" Woody asked. He'd come over to join them.

"The ones I've seen so far . . . by ginger, I like them very much," Drayton said.

"They're terrific," Theodosia said.

"You want me to e-mail these photos to you?" Woody asked. "You guys can take a look, maybe give input to Barbara on which ones are your favorites."

Drayton looked startled. "You want to e-mail them to me? Good gracious. I wouldn't know how . . ." He gave a helpless shrug and glanced toward Theodosia. "Theo . . . ?"

"Send the photos to me," Theodosia said. She pulled out one of her business cards and handed it to Woody. "My e-mail address is right there on the card."

Woody nodded and stuck her card in the pocket of his jeans. "Great. But give me a day or so. Tomorrow I have to run down to Savannah and shoot a big, fancy wedding at The Mansion on Forsyth Park." He rolled his eyes. "Can you believe it? This crazy bride who hired me is having *twelve* bridesmaids."

By the time Drayton's French Furet clock pealed out seven melodic chimes, all the guests had left. But the tables, chairs, and sofa hadn't quite been returned to their exact and proper places.

"The thing to do now is move," Drayton said, looking around.

"Don't worry," Theodosia said. "I'll help you put your home right again."

"And look. The stylist left *those* behind," Drayton said, indicating the pair of Staffordshire dogs that stared out at them, beady-eyed, from the mantle. "I suppose it's up to *me* to return these dogs to Earl Bullitt."

"There's no time like the present," Theodosia said. A spark of an idea had suddenly ignited in her brain.

"What are you talking about? It's . . ." Drayton glanced at his ancient Patek Phillipe. "Actually it's after seven. Bullitt's shop is probably locked up tight for the night."

"Hopefully not too tight."

"Theo . . ." Drayton said in a drawn out, questioning tone. "Pray tell, what are you thinking?"

"I think Earl Bullitt was trying like mad to maneuver us away from that room in his shop the other day." She gave a disdainful snort. "Storage room, my eye."

"Bullitt did act somewhat frantic when you tried to get in there and look around."

"What if he has the Navy Jack flag stashed in there?"

"What if we sneak in there and get caught?" Drayton asked.

Theodosia favored him with an angelic smile. "We'll say we're returning the Staffordshire dogs."

"An act of kindness," Drayton said. "Not a bad excuse. Actually, quite brilliant."

23

When they pulled up in front of Earl Bullitt's antiques shop the lights were still blazing inside.

"Look at this," Theodosia said. "Someone's still minding the store."

"I wonder who it is?" Drayton said. "I doubt that it's Bullitt himself at this late hour."

They got out of the car, Drayton gently cradling the Staffordshire dogs in his arms, and glanced up and down the street. Bullitt's Porsche was nowhere to be seen.

"Bullitt must have an employee who takes care of the store," Drayton said.

"Let's see if we can weasel our way in," Theodosia said. "Think you could help me with that?"

"This isn't my first rodeo," Drayton said.

The bell over the front door dinged as they walked in and startled a fifty-something woman with a frizzle of gray hair. She'd been frowning at something on the counter and turned with an almost fearful look on her face, momentarily forgetting the box she was packing.

"Oh!" the woman cried. "Didn't I lock that door?" She

looked harried. "I thought I did." She finally gazed directly at Theodosia and then Drayton. "I'm sorry but we're closed. And I need to rush off to . . ."

"Not a problem," Theodosia said, trying to project a friendly, nonthreatening vibe. "We just stopped by to return a pair of Staffordshire dogs that we borrowed from your employer for a photo shoot."

Drayton stepped forward and placed the dogs gently on the counter.

Tension on the woman's face drained immediately and she managed a smile. "I was wondering where those little darlings had run off to." Her voice dropped to a confidential whisper. "I had my fingers crossed that Mr. Bullitt hadn't sold the pair. I so love having them around. Mr. Bullitt is always telling me, 'Be careful, Mrs. Winkleman, don't fall in love with the merchandise because every single piece is for sale.'" She smiled. "But I do love these dogs."

"It's a good thing we caught you," Theodosia said, "so these sweet pups could come back to their rightful home."

Mrs. Winkleman gave an offhand wave. "I had to stay late anyway and pack up a parcel for Mr. Bullitt. He sold a pair of antique andirons to a customer down in Beaufort who's doing a total restoration on an old plantation house. Since we missed the last FedEx pickup, I promised Mr. Bullitt I'd run this package out to the airport. The FedEx office there accepts deliveries up until ten o'clock." She made a face. "But these darn things are made of cast iron, you know, and so heavy. Which is why I had to pack them in a reinforced box."

That was the tiny crack, the chink in the armor, that Theodosia had been hoping for.

"Why don't you finish your packing and we'll have Drayton carry that box out to your car," Theodosia suggested.

"I'd be most happy to help," Drayton said, jumping in. He was no dummy, he knew exactly what Theodosia was doing.

"Would you really?" Mrs. Winkleman looked thrilled. "That would be wonderful! These andirons are heavy as all get-out and I'm guessing the shipping's going to cost almost two hundred dollars. But I . . . Listen to me going on like this. I promise it won't take me more than two minutes to finish up. I'll just tape the box shut and make out a label."

"Take your time," Theodosia said. "We'll just look around."

Theodosia moseyed from counter to display case, keeping an eye out for the Navy Jack flag—or any flag for that matter. She didn't see a thing. There were oil paintings, brass figurines, antique china, jardinieres, clocks, and old tin signs, but nary a flag in sight. Maybe in that side room?

Theodosia raised her eyebrows at Drayton and he reacted right on cue.

"May I help you with that package now?" he asked.

"Yes," Mrs. Winkleman said. "I think I've . . . Yes, we're all set."

Drayton picked up the box while Mrs. Winkleman bustled in front of him like a tidy little hen. She held the door open for him and then led him to her car, a Ford Focus that was parked in front of the building.

Theodosia watched as they fussed about, deciding whether to wedge the box into the back seat or stash it in the trunk.

Good, Drayton is stalling. He's being a gentleman about it, but he's stalling.

Theodosia made a beeline for the side room. She grasped the doorknob, turned it, and . . . nothing happened.

The door to the mysterious room was locked.

Dipping a hand into her hobo bag, Theodosia pulled out her trusty Visa card. She'd used it once before to jiggle open a lock. Of course, if this was a dead bolt, the old credit card ploy wouldn't work. But this lock looked . . . doable.

Ever so carefully, Theodosia slid her card into the doorjamb. She angled it carefully and seesawed the card back and forth. She felt, more than heard, a little click. So hopefully it would . . . nope, no dice. The door still wouldn't open.

Theodosia tried again. This time she pushed her card farther in and worked it back and forth with an even gentler touch. She worked it for five, ten, and then twenty seconds, always keeping one eye on the front door. And then finally, like Indiana Jones touching just the right stone in a spooky old temple, the door swung open. Almost, but not quite, an invitation.

Theodosia dove inside.

It was clearly a storage room and filled with merchandise. She didn't know if these were new acquisitions or the dregs of the store. Didn't matter. She dug frantically through box after box, pulled open cupboard doors, searched under a pile of vintage topcoats. Nothing.

Okay. Where else?

Her searching eyes fell upon an old round-top trunk. She dropped to her knees, lifted the lid, and found an odd collection of dolls dressed in turn-of-the-century clothing. Not the most recent turn of the century, the one before it. From the musty interior of the trunk, the dolls' glassy eyes stared up at her as if to mock her.

Theodosia dropped the lid.

She heard the faint ding of the front door and jumped to her feet. She rushed out of the room, knowing she had only seconds to spare. She pulled the door closed behind her just as Mrs. Winkleman stepped into the shop.

"You see anything you like?" Mrs. Winkleman asked.

Theodosia's hand fell on the object closest to her. An absurd little glass lamp with a monkey curled around the base. "I'm pretty much loving this," she said.

"Isn't that adorable?" Mrs. Winkleman said.

"A remarkable piece," Drayton said. Theodosia was amazed he was able to keep a straight face.

"If you have your heart set on it," Mrs. Winkleman said, "I'll be sure to ask Mr. Bullitt what his best price might be."

"Please do that," Theodosia said. "And thank you."

Theodosia dropped Drayton off in front of his house.

"You want me to come in with you?" she asked. "Help set things straight?"

"Thank you for your kind offer, but no thank you," Drayton said. "You may not realize this about me, but I'm a bit fussy when it comes to arranging things."

"Noooo," Theodosia said, a smile in her voice.

"Okay, okay, I know when I'm being humored." Drayton got out of the car, gave her a backhand wave, and disappeared down his front walk.

Theodosia drove the few blocks to her house, resisting the temptation to take a late night drive past Donald Kingsley's house.

Theodosia bumped down her narrow alley, parked her car in her small garage, and walked across her patio. Halfway to her back door, a tiny creature was huddled in a puddle of light. Curious, Theodosia bent down to see what it was.

It was a little bluebird, technically an Eastern bluebird. Its feathers were bedraggled and the bird seemed to be breathing heavily.

Flew into a window? Had a nasty encounter with a hawk?

Whatever the reason, it couldn't stay out here. Some critter—a raccoon, an opossum, whatever—might come along and munch it for a snack.

Theodosia reached into her bag and pulled out a scarf. She placed it next to the little bird and gently scooped him into it. If the little bluebird was just stunned, he should recover in ten or fifteen minutes.

Once inside her kitchen, she placed the bluebird in a

cardboard box and covered it with a tea towel. Earl Grey watched her with what looked like deep concern.

"It's just a little bird that hit its head," she told him. "Probably be good as new in a few minutes."

Earl Grey wandered off while Theodosia brewed herself a cup of chamomile tea. She read the newspaper, puttered around her kitchen, and pretty much forgot about the box on the counter, until some fifteen minutes later when she heard the rustle of wings.

Peeking in, she saw that the bluebird had almost fully recovered.

Excellent.

She carried the box to the door, stepped outside, and pulled off the tea towel. Two seconds later the bluebird spread its wings and swooped up into a nearby magnolia tree.

Theodosia smiled to herself while silently bidding the little bird to take care.

24

❦

Friday morning and the skies over Charleston were still a mottled gray, but the rain had receded to a slight mist. If conditions continued to improve, Theodosia figured they might see a peep of sunshine. *Peep* being the operative word.

Theodosia fussed about the tea shop—Haley was in the kitchen, Drayton was searching through his tea trove—happy to be setting up the tables by herself this morning. She smoothed pink place mats onto her tables and pulled out cups and saucers in Royal Albert's Old Country Roses pattern. She figured the red roses and greenery would brighten everyone's day. Next came glass teapot warmers, tiny votive candles, flatware, and, finally, newly filled cream pitchers and sugar bowls. It felt good to be busy as the scent of cinnamon scones, jasmine tea, and fresh oranges slowly permeated the Indigo Tea Shop.

Still, the triple murder hung heavy over Theodosia's head. She supposed it was mostly because Angie had the most to lose and had begged her for help. And Theodosia, being a stickler for justice, for desperately wanting things to come to a logical conclusion, felt frustrated. Because that surely wasn't happening.

Strolling up to the front counter, Theodosia said, "It's a pity about last night, isn't it? I figured we might be onto something."

"A pity," Drayton echoed. He was standing there in deep contemplation, as if he was working out a new theory for particle physics. In reality, he was trying to decide between Earl Grey and an English breakfast tea.

"What's it going to be?" Theodosia asked. "The tea, I mean."

"I'm thinking the Earl Grey," Drayton said. "Haley tells me she's baking cinnamon scones and orange tea bread this morning, so it seems like a fine match."

"A match made in heaven."

BANG! BANG! BANG!

"Is the front door locked?" Drayton asked.

"Probably not. From when I went out to grab the *Post and Courier.*"

There was another loud bang and then the door snicked open a few inches.

"Hello?" Theodosia said.

The door opened wider and Bill Glass marched in, slick as you please. He wore his khaki photojournalist vest, a floppy Indiana Jones hat, and a smug smile on his face. He looked like he'd just been ousted from an illegal archaeological expedition but didn't care.

"I'm sorry, but we're not open for business yet," Theodosia said. She didn't want to deal with this loutish man so early in the morning.

Glass ignored her admonition. "I just heard the most interesting bit of news," he said, his voice slightly teasing.

Theodosia shook her head, but Drayton's curiosity rose up and got the best of him.

"What might that be?" Drayton asked.

"The police just released Charles Townsend," Glass said. "Like, ten minutes ago."

"What?" Theodosia stopped in her tracks. Stood there like Lot's wife turned to salt. Only, unlike Lot's wife, Theodosia was holding a teapot.

"Yup, Townsend's a free man," Glass said. "Free as a bird." He fluttered his fingers and made an annoying little twittering sound as he meandered over to the counter and set down his camera. "What I heard was this—the police admitted they made a mistake with Townsend and now claim to be looking elsewhere for the hot-air balloon killer." He poked a finger in Theodosia's direction. "So you better watch out, tea lady, there's still a vicious killer stalking our city."

"How did you find out about Townsend's release?" Drayton asked.

"I'm press," Glass said. "It's my job to know."

"You're not press," Theodosia said. "You publish a skunky little gossip rag."

"Which people in high places would kill to get their pictures in. Face it, honey, *you'd* love it if I did a feature story on you." Glass spread his arms wide. "I can see it now. Tea shop owner helps police solve baffling murder."

"Please stop," Theodosia said.

"You're upset because I hit a nerve." Glass winked at her. "You've got your own covert operation going, don't you?"

"I can't imagine what you're talking about," Theodosia said.

"We don't have time for any kind of amateur investigation," Drayton said in a haughty tone. "We're far too involved with our tea events."

"Yeah, right." Glass snorted.

For Theodosia, the news about Charles Townsend being released didn't come as good news. It meant that Harold wasn't off the hook at all. That he might be the next one to be taken in for questioning. But maybe not released.

Poor Angie. The bail bondsman might just take her B and B as collateral after all.

Glass snapped his fingers in front of Theodosia's face. "Hey, did you drift off to Planet X or something? How about comping me a cup of tea?"

"Drayton, why don't you give Mr. Glass a complimentary cup of tea," Theodosia said. "To go."

"Aw, you don't want me around?" Glass asked.

"Like I said, we're awfully busy," Theodosia said.

And they were busy. Once Bill Glass left, Haley ducked out of the kitchen, all jacked up about reviewing the menu for tomorrow's Beaux Arts Tea.

"We've already agreed on the scones, salads, and lobster bisque soup," Haley said. "But instead of serving the soup on its own, I'm thinking of adding a small accompaniment—a crostini topped with thin slices of London broil."

"You had me at London broil," Drayton said.

"I thought that might tweak your salivary glands," Haley said. "Which takes us to our entrée and dessert."

"Which we've already got locked down," Theodosia said.

"And we're still planning to serve champagne, right?" Haley asked. "Along with the tea?"

"I ordered a case of the good stuff," Theodosia said. "Genuine *methode champenoise.*"

Haley turned her gaze on Drayton. "Did you remember to order champagne glasses from the party rental place?"

"All taken care of," Drayton said. "And in my spare time, of which I have so little and you seem to have in abundance, I've also prepared a short talk on the beaux arts period."

"That ought to have them rolling in the aisles," Haley mumbled.

"Excuse me?" Drayton said.

"Nothing," Haley said as she scooted back into the kitchen.

Drayton shook his head while Theodosia just grinned at him. "Tea?" he said. "I brewed a pot of Japanese green tea as well."

"Don't mind if I do," Theodosia said.

Drayton reached under the counter and grabbed a tea-cup and saucer. Interestingly enough, it was the Chelsea Bird pattern by Royal Albert.

"That reminds me, I rescued a bluebird last night," Theodosia said.

"You what?"

"I found a little bluebird that had either flown into something or escaped the beak of some larger predator bird. Anyway, I brought the bird inside, let him come to his senses as he dried out, and then released him out-doors."

"That's almost like the story of *Niao-Yu* tea," Drayton said.

"I don't think I know that story."

"There was an old couple in China by the name of Ch'en who made their living gathering wild tea. One day they found an injured bird. They took the bird home, nursed it back to health, and then released it. A few days later, they heard a huge chatter and discovered that thousands of birds had perched in the trees surrounding their simple dwelling. When the birds flew away, the couple found their courtyard strewn with fragrant tea leaves that the birds had left—tea of a much finer quality than they had ever seen before. In fact, the birds left so much tea they were able to sell it and start a very prosperous tea business. So *Niao-Yu* tea literally means Left-by-the-Birds tea."

"And there really is a tea called Left-by-the-Birds?" Theodosia asked.

"I have a tin right here."

"I love it."

Drayton smiled. "Somehow I knew you would."

*   *   *

Maybe it was the warmer weather and the absence of rain, or the return of a lovely spring. Whatever was swirling about the ozone this morning caused the Indigo Tea Shop to suddenly get busy.

"It's all the tourists who are staying in the B and Bs," Drayton said to Theodosia. He was brewing pots of Fujian silver needle as well as pots of Chinese rose congou and Assam. "Lots of new folks have hit town for the weekend and are out and about exploring. Thank goodness the weather is much improved." He tapped an index finger against a blue-and-white teapot. "Theo, this Kertasarie Estate tea is for table six. But kindly take care. It's a tricky Indonesian black tea that requires an honest five minutes to steep."

Theodosia poured tea, ferried scones and tea bread, answered questions about teas versus tisanes (yes, all the Indigo Tea Shop's tisanes were caffeine free and made from fruits, flowers, and herbs). She also delivered extra pots of jam and Devonshire cream. When eleven thirty rolled around, they were hit with a new influx of customers—the luncheon crowd.

"I do believe we're going to make up for all the business we didn't have this past week," Theodosia said to Drayton.

"I hear you," he said. "But all in one day?" He was manning the phones and writing down take-out orders while he brewed and timed out pots of tea.

Thank goodness Haley's luncheon offerings were simple to serve. She'd prepared shrimp salad, hearty vegetable soup, grilled cheese sandwiches with apple and arugula, and something she called a scone slider.

"What's a scone slider?" Theodosia asked Haley as she picked up two soup orders.

"It's a Cheddar cheese scone stuffed with ham, white Cheddar, and honey mustard," Haley said.

"Did you just make that up?"

Haley gave her a shy glance. "Yeah. You like it?"

"I'm in awe."

Just when all the tables were occupied, when a bright-yellow horse-drawn jitney delivered yet another load of tourists to their front door, Delaine showed up.

She cut through the waiting crowd like the Titanic rushing to meet its destiny. Only instead of being shrouded in gray steel, she wore a perky pink jacket with white slacks.

"The-o-do-sia!" Delaine called out. "I don't need a table today but I *am* going to need two take-out lunches. Like, right away *s'il vous plaît*."

Theodosia had a teapot clutched in one hand and a tray full of luncheon salads balanced against one hip. "Talk to Drayton at the front counter. All take-out orders are going through Drayton today."

Delaine eyed the salads. "What are those yummy things? Shrimp salads? That's what I want."

"Talk to Drayton."

Theodosia delivered the salads, poured fresh cups of tea, and circled back to the front counter. "I take it you and Janine are eating in today?" she said to Delaine. Janine was Delaine's long-suffering assistant at Cotton Duck.

Delaine shook her head, causing her dangly diamond earrings to gently swish against her cheeks. "No, Janine's on vacation this week. Gone to visit her sister over in Walterboro." She wrinkled her nose. "Some nasty business about having a bunion removed." Then she brightened. "As luck would have it, my niece is in town visiting me. Well, actually, I'm hoping she'll stay on awhile. I can always use extra help on the sales floor."

"That sounds great, Delaine," Theodosia said. She glanced at the front door where six people were waiting.

"Do you think I could bring her to the Beaux Arts Tea tomorrow? My niece, I mean?"

"Absolutely," Theodosia said, heading for the crowd at

the front door, hoping to placate them. She called over her shoulder, "Tomorrow we'll have plenty of extra room."

But things have a way of working out and by one thirty, life at the Indigo Tea Shop had settled down. The tables were still filled to capacity, but the take-out orders had stopped flooding in and there weren't any more Nervous Nellies waiting at the front door.

"You hanging in there?" Theodosia asked Drayton. His bow tie was crooked and he looked as if he'd just run a half marathon.

"I think so. But, my goodness, that was a trial." Drayton sighed.

"That's what you said about your photo shoot yesterday."

"Did I? Hmm, I don't recall saying that."

"Face it, Drayton, you're a worrywart." Theodosia laughed.

"Noooo."

Theodosia held up a finger. "Still, you always accomplish your tasks with great style and finesse."

"Such a lovely backhanded compliment." The phone rang and Drayton heaved another sigh. "Please, let this not be another take-out order."

It wasn't.

"Call for you," Drayton said, handing the phone off to Theodosia. "I think it's Angie."

"Angie?" Theodosia said into the phone.

"I know this is last minute," Angie said. "But Harold and I were wondering if you could join us for dinner tonight? But a little later, maybe around eight o'clock?"

"You want to talk about . . . ?"

"No, I really don't," Angie said. "This would be more like a thank-you dinner. A thank-you for sticking your neck out for us."

"You don't have to do that."

"But I want to."

"Okay, that sounds lovely," Theodosia said. "I'll see you tonight. I look forward to it."

Not ten seconds after Theodosia hung up the phone, it rang again.

"Dear Lord," Drayton said. He snatched it up, listened, and handed it to Theodosia. "For you. Again."

"Hello?" she said.

Charles Townsend's anxious, breathy voice was suddenly in her ear. "It's urgent that I talk to you," he said.

Theodosia was instantly on alert. "Why? What's going on?" Obviously Townsend was freshly sprung from jail, just as Bill Glass had suggested.

"I don't want to breathe a single *word* over the phone," Townsend said. "In fact, I really don't even want to show my face at your tea shop. Maybe we could meet someplace nearby? Somewhere that's, like, extremely hush-hush and private."

"You're being awfully mysterious." *And scaring me a little bit, too.*

"I know I sound strange and I apologize for that. But I can't spill this over the phone, and I certainly don't want to do it with other people around." Townsend's words poured out as if a dam had suddenly burst. "I saw how caring and kind you were to Detective Tidwell the other night and you were nice to me, too. And before that, when you and Drayton came to see me, you weren't pushy and mean like some of the others. So I . . . I feel like I can trust you."

"Trust me with what?" Theodosia asked. This was a strange conversation.

"I have to tell you in person," Townsend said in a tight, strangled voice. "Can we meet somewhere? In secret?"

"How about I meet you in front of St. Philip's Church?" The church was just down the block from the Indigo Tea Shop. It was the historic edifice that bumped out into the street and had given Church Street its eponymous name.

"That's way too public. What if we met in back?"

"You mean in the graveyard?"

"Perfect," Townsend said.

Theodosia looked at her watch. "When?"

"Can you be there in twenty minutes?"

"Okay, um . . . yes. I'll see you there."

25

❧

"*I have to* run out," Theodosia said to Drayton once she'd hung up the phone.

"What's up?" Drayton asked matter-of-factly. He was stacking tea tins back on his shelves. Alphabetically, of course. And color coded.

"That was Charles Townsend. He wants to meet with me in secret."

Drayton stopped stacking. "Why don't I like the sound of that?"

"He says he has something important to tell me."

Drayton lifted a single eyebrow. "What? Something the police weren't able to beat out of him?"

"I don't think the police went *that* far."

"Could it be a confession?"

"I don't know," Theodosia said. "Townsend was quite mysterious about the whole thing."

"Maybe I should come with you."

"No. Townsend was specific in his request. He said he wanted to speak to me alone, in private. He practically begged me not to tell anyone else."

"Where are you supposed to meet him?" Drayton asked.

"St. Philip's Graveyard in about twenty minutes." Theodosia glanced at her watch. "Well, about eighteen minutes now."

"I still think I should come with you."

"How about if I put you on speed dial? If something feels the least bit hinky or threatening, I'll give you a quick call."

Drayton gave her a hard-eyed gaze. "Difficult to call with your head bashed in."

"That's not going to happen," Theodosia said.

"We hope."

Theodosia hurried along the path that circled around St. Philip's Church. It was the beginning of Gateway Walk, a four-block pathway that meandered through four different churchyards, moseyed past the Charleston Library Society, and ended up near the Gibbes Museum of Art. Along the way were countless pocket parks filled with flowers, fountains, and sculptures.

Today, however, Theodosia's ramble would be an abbreviated one. She was meeting Townsend in the antiquated cemetery directly behind St. Philip's Church. It was a historic old place where brigadier generals and signers of the Declaration of Independence were buried.

It was also a place of shadows and gloom, where tilting tombstones covered in dark moss looked like rows of rotted teeth. Many of the ancient tombs had sunk halfway into the ground and most of the mausoleums were chipped and pitted with age. Live oaks dripping with Spanish moss made sure the place remained dank and cool.

This was one of Charleston's so-called haunted spots. Several "ghost tours" stopped here and visitors were encouraged to try to commune with the dead and possibly even snap a photo that captured a faint outline of the cemetery's infamous "weeping woman" ghost.

This is where Drayton—and many others—had also witnessed slow-moving orbs.

Standing half-hidden behind a rounded tablet, on which names and dates were carved in French, Theodosia waited nervously for Charles Townsend. Branches rustled overhead, raindrops plipped and plopped, the wind snaking off the harbor sounded like a faint moan.

Theodosia had been waiting a good fifteen minutes and still hadn't seen hide nor hair of anyone or anything. No tourists, no ghosts, no Townsend.

How much longer should she wait? Theodosia wasn't sure. Maybe give it another ten minutes? It was turning cooler and streamers of fog drifted in, giving her surroundings an ethereal feel. Overhead was the occasional grumble of thunder.

It occurred to Theodosia that Charles Townsend might be so paranoid, so upset or obsessed by his employer's murder as well as his recent trip to jail, that he might have changed his mind and decided not to show up at all.

So be it. If that was the case, she'd just walk back to the tea shop. No harm done except some wasted time and energy.

Another five minutes ticked by without a trace of activity.

He isn't coming. Maybe he forgot? Or changed his mind?

Theodosia stepped around the tombstone, her feet crunching gravel underfoot. She took another couple of steps and heard . . . something.

Footsteps. Fast-moving footsteps. Someone running hard in her direction. Heading right toward her and really pounding away, as if their life depended on it.

Townsend?

Theodosia ducked back behind the tombstone and peered out, feeling a little nervous, a little fluttery. Yes, now Townsend came partially into view. He was running down the path, arms pumping, face bright red as a fire truck, cheeks puffed out as if he could barely draw another ragged breath. What was going on?

Theodosia stood up. "Charles? I was worried that you weren't . . ."

Townsend managed a quick glance over his shoulder and then snapped his head back in Theodosia's direction. Pure terror was written across his face as he scrambled toward her. "Watch out!" he screamed. "Get down!"

Wow. This poor guy is seriously nervous.

"Calm down," Theodosia said. "You're just being . . ."

BOOM!

A shot rang out, loud and thunderous, with enough firepower to wake the dead.

The word *paranoid* died on Theodosia's lips as she watched Townsend's entire body twist in midair and his face contort in agony. Then a spray of bright-red blood exploded from his left shoulder, as if it were happening in slow motion.

Townsend managed one more half stutter step and then faltered. A second later, he dropped in his tracks like a deer that had been nailed center of mass. Theodosia ducked down and waited tensely for another shot. When it didn't come, she scrambled for her cell phone. Hands shaking, heart beating wildly in her chest, she dialed 911.

Only when Theodosia heard the faint wail of a siren, some three minutes later, did she creep out from behind the tombstone to check on Townsend. He was lying where he'd fallen. Facedown, his entire body quivering. His shoulder was leaking blood like crazy and the fingers of one hand made crab-like motions in the white gravel.

Still alive but wounded.

Theodosia kicked it into high gear then. She whipped off her scarf, balled it up, and pressed it hard against Townsend's shoulder to try to stop the flow of blood.

"Help me," Townsend croaked. He turned his head so one glazed eye stared up at her.

"I called 911. You hear that siren? Try to hang on. Help should be here any minute."

"No, I mean . . ." Townsend groaned and the eye drooped shut.

Seconds later, a uniformed officer was bending over Townsend. Ten seconds after that, two EMTs arrived on the scene with medical equipment and a gurney. They wrapped his wound and did their standard emergency ABC life check: airway, breathing, and circulation. One of them pulled out a portable ventilator bag and got some oxygen flowing into Townsend.

While they worked on Townsend, the uniformed cop, whose name tag read T. MORROW, questioned Theodosia. She answered him as best she could. Who she was, why she was there, what she'd seen. Finally, she said, "You've got to call Detective Tidwell about this."

"Burt Tidwell?" Morrow said. "The head of RHD?" He meant the Robbery and Homicide Division.

"He's been in charge of this case," Theodosia said. She pointed to Townsend. "The man who just got shot here, Charles Townsend, he is . . . was . . . a kind of suspect in that hot-air balloon crash."

Morrow looked at her for a few long seconds and then said, "Holy crap, lady. Seriously?"

Theodosia nodded. "Call Tidwell. He'll fill you in."

It wasn't until the EMTs loaded Townsend into the ambulance, and the ambulance took off with a *whoop-whoop* burst of its siren, that Theodosia took a deep breath. She wondered what it was that Townsend had been so all-fired-up about? Just what had he been so anxious to tell her? And who on earth had shot him?

26

❧

"How was your meeting with Charles Townsend?" Drayton asked Theodosia when she returned to the shop.

Theodosia stopped at the front counter and gazed at him. She was feeling unsettled and more than a little freaked out.

"What?" he said.

"There was no meeting."

"Just as I figured." Drayton nodded sagely. "Townsend chickened out."

"No, he was shot."

Drayton's lips twitched into an almost-smile and he gave a low chuckle. "You don't have to make up crazy stories for me, Theo. I never thought the fellow would show in the first place. He was simply playing . . . silly games."

Theodosia's voice rose. "Drayton, the man was shot. Literally. One second I was standing in the cemetery watching Charles Townsend run toward me, the next second there was a sharp crack and blood started gushing from a shoulder wound."

Drayton wagged his head in a sort of double take. But he still looked hesitant, as if he didn't believe her. "Shot?" he said.

"With a bullet. You know, bang bang?"

Right before Theodosia's eyes, Drayton's face morphed from disbelief to stunned. "Great Caesar's ghost, tell me the whole thing!" he cried. "Tell me what happened!"

So Theodosia told him about waiting in the cemetery, hearing the frantic *thud-thump* of running footsteps, seeing the fear on Townsend's face, and then watching him jerk and twist like a game bird who'd been hit with a load of buckshot.

"Then what did you do?" Drayton asked.

Theodosia shrugged. "What could I do? I dove behind a tombstone so *I* didn't get shot and called 911. Hunkered there until the police showed up. And an ambulance."

"Did you see who shot him?"

"No I did not. You know how spooky and shrouded with foliage that place is. And the fog didn't help, either."

"Is Townsend . . . is he *dead*?"

"Whoever it was just winged him. He'll live."

"Theo!" Now Drayton's eyes bugged out like an animated cartoon character. "You're talking as if this was an episode of *Wyatt Earp*. But . . . wait, all of this really happened?"

"Cross my heart. Somebody took a shot at Townsend just as we were about to meet up. I couldn't make this stuff up if I wanted to."

"Who do you *think* shot him?"

"If I had to venture a guess," Theodosia said, "I'd say it was someone who didn't want Townsend talking to me." She drew a deep breath and then blew it out, feeling a glint of fear. "Someone who almost pulled off a fourth murder."

Theodosia was still shaking, but she managed to show up at WCSC-TV right on time.

"Theodosia Browning to see Alicia Kellig," she said to the gum-chewing receptionist who sat at their swoopy, white front desk. The rest of the lobby was white as well: white chairs, tables, and lamps. The only spot of color was a large, shaggy, purple-and-orange rug. She supposed the place was intended to look industrial chic but it looked more like a set out of *2001: A Space Odyssey.*

"Do you have an appointment?" the receptionist asked.

"Actually, Alicia called me to do a quick on-air segment for your Action Auction."

"Oh," the girl said, reaching to hit a button on her console. "That's different. That makes you talent."

Theodosia smiled. "I wouldn't go that far."

The receptionist mumbled something into her headset and said, "Okay, I'll tell her." She turned to Theodosia. "Do you know where Studio B is? Right down this corridor and . . ."

"I think I can find it, yes."

"Alicia said she'd meet you there."

Theodosia walked down the hallway, amused by all the colorful, severely retouched photos of on-air personnel that were hanging on the walls. Here was Weston Keyes, the genial host of *Charleston Today*, wearing an inch of pancake makeup and a pound of pomade. And there was Chip Monson, one of the evening sports anchors, with sparkling white teeth, a golfer's tan, and more hair than anyone had a right to.

Just past the lunchroom, where a security guard was slouched in a chair eating a donut and studying his cell phone, Theodosia arrived at Studio B. Large red letters on the door said CLOSED SET, ABSOLUTELY NO ENTRY, but she went in anyway.

And there was Alicia, clipboard in hand and wearing an earpiece. "Girl, you made it!" she whispered.

I almost didn't, Theodosia thought to herself and then said, "Thanks again for inviting me."

"Thanks for donating such good stuff," Alicia said.

White-blond, super short hair framed her wide-set eyes that were tinged with pink mascara. Her slight figure was encased in skintight jeans and a white T-shirt that said GUCCI GIRL.

Theodosia had always thought of a producer as a frazzled, middle-aged TV veteran who ran around constantly trying to keep things organized. Now it looked as if her image was slightly out of date. Well . . . good.

Theodosia glanced about the enormous studio. It was dimly lit, with cameras and dollies parked everywhere, and thick rubber cables snaking underfoot. At the far end of the studio was a brightly lit row of tables that held all manner of auction items: Instant Pots, a paddleboard, luggage, an Oriental carpet, some kind of home Pilates system, an antique clock, a cookware set, and, of course, Theodosia's tea and teapots. A perky female host was facing a camera, talking up the merits of a matching set of zebra-striped luggage.

"And when you return home from your fabulous vacation," the host cooed, "each piece of luggage nests right inside the other. So hurry up and call those bids in right now!"

"This is going out live?" Theodosia asked.

Alicia nodded as she touched a finger to her lips. "Come this way. We'll get you on next."

Theodosia followed Alicia toward the long table that was mounded with Action Auction items. The on-air host saw them coming and quickly wrapped up her presentation. "Stick around, because when we come back we're going to talk about the most exquisite tea and teapots you could ever imagine!"

The camera pulled back and the cameraman, a pear-shaped man in crepe-soled shoes, said, "And we're out, Josie."

The host, Josie, took a step back and fanned herself. "Whew," she said. "Hot under those lights." She was in her early thirties, super skinny, with an extremely pale complexion and long, dark hair with a skunk stripe on one side. As a makeup artist hurried over to give her a touch-up, Josie said, "Use the absolute whitest, lightest powder you've got. No color except on my lips."

While Josie was having her lips lined, her face powdered to a corpse-like pallor, and her hair vigorously poufed, a soundman crept in and clipped a tiny microphone to Theodosia's jacket lapel.

Once Josie had been beautified (embalmed?), she turned a bright, TV smile on Theodosia. "You're my tea lady?"

"That's me," Theodosia said.

"Come on around here and stand next to me," Josie said. She peered out at the cameraman. "Frankie, we're going to want to open and hold with a two-shot, then do a tracking shot into the teapot." She glanced at Theodosia. "You ready to give us the poop?"

"This particular teapot is made by Shelley, which is . . ."

"Whoa. You don't have to sell *me*," Josie chuckled. "Just worry about pitching it to our TV audience."

"Gulp."

"You'll be fine," Josie said.

"Theodosia's done this before," Alicia said. "She's a natural."

Two minutes later, nerves fizzing, Theodosia was selling it like her life depended on it. She told the TV audience about the Shelley teapot in the Melody pattern and sang sweet siren songs about Drayton's new house blends, his Imperial Oolong and Chocolate Cherry Paradise tea.

"And these particular teas are blended right there in your tea shop? The Indigo Tea Shop?" Josie asked.

Theodosia nodded. "Absolutely. We're right over on Church Street and stock at least two hundred different varieties of tea."

Theodosia's segment was over before she could say Egyptian chamomile spice.

"Well done," Josie proclaimed.

"Thank you," Alicia said. She touched a hand to her

earpiece. "I'm getting word from our call center that bids are coming in."

"Already?" Theodosia asked as the sound guy reached in and unclipped her mike.

"Don't you just love live TV?" Alicia said. "It scares us half to death, which is why we hardly ever do it. Except for the news and weather, of course. And if we could pretape that, we would."

"Live TV is kind of thrilling," Theodosia said. "Like walking a tightrope." Her palms felt sweaty and her heart was still pounding. But in a good way.

"Thank you again," Alicia said as she walked Theodosia through the studio. "Hope to see you soon." Just as Alicia pushed open the door to the outside corridor, a man eased his way in. "Hey, you must be my four forty-five." She clicked her pen and pointed it at him. "The antique clock, right?"

"Right," said the man, which caused Theodosia to give him a startled glance.

"Tod Slawson?" Theodosia said. "What are you doing here?"

Slawson gave her a lazy grin and pointed at Alicia. "Just like she said, I'm her four forty-five."

"You donated a piece to the auction?" Theodosia asked.

"A Biedermeier mantel clock," Alicia said. "And we are scheduled to go on . . ." She glanced at her clipboard and grabbed Slawson by the sleeve. "Right now!"

Just as Theodosia was leaving the building, she ran smack-dab into Dale Dickerson, the roving TV reporter. She gave him a friendly, neutral smile, while Dickerson fairly beamed at her.

"What are *you* doing here?" Dickerson boomed. He looked coiffed and buffed and ready to leap in front of a camera.

"Just a quick on-air thing for your Action Auction," Theodosia said.

"You donated something?"

"A teapot."

"Aren't you a sweetheart," Dickerson said. He was blocking the doorway, trying his best not to let her get past him. "It's so great that our paths crossed again!"

Ever since he'd started flirting with her, Theodosia wondered if Dickerson was interested in *her* or in trying to worm a few more details out of her for his story.

"It was nice seeing you," Theodosia said as she tried to ease her way past him.

"Hey, don't be in such a hurry. Have you got time for a cup of coffee . . . I'm sorry, tea? Or we could go somewhere and have a drink if you'd like."

"Sorry, but I have to be going."

Dickerson leaned toward her, not exactly invading her space, but certainly getting close. "I'd like to see you again," he said.

"Again? We've barely seen each other a first time."

"You know what I mean. I feel like we have a genuine connection."

"Mr. Dickerson," Theodosia said in a mock formal tone, "are you trying to pry more information from me about the crash?"

"No!"

Theodosia smiled. "I do believe you are."

Dickerson looked supremely disappointed.

"Another time then," Theodosia said, wincing because she really didn't want to encourage him, but she didn't want to be impolite, either.

Breathing a sigh of relief, Theodosia walked across the parking lot and climbed into her Jeep. Just as she was about to start her engine, her cell phone rang.

She scrambled to dig it out of her purse. "Hello?" She was expecting it to be Drayton asking how her TV gig had gone.

Big surprise. It was Tidwell.

"I think you'll be interested in what has become a radical new development," Tidwell said without any sort of introduction or preamble. "We have a confession. Granted it's a trifle overwrought, but it's a confession nonetheless."

"What are you talking about?" Theodosia stammered. *What was Tidwell talking about?* "A confession from whom?" she asked.

"Your little friend Charles Townsend."

Theodosia dropped the phone to her chest. *Oh dear Lord, I knew it all along. Townsend was the one who caused the hot-air balloon crash that killed those three people. The idea's been pinging around in my subconscious all week long. Only I didn't listen carefully enough. I didn't do anything about it.*

Theodosia recovered seconds later and said, "Townsend caused the hot-air balloon crash? He drove his drone right into it?"

"No, he did not," Tidwell said.

"Wait a minute," Theodosia said. "I'm confused then. What exactly is Townsend confessing to?"

"It's complicated," Tidwell said. "Better you just get yourself over here to Mercy Hospital."

27

❧

It was rush hour, so traffic was in a snarl all up and down Broad Street. It took a bit of creative navigation, but Theodosia finally arrived at Mercy Hospital, circled the parking lot twice, and managed to find the only available parking space. She walked through the automatic door into the hospital, mindful of the people on crutches and in wheelchairs, and headed for the front desk. The information desk.

But before she could inquire about Charles Townsend's room number, a dark-haired plainclothes policeman spotted her and hurried toward her. Leaning in, he said, "Miss Browning?"

Theodosia straightened up. "Yes?"

"Detective Tidwell asked me to send you up to room four fifteen."

"That's where . . . ?"

"Yes, ma'am."

Theodosia rode up in the elevator with two orderlies and a laundry cart, wondering the whole time what kind of confession Charles Townsend had poured out to Tidwell.

Was that what he'd wanted to tell her in the cemetery this afternoon? To spill his guts? About . . . what?

If Townsend *wasn't* the one who'd murdered Don Kingsley and company, then what exactly was the big crime he was confessing to? Theodosia couldn't imagine what it could be. An unpaid speeding ticket? Cheating on his SAT test? Falsifying a résumé? Seriously, Townsend was a fairly young guy so how bad could it be?

Well, it was apparently bad enough because Tidwell had shackled one of Townsend's arms to the railing of his hospital bed.

Theodosia figured it had to be Townsend's good arm, right? Or could Tidwell be that much of a sadist?

Tidwell stood up when Theodosia entered the hospital room. Townsend just grimaced in her direction and made a dull clank.

"Good, you've arrived," Tidwell said. "About time."

"I came as fast as I could. It's rush hour out there in case you hadn't noticed," Theodosia said.

"There's little time to waste, so I prefer we get right down to business," Tidwell said.

"What exactly are we getting down to?" Theodosia asked.

Tidwell stared at her. "Imagine my utter surprise when I found out that young Mr. Townsend here had been shot," he said. "And that it happened on his way to meet you."

Theodosia met his gaze evenly. "I didn't think it was supposed to be a social call."

"I dare say it wasn't," Tidwell said. "Yet you continue to insinuate yourself into any number of bizarre situations surrounding this case. And since you've been so blasted *involved* in what has become a thorn-in-the-side homicide for me, I wanted you to hear Townsend's confession directly from the horse's mouth."

"I guess that makes me the horse," Townsend said, licking his lips and finally speaking up. His voice was choked with emotion and his face looked pinched and ashen against the flimsy white sheets. Part of a large bandage stuck out from the rounded collar of his pale-blue hospital gown.

"How's your shoulder?" Theodosia asked him. She was wary of Townsend, but felt sorry for him, too.

"Terrible," Townsend said. "Hurts like crazy."

Tidwell ignored their exchange. "You are now going to relate to us your side of the story, Mr. Townsend. While I record every single dulcet tone you utter." Tidwell held up a small tape recorder and waggled it in Townsend's face. Then he clicked it on and spoke into the microphone, noting the time, date, place, and names of the three people present. When he played the recording back, his voice sounded tinny but audible. "Good, it's working. Mr. Townsend, you may proceed. Tell us your tale of woe and don't leave out any glaring details. Realize, too, that this is not the time to jerk us around or try to curry sympathy. Those tactics won't work with me."

Me neither, Theodosia told herself.

Townsend struggled to sit up in bed. "Can you at least take this handcuff off me?"

"Not a chance," Tidwell said. He fiddled with one of the tape recorder's knobs and waited.

Theodosia sat down in an ugly peach-colored vinyl chair between the window and the bed, anxious to hear Townsend's confession, whatever it may be.

"I'm no killer," Townsend started out in a barely audible, creaky voice. Theodosia thought he sounded like the *Man in the Iron Mask*. Like he'd been locked up in a dungeon and hadn't uttered a word in twenty years.

"Go on," Tidwell prodded.

"I loved working for Don Kingsley, he was a good guy, a real gentleman." Townsend coughed, reached for his glass of water, and took a long sip. His hand shook as he put it back and water dribbled down his chin and onto his gown. Finally, he resumed. "Mr. Kingsley was giving me more and more responsibility with his collection. He was talking about establishing an honest-to-goodness museum. It was all rather exciting, and I figured I had a real future there. So when the hot-air balloon exploded and it was obvious there were no survivors, I went into absolute shock. I felt like I had died, too. And I had no idea what to do or where to turn." Townsend's face was beaded with sweat, his eyes rolling back and forth as if he were experiencing excruciating pain.

"Tape's rolling," Tidwell said.

"Afterward," Townsend continued, "a few hours later, when I returned to the mansion, I wandered through the place, just going from room to room. It felt so empty and forlorn. And I felt absolutely hopeless, as if *my* life had ended, too. And then . . ."

"And then?" Theodosia said, leaning forward in her chair.

Townsend's face took on an almost cunning look. "And then . . . I don't know *why* I did it . . . but I took the flag and hid it upstairs in the attic. Way back in a dusty old part where nobody would ever find it."

"Just to be absolutely clear, you *stole* Mr. Kingsley's Navy Jack flag," Tidwell said.

Townsend hung his head forward and whispered, "Yes."

"Louder, please," Tidwell said.

"Yes, I took the flag," Townsend said.

"So *you* have the missing Navy Jack?" Theodosia asked.

Townsend shook his head miserably. "That's the terrible problem. I *don't* have the flag anymore. Someone stole it from me!"

Theodosia stood up. "What are you talking about? Who stole it?" She was knocked for a loop by this revelation and practically shouted at Townsend.

"I don't know who stole it!" Townsend cried. "Someone broke into the mansion and accosted me at gunpoint.

Threatened me, told me they'd *kill* me if I didn't hand over the flag. So I did. I had to. You can't believe how terrified I was!"

"And when exactly did this holdup occur?" Tidwell asked.

"You know when," Townsend said, ducking his head and giving Tidwell a nervous, guilty look. "It was Wednesday night. Right before you got hit on the head and you and Miss Browning showed up at the back door."

"You see?" Tidwell said to Theodosia.

Theodosia blinked. "My goodness but this is strange." She was shocked. She hadn't seen this coming at all.

"And you can keep asking and asking, but I don't know who the thief was!" Townsend shouted, nearly in tears. "Whoever it was wore a balaclava—a kind of black ski mask—so I couldn't see their face or hair. And they spoke through one of those voice things."

"A voice changer?" Theodosia said. "So they could alter and disguise their real voice?"

"Yes!" Townsend cried.

The door to Townsend's room opened and a nurse stuck her head in. "Everything okay in here?" she asked.

"Fine. Please leave," Tidwell said. He moved his chair closer to Townsend and his expression hardened. "Young man, were you the one who struck me on the back of the head while I was investigating outside the Kingsley mansion?"

"What?" Townsend looked astonished. "No! I figure it had to be the same person who stole the flag. After they threatened me, they ran out the back door and must have encountered you!"

"This is all rather confusing," Tidwell said.

"Maybe you got hit harder than you thought," Theodosia said. She sat back down again and said, "So let me get this straight. You were threatened by . . . someone with a gun. At which point you turned over the Navy Jack flag to them. And then this same mystery person rushed out and, in trying to get away, struck Detective Tidwell on the head?"

"Probably," Townsend said. "I mean, that scenario *sounds* right."

"Why didn't you say something when I brought Detective Tidwell to the back door? When he limped in and I asked you for help?" Theodosia asked. "That's the point at which we could have *done* something!"

"I was terrified and not thinking straight!" Townsend cried. "I'd just been threatened with bodily harm."

"You're sure you weren't covering up for someone else?" Theodosia asked.

"Of course not!"

"So our desperate killer is still out there," Tidwell said. "And now it turns out our killer is also a thief."

"I suppose that's it in a nutshell," Theodosia said. "Which puts us back to square one." But even as she said that, a random thought streaked through her brain. *Unless somehow . . . somewhere . . . there's a second person involved.*

Theodosia had just enough time to get to the Featherbed House for dinner. She pulled to the curb some fifty feet from the front door and sat there thinking. Her engine ticked down as she wondered if she should tell Angie and Harold about Charles Townsend's hospital bed confession.

She was still wondering about it when she walked into the lobby.

"Checking in?" the young woman behind the front desk asked.

Theodosia touched a hand to her chest. "I'm Theodosia Browning. I'm supposed to be joining Angie and Harold for dinner tonight."

"Of course," said the young woman. "Angie told me you were coming. Right this way."

Theodosia was led through the ample, elegant lobby

where guests sipped glasses of sherry, lounged on sofas and chairs, and browsed through an extensive library of books on Charleston history.

"In here," the young woman said. "The breakfast room."

"Thank you," Theodosia said. The white linen-clad table was set with service for three. Candles glowed and soft music played.

"Theo," Angie said from behind her. "I'm so glad you could make it."

Theodosia turned and gave Angie a warm hug. "And I'm so glad you invited me. This looks lovely."

"If your young man had been in town, I would have invited him, too."

"Pete will be back tomorrow," Theodosia said.

"You must be happy about that."

"You have no idea."

A door at the far end of the room creaked open and Harold appeared with a tray of appetizers. "Talk about timing," he said. "These stuffed mushroom caps just came out of the oven."

They all sat down then as Angie poured glasses of red wine and Harold served his baked mushrooms sprinkled with bread crumbs and Romano cheese.

Dinner was lovely. Angie brought out a second course of angel-hair pasta swirled in a light lemon and fresh herb sauce—what Harold called a *segundo*. Then a main course of grilled pork medallions and Broccolini was served. Conversation was easy and upbeat. The missing drone was not mentioned. Nor were the deaths of Don Kingsley and his fellow hot-air balloonists, or the fact that Harold had been summarily fired from his job at SyncSoft.

"This is a wonderful treat," Theodosia remarked. "Usually I'm the one who's serving food and then dashing back into the kitchen to grab more."

"Harold's become quite the food service manager," Angie said. "He's completely updated our breakfast menu . . ."

"We've added crepes," Harold said. "Turns out they're

not all that hard to make. The trick is using a blue steel pan and then seasoning it correctly." He ducked his head. "I meant seasoning the pan, not the crepes."

"And he's been handling all our food ordering," Angie finished.

"I take it you're still keeping your complimentary wine and cheese each evening?" Theodosia asked.

"That's squarely in Teddy's wheelhouse, so I dare not touch it." Harold laughed.

It wasn't until Harold brought out dessert—raspberry tortes—that the fateful balloon crash was finally mentioned.

"I want to thank you for all you've done," Angie said to Theodosia. "Standing up against that awful Detective Tidwell and trying to ferret out suspects. But I've got to ask . . . Have you learned anything more?"

Theodosia was about to tell her about Townsend getting shot in the cemetery and his subsequent revelation from his hospital bed. Then she stopped. Hushed herself. Instead, she shook her head.

"I'm afraid," Theodosia said, "that I'm just as much in the dark as you are."

She wasn't going to mention the flag being stolen for a second time. Because, after all, who knew who'd been wearing that balaclava? And carrying a pistol?

Earl Grey scrambled to his feet when Theodosia came flying through the back door. "Did Mrs. Barry feed you?" She glanced at Earl Grey's stainless steel dog bowl where a few hunks of kibble remained. "Oh, good. She was here."

The dog walked over to her and poked her with his muzzle. *Give me a pet, why don't ya?*

"You are such a dear boy," Theodosia crooned to him. She cupped Earl Grey's head in her hands and gently tugged his ears. "Have I told you how much I love you?"

"Rrowrr." *Tell me again.*

"How about a jerky treat?" Theodosia pulled the treat bag out of the cupboard and fed one to Earl Grey just as the phone rang.

It was Pete Riley.

"You sound like you're close by," Theodosia told him. "Did you catch an early flight? Are you by any chance back in Charleston?" *Hope, hope.*

"Dóes *fantasizing* about being back with you count?"

"It's nice, but certainly not as good as the real thing."

"But I am in my hotel room packing," Riley said.

"So you'll be back tomorrow for sure?"

"I'm catching the three o'clock plane out of here."

"Mmm, not until then." Theodosia's brows pinched together. "That means you'll be arriving fairly late."

"Isn't dining late the fashionable thing to do?" Riley asked.

Theodosia smiled to herself. "What exactly did you have in mind?"

"I could stop at Harris Teeter for groceries on my way home and then whip up my famous brown butter sea scallops."

"You're on." Riley was no Ina Garten, she knew that. Still, this was a man who owned a mortar and pestle and he'd once cooked scrumptious crab cakes for her. So there were positive signs that he might harbor some fine culinary skills along with his detecting skills.

"Come over to my place tomorrow night around nine," Riley said. "And I'll have everything ready. Wine chilled, candles lit, the whole romantic thing. Bring Earl Grey, too. I'm dying to see him, though not as much as I'm looking forward to seeing you."

"Whew, I thought I might be playing second fiddle for a moment." Then Theodosia hesitated. She didn't want to tell Riley how deeply immersed she was in the killer drone case, but was curious if Tidwell had tapped him for a second opinion. "I was wondering . . . how much have you been briefed on this drone thing?"

"Bits and pieces. I've accessed a few reports on my laptop and skimmed through them. Now I'm going to read through all of the police reports and interviews, see if a fresh pair of eyes can help figure something out."

Theodosia nodded, though she knew he couldn't see her. "Bless you."

"I'll see you tomorrow night, sweetheart."

Theodosia went upstairs and puttered around. She changed into comfy clothes, fluffed Earl Grey's upstairs bed (yes, he had two beds), and ran a finger down an enormous stack of books that she'd just *had* to have but hadn't gotten around to reading yet.

Outside, trees whispered and shuddered while lightning slashed across the night sky—the storm making a return engagement. Theodosia glanced out the window as another flash turned the landscape into a stark black-and-white image, like a reverse negative. And, just for an instant, she thought she saw a face looking up at her. Then the world went completely dark. She hovered uneasily at the window until the next lightning flash lit up her side yard. There was nobody there.

Just nerves, she told herself. Just nerves.

Flopping down in her cushy armchair, Theodosia turned on the TV. The late news was on and, interestingly enough, so was Detective Tidwell. He was standing next to the mayor at a press conference that had clearly taken place just a few hours earlier. Tidwell's posture was stiff and he didn't look one bit happy. Then again, nobody looked particularly happy. Not Tidwell, not the mayor, not the PR flunky who was trying to inchworm his way into the photo op.

Theodosia wondered if Tidwell had talked about the missing flag on TV and decided he probably hadn't. It would muddy the water too much. Besides, the press was rabid for details about the investigation into the hot-air balloon crash.

The mayor, looking grim and slightly frantic, as if a

pack of jackals was slavering after him (which they were), promised that the triple homicide would be solved in a matter of days.

Tidwell flinched visibly at the mayor's words. He obviously didn't think it would be that easy.

Neither did Theodosia.

28

❦

Wonder of wonders, the sun was out. Well, technically it had made a guest appearance for all of five minutes on this Saturday morning. Still, it was a huge improvement. The sky was definitely brighter with an occasional hint of blue breaking through. The breeze off Charleston Harbor was pleasant and tinged with warmth.

Theodosia, who'd shown up bright and early at the Portman Mansion, along with Drayton and Haley, figured this nicer weather heralded abundant good luck for their Beaux Arts Tea.

"You're sure those gold tablecloths are appropriate?" Haley asked. They were clustered in the dining room and had just draped a single table to test Drayton's design and color scheme.

"They're perfect," Drayton said. "Spot-on, in fact. You realize we're also using brocade place mats and will have huge bouquets of white roses set on top of octagonal mirrors for our centerpieces."

"All that plus tea accoutrements and candles?" Haley asked.

Drayton smiled. "I'm putting white tapers in those gilded cherub candelabras that you adore so much."

Haley made a face. "If you throw those ghastly, grinning little celestial beings into the mix, that's going to make for an awful lot of ornament." She pushed a hank of blond hair back behind her ear and squinted at him. "Maybe too much?"

"Consider it embellishment, not merely ornament," Drayton said. "There's a world of difference between the two. What we're striving to achieve today is rich, decorative detail, layered with gilt and gold. We want our table décor to hold true to our beaux arts theme."

Haley curled a lip. She still wasn't convinced. "It still looks like the last dregs of the Austro-Hungarian Empire to me."

"I know you're a shabby chic kind of girl." Drayton chuckled. "And next time we need quaint patterned linens and paint-spattered wooden chairs, I promise I'll look to you for expertise."

Theodosia was unpacking their Sevres china, slightly bemused at the way Drayton and Haley were going back and forth. They didn't exactly fight as much as they quibbled with each other. It was kind of like watching a hot dose of *Housewives* reality TV.

"While you two layer on the schmaltz, I'm going to get cracking in the kitchen," Haley said.

"Do you need any help?" Theodosia asked. She was mindful that this was a big undertaking for all of them.

"Nope." Haley sounded confident. "Miss Dimple should be arriving any minute. But fear not, I'll yell if I need help."

Once Haley had disappeared, Theodosia said, "I've got to bring you up to speed on something that happened."

"Hmm?" Drayton said. He was focused on polishing the silverware. Or, rather, repolishing it and buffing each piece with a soft cloth so it shone even more brilliantly.

"I have to tell you about last night."

Drayton stopped polishing and stared at her. "What happened last night?"

Theodosia told him about being called to the hospital, hearing Charles Townsend's confession about *stealing* the flag, and then Townsend's blow-by-blow description of subsequently being *robbed* of the flag himself.

"Townsend was actually robbed?" Drayton asked. "At gunpoint?"

"That's what he claims." Then Theodosia told Drayton about the rest of her evening. About how, right after the hospital visit, she'd run over to Angie and Harold's for dinner.

"Sounds like you had yourself a nice drama-filled evening," Drayton said. "But the big question is, did you spill the beans to Angie and Harold about Townsend's flag confession?"

"No, I didn't. Because now it seems like a somewhat separate issue," Theodosia said.

"Separate from the hot-air balloon crash?"

"Yes."

Drayton thought for a few moments. "You believe that Townsend, in a moment of self-induced pity after the balloon crash, stole the Navy Jack flag . . ." He paused. "Which in turn was stolen from him a few days later."

"That's what Townsend claims and the events certainly sound plausible enough," Theodosia said.

Drayton held up a hand. "And then whoever chased and shot Townsend yesterday did so because they feared that Townsend was going to confess the flag heist to you?"

"I guess so. Although Townsend didn't exactly phrase it that way." Theodosia frowned. "I guess I kind of assumed . . ."

"The problem I see," Drayton said, "is that somebody—some third party, possibly the killer—knows that you're involved. That's definitely not good."

"I hear you," Theodosia said.

"So now we're fairly sure that someone other than

Townsend was responsible for bringing down the hot-air balloon."

Theodosia touched a hand to her cheek. "That's what I'm thinking. That Townsend is off the hook as far as the triple homicide is concerned."

"But he's *on* the hook for the flag. And so is the person who stole it after he stole it."

"Maybe it was the *killer* who came back and held Townsend up at gunpoint to steal the flag. Because that was his aim all along—to get his sticky hands on that flag," Theodosia said.

"This situation gets more and more convoluted," Drayton said.

"I know. I keep thinking I should take Detective Tidwell's advice and bow out."

"You mean bow out of the investigation?"

"That's right," Theodosia said.

Drayton shook his head. "You can't do that."

"Why not?"

"Because we need to find that flag. The Navy Jack. It's a sacred, hallowed piece of history and I don't want some desperate criminal to profit by it. Truth is, I'd love to see that flag recovered and then convince Tawney to donate it to the Heritage Society."

"What if Tawney was the one who stole it?" Theodosia asked.

Drayton's face clouded. "Then we've got a problem."

Miss Chatfield, the event coordinator, was suitably impressed with their table décor.

"Wonderful," Miss Chatfield said, practically clapping her hands. "So elegant and refined."

"We planned our table decorations to play off the architectural elements of your fine mansion," Drayton told her. He was laying it on as thick as meringue.

"And what may I ask will be displayed on these lovely

easels?" Miss Chatfield asked. Drayton had hauled in three borrowed wooden easels and placed them strategically around the dining room.

"Oil paintings," Theodosia said. She was just carrying in one of the paintings when she heard Miss Chatfield ask her question.

Drayton dashed over to help Theodosia. "Let me give you a hand with that. That gilt frame looks awfully heavy."

Miss Chatfield's eyes widened as Drayton gently unwrapped the painting and placed it on one of the easels. It gleamed under the light of the room's chandelier.

"My goodness but you pulled out all the stops," Miss Chatfield said. "Did you borrow your paintings from the Gibbes Museum or . . . ?"

"The Dolce Gallery over on Church Street," Theodosia said. "Tom Ritter, the gallery owner, let us pick out three works that had a late nineteenth-century beaux arts feel."

"Your tea is going to be fanciful as well as amazing," Miss Chatfield said. "I'm going to run and grab my camera so I can capture a few shots of this table décor. It may serve as inspiration to other potential clients who plan to hold an event here."

Just as they finished carrying in the paintings and Theodosia was busily arranging long-stemmed white roses in silver teapots, Haley came back in from the kitchen carrying a plate. Miss Dimple was with her. She'd arrived on time as promised.

"Teapots instead of vases, huh?" Haley said as she studied the tables. She'd changed into a black blouse and skirt with a frilly white apron.

"I thought they might be kind of fun," Theodosia said. "We hardly ever use these really large teapots."

"Everything looks beautiful." Miss Dimple beamed. "And I really love the paintings. They lend such a Parisian art gallery feel."

"Are you ready to help serve, dear lady?" Drayton asked Miss Dimple. "It promises to be a busy day."

"I'm ready as ever," Miss Dimple said, giving him a slow wink. Her frilly white apron was worn over a simple black dress.

"What have you got there?" Theodosia asked Haley. "Something delicious to tempt us with?"

"I wanted to show you guys our dessert cookies." Haley tipped her plate so everyone could see. "Vanilla tea cookies piped with gold trim and a sugary Napoleon bee in the center."

"Now this would definitely fit in the sugar arts category," Theodosia said.

Haley bobbed her head. "I think so. Cool, huh?"

"Beyond," Miss Dimple said.

Drayton and Miss Dimple fussed with the tables, making tiny adjustments here and there, while Haley helped Theodosia finish arranging the floral bouquets.

When they were all done, when the plates, teacups, and crystal were perfectly set and sparkling in the light, Drayton glanced around and bobbed his head. He was pleased. "Alright now, we need to synchronize our watches."

"Why?" Haley asked. "Will we be blowing up a bridge?"

Theodosia and Miss Dimple burst out laughing while Drayton tried not to smile. Didn't work.

"Gotcha," Haley said to him. "I gotcha good this time."

"Yes, you did," Drayton said.

"Do you two need any help with the food?" Theodosia asked Haley and Miss Dimple. They were zeroing in on eleven o'clock. Their guests would be arriving precisely at twelve.

"Nope," Haley said. "Miss Dimple and I have it covered."

"Can I at least come back and take a peek?"

"Of course," Haley said.

Theodosia followed them into the kitchen where scones baked and lobster bisque simmered. Just as she was admiring Haley's cookies again, the ornate wall phone rang.

"I hope it isn't one of your guests calling to cancel," Miss Dimple said.

Haley picked up the phone and listened for a few seconds. Then she rolled her eyes and handed the receiver to Theodosia. "For you," she said. "I guess."

"Who is it?" Theodosia whispered.

Haley frowned and shook her head. "Don't know. It's either a hysterical woman or someone's playing badminton with a squawking chicken. I could barely make out what she was saying."

Theodosia took the call with some trepidation. "Hello?"

"Theodosia!" came a loud, high-pitched screech. "I need you to come over here immediately!"

"Who is this?"

"It's Tawney. Tawney Kingsley. I need your help. I'm *desperate!*"

"Tawney, I'm desperate myself. I'm an hour away from seating fifty-seven . . . almost sixty guests for my ultra-fancy Beaux Arts Tea. Now, I don't doubt that you have a major problem on your hands, but could you possibly ask someone else to lend a hand? I'm just not . . ."

"Pleeease!" Tawney implored. "I need your cool head. I'm smack-dab in the middle of a gigantic emergency . . . life and death, actually. You see, I just received a . . . an extremely bizarre delivery. Or at least I *think* I did."

"I'm sorry, I have no idea what you're talking about." Haley was right, the poor woman sounded absolutely bedbugs.

"Don't you want to get to the bottom of this hot-air balloon murder?" Tawney yelped.

Those were the words that stopped Theodosia from hanging up and writing this off as a frivolous call from an overwrought, probably overindulged woman. "Well . . . yes," she said. "Of course I do."

"Then get over here!"

* * *

A tearful Tawney met Theodosia at the front door of her soon-to-be ultra-fancy bed-and-breakfast. She wore an embroidered pink crepe dress that was probably Gucci, but her complexion was blotchy, her hair as frizzled as a Medusa, and she was in the middle of an ugly cry.

"You came!" Tawney cried. "Thank goodness!"

"What's the problem?" Theodosia asked. She wanted to figure out what Tawney's problem was and then hand it off to someone who could actually help. One and done and back to her tea. "You said there was some kind of weird delivery?"

"Not just weird, horrible!" Tawney cried. "Cruel, in fact!"

"Whatever it is, I'm sure we can send it back. Did you call FedEx or . . ."

"No! This box didn't come from any *reputable* delivery service," Tawney shrieked.

"When did it arrive?" Theodosia asked.

Tawney's teeth chattered as she shook her head frantically. "I don't know. It just showed up this morning. I've gotten so many deliveries lately I can barely keep track of them."

"Maybe you'd better just show me this mysterious package," Theodosia said.

Tawney waggled a finger. "In here. In the side parlor. I dragged the cardboard box in here because I thought my Italian towel warmers had arrived. Little did I know."

Theodosia followed Tawney into the parlor where a large cardboard box sat in the center of the room. Brown tape had been pulled away and the box had been partially ripped open.

Tawney pointed at it. "I didn't . . . I don't know what to do," she said tearfully. "Maybe you can figure something out."

Theodosia glanced at Tawney as she walked over to

the box. Something in that box had made Tawney come completely unhinged. *No, she's not just unhinged, the woman acts like she's scared to death. So what could it be?*

Theodosia took a deep breath and leaned forward. She folded back a top flap and gingerly peeked into the large box as if she were expecting an angry clown with red-rimmed eyes and vicious teeth to leap out at her.

It was worse.

Inside was a pile of shattered metal.

"Is that what I think it is?" Tawney asked in a frightened, little girl voice.

Theodosia was too shocked to answer. Her heart thudded inside her chest as she continued to stare into the box. Tawney's voice sounded like it was a million miles away as she fought against the sudden pounding in her head and struggled to recover her bearings. Because just from her initial glance, Theodosia was pretty sure she knew what it was. But she couldn't imagine why it had been delivered here. Or who had delivered it.

"It's the drone," Theodosia said. Her throat felt dry and constricted, as if someone had wound a cord around it. "It's the killer drone."

29

It took forever for Theodosia to talk her way through the gatekeepers at police headquarters and get Detective Tidwell on the line. But once she was talking to him, once she told him about Tawney's bizarre delivery, Tidwell was suddenly on full alert.

"Don't touch anything in that box," Tidwell roared. "Don't allow anyone into that house, don't let anyone leave the premises. Do you hear me, Miss Browning? Am I making myself clear?"

"Crystal clear," Theodosia told him. "You're coming over then?"

"Yes, I'm going to . . . I'm on my way." There was more shouting and then the phone slammed in her ear.

When Tidwell did show up, some ten minutes later, he arrived in a blaze of strobing lights and shrieking sirens.

"Oh dear," Tawney fretted as they pulled back the curtains and peered out the front window. "What will the neighbors think?"

"That probably shouldn't be your biggest worry right now," Theodosia said.

A thunder of footsteps on the veranda sent them scurrying to answer the front door.

"Where is it?" were Tidwell's first words. His face was bright red, his jowls shook, and his nostrils quivered. He looked like a bluetick hound who'd just scented a passel of opossums.

"Follow me," Theodosia said, leading Tidwell, his contingent of two uniformed officers, and Archie Banks, his crackerjack crime scene guy, into the parlor. Tawney followed behind, trying her best to run on four-inch stilettos while making urgent little bleats.

Tidwell peered into the cardboard box, hesitated for a moment, and then stepped back. "I need photographs of everything," he shouted. "Fingerprints as well. Check that delivery label and any trace evidence that might be in the box."

His team immediately snapped to attention and got busy.

"Do you want me to string crime scene tape across the front of the house?" one of the officers asked.

"No," Tawney said.

"Do it," Tidwell said. His beady eyes roved about the room where they finally landed on Theodosia and Tawney. "We need to talk." It wasn't simply a declarative sentence, it was a direct order.

"This way," Theodosia said. She led Tidwell across the center hallway and into a second parlor. It was jammed with more brocade furniture than Louis XVI and Marie Antoinette had ever imagined possible, but at least it was a place to sit down.

Once the three of them were perched on four-hundred-dollar silk and velvet pillows, Tidwell licked his lips and said, "Tell me the circumstances. Don't leave anything out."

Theodosia gave Tawney an encouraging nod. "Tawney? Go ahead."

In a halting, hiccuping speech, Tawney told Detective Tidwell about the box showing up on her front step, her dragging it inside, and then opening it to discover the remnants of the dreaded drone.

"I thought it was my heated towel racks," she said in a quavering voice.

"Towel racks?" Tidwell looked puzzled. "Heated?"

"Sounds nice, doesn't it?" Theodosia said.

Tidwell ignored her.

"Someone," he said, "is determined to stir up a ridiculous amount of trouble." He focused his fierce gaze directly on Tawney. "Am I to believe, Mrs. Kingsley, that you're telling me the absolute truth about this cardboard box magically appearing on your doorstep?"

"I wouldn't lie to you!" Tawney squeaked.

"Most suspects lie their fool heads off," Tidwell muttered. "Why should you be any different?"

"I'm a suspect?" Tawney's mouth flew open in surprise.

"If you could have heard her," Theodosia said. "If you could have *seen* how frantic Tawney was . . ."

"I was kapow out of my mind!" Tawney cried. She tapped a finger against her forehead to underscore her words.

"For all I know you may be an extremely skilled actress," Tidwell said.

"I'm not," Tawney said. "I'm terrible. My junior year in high school we did *Guys and Dolls* and our drama teacher, Mr. Langsweirdt, kicked me out of the play."

Tidwell leaned back in his chair and stared at her. Somehow, her ditziness had registered with him. "No, I don't believe you are acting, Mrs. Kingsley. But someone . . . quite probably your husband's killer . . . is following this investigation closely. And doing his best to toy with us and try to knock us off track."

"But who?" Theodosia asked. "It can't be Charles Townsend as we first suspected. I mean, he didn't orchestrate the drone showing up. He's probably still in the hospital . . ."

"Townsend is in the hospital?" Tawney looked shocked. "What happened?"

"Somebody shot him," Theodosia told her.

Tawney's eyes widened in shock, while her pupils seemed to contract. "They *shot* him? Someone shot Charles? Dear Lord, what if *I'm* next? What if the killer tries to shoot me, too?" She put a hand to her mouth as if to stifle a sob. "I don't want to be a shooting victim," she cried in what appeared to be genuine anguish.

"It's highly doubtful that you shall be," Tidwell said. He rubbed the back of his hand against his bristly cheek. Now he looked anxious and preoccupied. "What I need to do is question Townsend again. On the off chance he may have an accomplice."

"You don't think Townsend's story holds water?" Theodosia asked. "You did last night." She glanced at her watch. She had fifteen minutes left before her Beaux Arts Tea got underway and the secret sipper showed up. She had to get moving.

Tidwell shrugged. "I don't have any cut-and-dried answers just yet. I'm obviously still investigating."

"Well, hurry it up, will you?" Theodosia said in a slightly acerbic tone. "And would you kindly ask one of the officers to move your Crown Vic? It's blocking my car."

"What in heaven's name happened to you?" Drayton asked when Theodosia finally returned to the Portman Mansion. "Where did you disappear to? I thought you'd been kidnapped by a band of roving troubadours. I've been tearing my hair out." He looked frantic and his bow tie was askew.

"I'll tell you later," Theodosia promised him. She was breathless from rushing around, feeling frantic about the tea party. "But I guarantee it's something big."

Drayton's eyes drilled into her. "Big as in majorly serious and having to do with the recent murders?"

Theodosia nodded.

Drayton put his hands on his hips. "Then I insist you spill the beans *tout de suite*."

"Okay," Theodosia relented. "Here's the deal. Somebody boxed up the killer drone and shipped it to Tawney's B and B."

Drayton's mouth opened, but not a single solitary word came out. Finally, he cleared his throat and said in hushed tones, "Theo, you can't be serious."

"I am. That's where I ran off to." She reached up and straightened his bow tie.

"That's where . . . I mean . . . you actually *saw* this drone with your own eyes?" Drayton asked.

"What I saw was a bunch of jumbled metal parts lying inside a box, but there were enough pieces so you could tell what it was—what it had been, anyway—a drone."

Drayton was suddenly jazzed with excitement. "Do you think it was the actual drone that took down the hot-air balloon? That killed Tawney's husband and his cohorts? Theo, you can't be serious."

"I saw the stupid thing with my own eyes. Lots of shiny metal basically smashed and crumpled. So I'm guessing it probably *was* the same drone that crashed into Donald Kingsley's hot-air balloon."

"That's astonishing. Why would . . . who would . . . ?" Drayton fumbled to find the right words. "Could this have been Tawney's clever but obtuse way of confessing to her husband's murder?"

"I thought about that, I really did. But, Drayton, if you could have seen the look on Tawney's face. She was rocked to the core. The poor woman was shattered!"

"She could also be a fantastic actress," Drayton said.

"That's exactly what Tidwell said."

"He was there?"

"I had to call him. What choice did I have?" Theodosia said.

"Probably none at that point." Drayton looked thoughtful. "Sending the drone to Tawney sounds like the kind of nasty prank Earl Bullitt would pull."

Theodosia cocked a finger at him. "Now *that* hadn't occurred to me. But you're right. It does sound like his kind of rotten, taunting stunt."

They batted the idea of Tawney masterminding the drone attack back and forth. Of Earl Bullitt doing it. Then asked themselves whether Tod Slawson or Harold Affolter could be responsible. But they never came to any firm conclusion and there wasn't any more time for speculation, because at twelve o'clock sharp, the doorbell rang—a long series of melodic chimes that pealed like church bells. And by the time Theodosia and Drayton went to answer the door, a half dozen women all dressed in pastel dresses and suits—and wearing elaborate hats and fascinators—were waiting expectantly.

Drayton immediately shifted into genteel host mode. He welcomed all the guests, sprinkling compliments like fairy dust. Then he led the ladies, arm in arm, into the magnificent dining room. Of course, his "tablescapes" were greatly *oohed* and *aahed* over and he humbly accepted their excited praise.

Then it was back to the front door to greet the next round of guests. Drayton did more gallant gushing while Theodosia ticked off names from her checklist. She wanted to make sure that Haley and Miss Dimple had an exact head count for the entrées. Yes, she wanted to think about the drone some more, but reality had intruded. Like it usually did.

All the guests were seated at the half dozen large, round tables, and Drayton and Miss Dimple were pouring tea, when Delaine Dish finally showed up. She grabbed Theodosia, administered the requisite air kisses so she wouldn't smear her makeup, and immediately began exclaiming over the Portman Mansion.

"Isn't this place *splendiferous*!" Delaine cried, talking in her usual italics and exclamation marks. "And you've attracted a *huge* crowd for your lovely Beaux Arts Tea today. Oh my, will you take a look at the décor on those tables—what a fabulous array of glitz and glam!"

"Drayton pretty much art directed the whole thing," Theodosia told her.

"Oh, Theo," Delaine said, almost as an afterthought. "You remember my dear sister, Nadine, from New York, don't you?"

"I certainly do," Theodosia said. She recalled that Nadine had presented a bit of a problem on her last visit. Nadine was, to put it bluntly, a kleptomaniac. Theodosia looked around worriedly. "Did she . . . did you bring Nadine along as well?" *Please no.*

"Unfortunately, Nadine wasn't able to make it. She's tied up with some legal matters at the moment. But as I mentioned to you earlier, I brought her daughter as my guest." Delaine turned and pulled a young woman to the forefront. "Theo, I want you to meet Bettina, my sweet, darling niece."

"Wonderful to meet you," said a relieved Theodosia. *At least the candlesticks won't get clipped.* Bettina had luminous brown eyes and curly brown hair. Her angular but interesting face had a sharp nose and she wore a clingy knit dress in a pale peach that showed off her skinny hip bones to perfection.

"Scrumptious dress you're wearing," Theodosia said.

Bettina smiled. "Thank you."

"Bettina will be working right alongside me at Cotton Duck," Delaine explained. "She recently graduated from the Fashion Institute of Technology in New York with a degree in marketing. So I expect big things from her."

Bettina blushed prettily. "Nice to meet you, Miss Browning. Delaine has told me so much about you, about what dear close friends the two of you are."

Are we really? Theodosia wondered.

"The thing is, I'm pretty much a neophyte when it comes to retail," Bettina said. "Most everything I know so far I've learned in a classroom, but Aunt Delaine is such an experienced pro." She gripped Delaine's arm and gazed fondly at her. "So I'm counting on Aunt Delaine to teach me the critical ins and outs of fashion merchandising and sales."

"Remember, dear, that I asked you to call me Delaine?" Delaine's tone was slightly cool. "I prefer to think of us as contemporaries." She gave a little shudder. "Honestly," she trilled, "a title like *aunt* makes a person sound positively *ancient*."

The Beaux Arts Tea had also been advertised as a champagne tea. So, of course, champagne corks began to pop almost immediately.

Drayton poured bottles of bubbly with great flourish and explained the difference between the champagne flutes they were using versus the traditional *coupes*, or cup-shaped, glasses.

"*Coupes* were the choice of champagne drinkers for many years," Drayton said, "until a few clever glassware manufacturers designed the flute. This tall, narrow glass reduced the surface area to help preserve carbonation."

"In other words, more bubbles," one woman offered with a laugh.

"Exactly," Drayton said. "*Coupes* enjoyed a fine tradition for many years as did the art of sabering a champagne bottle." He picked up a bottle to demonstrate. "Sabering began when Napoleon's officers wanted to celebrate a victory. They pulled out their sabers, ran them swiftly along the side of the bottle, and—*clink!*—popped off the top."

An excited murmur ran through the crowd.

Drayton continued. "Then you had to drink your bottle *very* carefully." He stood smiling, tall and erect, heels together, like a ballet master. "Of course, there's another champagne I want to tell you about. Darjeeling, often called the champagne of teas."

At Drayton's cue, Theodosia and Miss Dimple began rounding the tables and pouring refills.

"This is the tea we served initially when you first sat down. A first-flush Darjeeling, picked in spring, that delivers a light, bright flavor and a floral fragrance." Drayton gave a small bow. "And now that we've got you half-tipsy on tea, champagne, and knowledge, I'd like to introduce our hostess, Miss Theodosia Browning."

There was more applause as Theodosia walked to the center of the room.

"Welcome, everyone, to our first-ever Beaux Arts Tea," Theodosia said. "We chose to hold it in this elegant mansion instead of the Indigo Tea Shop in order to give you the full impact of a fancy French-inspired tea." She smiled at her friend, Helen Winder, who was seated a few feet away from her. "And the Portman Mansion also has a larger kitchen, which means we can serve a greatly expanded menu."

Now there was excited applause.

"So let's get to it, shall we?" Theodosia said. "Our first course consists of eggnog scones served with strawberry butter and Devonshire cream. Following that, will be our *salade Josephine*, a mixture of spring greens topped with toasted pecans, dried cranberries, blue cheese crumbles, and sliced pears. Then, as a sort of mid-luncheon amuse-bouche, we have a small cup of lobster bisque with a surprise crostini. And I hope you'll still be hungry for our main course of chicken *Francoise*. These are grilled chicken breasts with tomatoes, basil, and pesto aioli served on a toasted mini baguette. For dessert . . ." Theodosia hesitated, a definite twinkle in her eye. "Well, I think we'll reveal that a little later."

And they were off and running.

Theodosia and Miss Dimple brought out the scones, Drayton poured tea and worked the tables like a pro, and Haley remained in the kitchen, tossing the salad and then plating it just so.

By the time the salad and lobster bisque had been served, Theodosia knew she had a hit on her hands. "We're golden," she told Drayton. "Everything is going beautifully."

"But have you figured out who our secret sipper is?" Drayton asked. "Perhaps the blonde in the beehive fascinator?"

"I'll make the rounds and chat with our guests. See if I can figure it out."

"Will you be doing a super fancy tea like this every year?" her friend Bonnie Tracy asked as Theodosia approached her table.

"How about holding a fancy autumn tea here?" another friend inquired.

"Oh, but Theodosia should host a holiday tea," said Mrs. Pomeroy, another one of her regulars.

"But we adore going to the Indigo Tea Shop," Jill Biatek put in. "That's what my daughter Kristen and I love best. It's such a charming, cozy place."

"Not to worry," Theodosia assured them. "We're always going to have special tea events at the Indigo Tea Shop. Probably one or two a week."

That seemed to make all their guests happy. But she still hadn't spotted their secret sipper. Hmm.

30

❧

Theodosia hurried into the kitchen to give Haley an update. "Our guests are absolutely stark raving delighted with your food," Theodosia said. "You should probably come out and take a bow."

"You take a bow," Haley said as she continued working. "I've got to scoop my chocolate mousse into crystal bowls and accent them with cookies and candied flowers." She glanced up from the stove. "Have you told our guests what we're serving for dessert?"

"Not yet. I thought we'd leave it as a surprise."

"Works for me."

Out in the main dining room, Drayton and Miss Dimple were pouring rounds of gingerbread orange tea, a special dessert tea, as well as one of Drayton's famous house blends.

"As you know," Drayton said, his voice rising in an almost oratorical manner, "the beaux arts style is closely associated with the École des Beaux-Arts in Paris. This style of classicism mixed with opulence prevailed in Paris in the late nineteenth century and quickly spread throughout Europe and America. The ornateness combined with delicate balance became a founding principal in architecture, gardens and landscaping, painting, and home décor."

That was Theodosia's cue to enter the dining room bearing an enormous silver tray.

"Which is why," Theodosia said, as heads turned her way, "our Beaux Arts Tea dessert consists of a classic chocolate mousse, a special sugar cookie, and candied edible flowers." She tilted her tray carefully for everyone to see. "Now I ask you, could there be anything more elegant, decadent, and rich than this?"

Needless to say, dessert proved to be an enormous success. Spoons scraped the bottoms of parfait bowls and a few cookies were wrapped in foil and deposited in fancy handbags to be taken home for later.

Delaine grabbed Theodosia's arm just as she swung past her, pouring a final refill of tea. "This was just spectacular," Delaine purred. "And I absolutely adore this venue."

"It's kind of perfect, isn't it?" Theodosia said.

She fluttered her eyelashes. "This is the kind of place a girl could get married in."

"How's that going by the way?" Theodosia wondered if Delaine was still head over teakettle for Tod Slawson. "Are you still dreaming of a future with Tod?" *Who I still think of as a sort of suspect.*

"Maybe." Delaine frowned. "The funny thing is, sometimes when you get what you want, you don't want it anymore."

Really, Delaine?

Theodosia patted Delaine gently on the shoulder and said, "You're a smart girl. I'm sure you'll figure it out."

Once the guests had departed, once the tables were cleared and the dishes either stacked in the dishwasher or handwashed by Miss Dimple, Drayton collapsed in an easy chair in the Portman Mansion's cozy library.

"I'm getting too old for this," Drayton said. "One of these days you're going to have to find yourself a younger man."

"I already have." Theodosia smiled.

Drayton rolled his eyes. "You know what I mean. To work in the tea shop. To help you host major events."

"Unless I'm mistaken, you were the Energizer Bunny today. You ran around all morning and afternoon, decorating, greeting guests, pouring tea, serving any number of courses, and still found time to answer a million miscellaneous questions about tea and tea brewing. Your energy level was heroic."

"Yes, but . . ." Drayton looked past Theodosia. "Say now, what lovely treat do we have here?"

Haley and Miss Dimple walked into the library. Both were grinning from ear to ear and Haley was holding a tray with four champagne flutes filled to the brim with golden champagne.

"I thought we deserved this," Haley said. "A post-party pick-me-up."

"A dram of bubbly to celebrate our success," Drayton said, brightening immediately. "Good thing we had some champagne left over."

"Good thing Theodosia stashed an extra bottle in the vegetable drawer," Haley said.

They each took a glass of champagne and held it up.

"What are we toasting?" Miss Dimple asked.

"Good spirits," Haley said.

Theodosia smiled. "Good friends."

"And may the angels protect us and heaven accept us," Drayton said.

They clinked their glasses together and took a sip.

"My, that's delicious," Miss Dimple said. "And quite bracing I might add." Which gave them all a giggle.

Theodosia was gathering up the linen napkins and tablecloths, when her cell phone made a musical riff from inside her apron pocket. She pulled it out, glanced at the screen, and smiled. Woody Hovel, the photographer, had e-mailed her the photos from Drayton's photo shoot.

"Guess what just popped up on my phone," Theodosia said as she walked into the library where Drayton was flipping through a book on Charleston's maritime heritage.

He looked up. "Someone called to complain?"

"Hardly. Your photos arrived." She started thumbing through them, perusing the first few shots. And did they ever look good.

"I'm afraid to ask," Drayton said. "But how did they turn out?"

"Are you kidding?" Theodosia said, still flipping through them. "Most of these shots are spectacular."

"Truly?" Drayton sounded as if he didn't believe her.

"Come on, you know how gorgeous your house is. Now all the readers of *Southern Interiors Magazine* will be swept off their feet by it, too. Here." Theodosia passed her phone to Drayton. "See for yourself."

Drayton scanned a few of the photos, his mouth working silently. Was it approval? Disapproval? "These are actually quite decent," he said finally. "There are a couple of shots here that show off the fireplace and the seascape hanging above it to perfection."

"See? I told you the photo shoot was going to turn out great," Theodosia said. "Take a look at some of the other photos." She showed Drayton how to scroll through the photos.

Drayton scrolled along gingerly, making random comments as he went along. "Yes, yes, I like that. Oh dear, that one's not quite perfect. But look here, this one is lovely."

"Take a look at the dining room shots," Theodosia said.

Drayton touched a finger to the screen and nothing happened. "Here, you find them for me," he said. "I'm all fumble fingers with this thing."

Theodosia took back her iPhone and scrolled to the dining room shots. She passed the phone back to him.

"See how fabulous it looks? Your Limoges on the table, the candles flickering, the crystal chandelier overhead . . ."

"It does look moody and elegant," he said.

"I told you there was nothing to worry about. Almost any of these shots will work well in a magazine layout."

"What's this?" Drayton asked. His index finger tapped the edge of the screen.

"What's what?"

"On the dining room window just to the left of the curtains. There's some sort of fuzzy blur. Drat. That would have been a lovely photo."

"Let me see," Theodosia said. She took back the phone and studied the shot. Then she spread it with her fingers to enlarge it.

"I didn't know you could do that with a picture," Drayton said. "Now do you see that strange blur? Do you think it can be removed? Not airbrushed—I know that's old school. But what do they call that digital technique . . . you photo-shape it?"

"Photoshop. But, what you're seeing isn't a blur. It looks more like . . ." Theodosia sucked in a glut of air and then released it slowly.

"What?" Drayton asked. "Problem?"

"You're going to think I'm absolutely bonkers, but it looks like a face. Like someone was standing outside your house and pressing their face tight against the window so they could look in."

"Who would do that?"

"Someone who's extremely curious," Theodosia said. *Or someone who meant to harm us?*

"Whose face could it be?" Drayton asked again.

"I don't know. It's difficult to tell with an image this small."

"Can you enlarge it some more?"

"Let me see what I can do." Theodosia fussed with the image, touching the screen and trying to expand it a little more. "Is that any better?" She passed her phone to Drayton.

Drayton studied it. "Not really." Then, "Well, it does kind of look like a woman."

"Let me see again."

"Do you think it could be Tawney?" Drayton asked.

Theodosia shook her head. She didn't think so. She just hoped it wasn't Angie Congdon.

"This is weird," Drayton said. "In fact, it gives me chills to know that someone was standing outside and watching us."

"If we really want to enhance this photo, we're going to have to go to the Indigo Tea Shop and punch this image up on my iMac."

Drayton frowned. "That does seem like a bother."

But Theodosia's mind was humming and alarm bells were starting to clang.

"No, Drayton, I think we *should* take a closer look. I've got a funny feeling about this."

"Good funny or bad funny?" Drayton asked. Then he suddenly turned serious himself. "Wait just one minute. Is this the ghostly presence Madame Poporov talked about?"

"I don't know, Drayton. That's what we need to find out."

31

❧

Though the café part of the Indigo Tea Shop was dark, a light burned in the back office where Theodosia and Drayton sat staring at her computer. Theodosia had enlarged the face in the window as much as she possibly could while leaving the image still readable.

"It's still awfully blurry," Drayton said.

"Maybe I enlarged it too much," Theodosia said. "Let me try to tighten it up." She manipulated the image using her mouse. "Okay, there. Jeepers, look at the ears. Could that be Earl Bullitt?"

Drayton stared at the slightly reduced image. "I was thinking it might be Tawney Kingsley because it kind of looks like her hair. If it is her, then she was lying through her teeth to you this morning, trying to sucker you in."

"That would point to Tawney being the killer then," Theodosia said. "It would mean that she murdered her own husband as well as two innocent passengers on that hot-air balloon. But . . ." Theodosia was seriously flummoxed. "It would also mean that Tawney lied quite skillfully to Tidwell. Because after all was said and done this morning, I got the feeling he believed her."

"Tawney might have wrapped him around her little finger," Drayton said. He leaned back in his chair, thinking. "Of course, the image is not all that distinct. It could be someone else."

Theodosia worried her upper teeth against her lower lip. "Maybe you should just come out and say it."

"Okay, I will. That could also be Angie Congdon's face. If she's utterly desperate, if she's covering up for Harold . . . then she's probably looking for some way to get him off the hook."

"What if it's a man wearing some type of disguise?" Theodosia asked. "Then it really could be Earl Bullitt or Tod Slawson wearing some kind of head covering."

"That would be strange," Drayton said, "but not out of the question. Especially if someone was desperate to keep a keen eye on us."

"Because we've been investigating," Theodosia said slowly.

"Poking our nose in," Drayton said. "Where it doesn't belong. A lot of people *know* we've been involved."

"There's another person who's squarely in the mix as well."

Drayton looked at her, puzzled. "Who's that?"

"Brooklyn Vance," Theodosia said.

"That lovely museum lady?" Drayton touched a finger to his bow tie. "How could you say such a thing?"

"Because that lovely museum lady was also trying to get her hands on the Navy Jack flag."

They both peered at the face on the screen, trying to fathom who it might be. Finally, after squinting so hard her eyes felt scratchy, Theodosia said, "You know, this really *could* be Brooklyn."

"Hmm." Drayton leaned back in his chair and stared straight ahead, as if the microprocessor in his brain had started to click away on something.

"Was that a good *hmm* or a bad *hmm*?" Theodosia asked. She didn't know if Drayton had discounted her statement or was weighing it carefully.

Finally, Drayton said, "I've got a bad feeling about this."

"As do I," Theodosia said.

"It would be an impossible long shot . . ."

"But long shots sometimes come in first . . ."

"Yes, they do," Drayton said. "So it might be . . . it could be . . . Brooklyn."

"But we'd have to be absolutely sure before we pointed a finger or made any accusations against her."

Drayton gave Theodosia a cryptic look. "How would we go about checking her story?"

"Brooklyn claimed to be the daughter of Colonel Joshua Vance, am I right?"

"She did," Drayton said. "Though Colonel Vance has an absolute sterling reputation."

"Good for him. Let's give him a call."

"Right now? I really hate to disturb the man," Drayton said.

"Drayton, we *have* to call him. If we're suspicious of Brooklyn—and it looks as though we're together on this—then we have to know for sure!"

"How would we go about finding his number?"

"Internet," Theodosia said. "The stalker's best friend."

A few clicks later and they'd found Colonel Joshua Vance's phone number.

"What am I supposed to ask him?" Drayton hissed as he dialed the number. He wasn't just hesitant, he had developed seriously cold feet.

"Tell Colonel Vance that you're trying to get hold of his daughter. Say it's an emergency. Um . . . concerning a piece of artwork at the museum she works for in Wilmington."

"That could work," Drayton said.

Theodosia listened with bated breath as Drayton introduced himself, gave a fast little spiel about art at the Heritage Society, and then asked about Brooklyn Vance. Drayton listened for a few more moments, thanked the Colonel profusely, apologized for disturbing him, and hung up.

"Well?" Theodosia asked. She was hanging on pins and needles.

Drayton's face registered shock as he stared at her. "There is no daughter."

"I knew it!" Theodosia whooped. "I'll bet there's no Keystone Museum, either."

"We have to be absolutely sure about that. There could be another family named Vance, after all."

"Doubtful," Theodosia said. "But let's check." She googled Keystone Museum in Wilmington, North Carolina. And found nothing. Tried to locate a website. Again, nothing came up.

"Nothing at all?" Drayton asked.

"Nada."

"Maybe because the museum hasn't opened yet?"

"But something should have popped up. It would have been written about in the local papers. A new museum is a really big deal. *Someone* would have reported on it."

"You'd think so," Drayton said.

"Wait a minute. Brooklyn gave me her business card," Theodosia said.

"Do you still have it?"

Theodosia dug into her wallet. "Yes, here it is."

"Dial the number," Drayton said. "See who answers."

Theodosia dialed and listened while it rang. *Maybe Brooklyn is on the up and up after all?*

The phone picked up on the other end.

"Napoli Pizza."

Theodosia hung up the phone. "Napoli Pizza," she said. Her voice felt hollow to her own ears.

"So the number's a fake." Drayton's eyes burned into hers.

"She's a sham and so is her story." Theodosia wasn't

sure if she was feeling anger or a strange relief that the murder mystery was partially solved.

"So what now?" Drayton was looking for Theodosia to take the lead.

But Theodosia wasn't sure what their next step should be. "Do you think we have enough evidence to call Detective Tidwell?"

"I'm not sure we have *any* evidence," Drayton said. "All we know is that Brooklyn's a phony. After that, we're just limping along on wild hunches and suppositions."

"But we've got this photograph." Theodosia tapped her computer screen. "An image that's strangely spooky but just might lead us down the right path."

"She knew about the flag," Theodosia said to Tidwell once she'd run through a quick version of Drayton's and her suspicions about Brooklyn Vance. And she told him about the shadowy face that had popped up in the photograph— the face that the longer she stared at, looked decidedly more like Brooklyn.

"And you say she's involved in the art world?" Tidwell asked. "I remember hearing the Vance woman's name mentioned, but I wasn't the one who interviewed her."

"Brooklyn Vance claims to have had a career in art. Which leads me to a somewhat strange question. You used to be an FBI agent. Doesn't the FBI have some kind of art heist squad?"

"You mean the FBI's dedicated Art Crime Team?"

"That's a real thing? Perfect. We surely could use their help. And yours, too." Theodosia paused. "In fact, what are you doing right now?"

"Getting ready to slip into a nice dry martini," Tidwell said.

"Could you forgo your drink for now and come over to the tea shop? Take a look at this photo? It would mean an awful lot to us."

A long silence spun out before Tidwell replied. "If I must."

Tidwell showed up at the Indigo Tea Shop some twenty minutes later, clutching a laptop and looking off-duty rumpled in a pair of ill-fitting khaki slacks and a brown jacket that billowed about his frame. His lips were set in a straight line as though he was unhappy about being called out on a Saturday night, which he undoubtedly was.

"Internet connection," were Tidwell's first words.

"In my office," Theodosia said. She led him through the darkened tea shop and into her office.

Drayton stood up hastily and said, "Thank you for coming."

Tidwell answered with a shrug and a grunt.

Theodosia hoped this wasn't going to turn into a conversation of monosyllabic proportions.

It didn't.

"You realize," Tidwell said as they fumbled with cords and plug-ins and finally established an Internet connection for his laptop, "that when the Navy Jack flag disappeared from Don Kingsley's home, I immediately checked the FBI's National Stolen Art File."

"But the flag wouldn't have popped up at that point," Theodosia said. "It was too soon. We really didn't know it had gone missing a second time until Charles Townsend's confession last night."

"Thank you for pointing that out to me," Tidwell said in a facetious tone. He dropped into her desk chair, straining the side rails and causing the chair to emit a low groan.

Theodosia prayed that he hadn't permanently disabled her chair.

Tidwell's chubby fingers poked at his computer keys, almost a hunt and peck mode of typing. He called up the FBI website, then entered a long string of numbers and letters—his password code. A whirling ball occupied center screen for a few moments and then, voilà, they were in.

"Are you checking stolen art or known suspects?" Theodosia asked.

"Suspects obviously," Tidwell said. "I'm guessing there aren't that many women in the database."

Surprisingly, there were almost a hundred.

"We need to narrow this down by parameters," Tidwell said. "Age, hair color, that sort of thing."

"I'd say between thirty and thirty-five," Theodosia said. "Dark hair."

"Last known address?"

Theodosia shrugged. "Wilmington? I don't know. That was probably just a ruse."

"People often base their fictional alibis on partial truths," Tidwell said. He tapped away some more until five grainy pictures appeared. "Take a look at these possible candidates."

Theodosia and Drayton leaned over his broad shoulders and stared at the screen.

"Whoa," Theodosia said. It wasn't quite a gasp, but almost. One of the photos looked suspiciously like Brooklyn Vance, only with shorter hair.

"Which one caught your eye?" Tidwell asked.

"The woman in the middle," Theodosia said.

"Is that her?" Drayton squinted at the photos on Tidwell's laptop.

"Look," Theodosia said, pointing to the blur on her own computer screen. "The pictures are different enough. Her hair is lighter and wispier in the FBI photo and now it's dark and worn much longer. But take a look at the curve of her cheekbone, the slightly pointed chin."

"Sweet Fanny Adams, I think you're right," Drayton exclaimed. "It's practically a match."

"Did either of you see the movie *Catch Me If You Can*?" Tidwell asked.

"With Leonardo DiCaprio playing the impostor," Theodosia said. "Figuring out bank routing systems and cashing millions of dollars in phony checks."

"And using phony identities," Tidwell said. He reached forward and hesitated, and then tapped the screen. "I'll bet you anything that's our girl."

They moved into the tea room then, where Drayton brewed a pot of Indian spice tea and Theodosia put out a plate of leftover raspberry scones that she'd grabbed from the freezer and heated up.

"So now that we think our killer might be Brooklyn, how do we go about finding her?" Theodosia asked.

Tidwell blew on his cup of tea and then took a small sip. "Brooklyn Vance is obviously from out of town. So where has she been staying?"

"No clue," Drayton said. "It's going to be like looking for a needle in a haystack. If she's still in town."

"Then we've got to narrow that haystack down to a single bale," Tidwell said. He grabbed one of the scones, took a large bite, and chewed thoughtfully.

"What if . . . what if Brooklyn was staying at the Featherbed House?" Theodosia ventured.

"Is that a wild guess out of the clear blue or do you know something we don't?" Tidwell asked.

Theodosia tried to dredge up an image from a few days ago. It swam up in her memory, circled around, and dove back down again into the netherworld. She focused harder and let it slowly rise to the surface again. "Okay, the first time I ever laid eyes on Brooklyn Vance was when she was leaving Tawney Kingsley's B and B and heading in the *direction* of the Featherbed House."

"If Brooklyn was staying there," Drayton said, "it might have put her right in the catbird seat. She might have been privy to all sorts of rumors and critical information."

"Like who are the main suspects and has the blame

shifted to Harold Affolter yet?" Theodosia said. "And what new information Angie had picked up?"

"Remember at the funeral lunch, when Brooklyn started getting cozy with Earl Bullitt?" Drayton said.

Theodosia remembered it well. "I'll bet you anything that was Brooklyn taking the pulse of the investigation."

Tidwell scarfed down his final bite of scone and smacked his lips. But he didn't look like his usual satisfied scone-eating self. He looked unhappy, as if he'd been badly snookered. "And to think," he said, "she was right there under our noses all along."

32

❧

They rode to the Featherbed House in Tidwell's practically obsolete Crown Victoria. It was the color of cheap Burgundy wine, the springs were shot, and it carried a faint aroma of motor oil and spilled coffee. But good coffee, probably a French roast.

Tidwell loved the car; it was his baby. As his radio buzzed frantically with static and police alerts, he called ahead and requested that two squads meet them at Angie's B and B. When they arrived, four uniformed SWAT officers were waiting outside on the sidewalk.

In their dark uniforms, Theodosia thought they looked like a SEAL Team ready to make a major assault on Fallujah. Still, Brooklyn was armed and dangerous, so it was nice to have some firepower for backup.

Theodosia ran up the front steps of the Featherbed House and into the lobby. She looked around, saw a half dozen guests sipping wine and helping themselves to a table filled with hors d'oeuvres. The last thing Theodosia wanted to do was disturb the guests' peace and quiet, but then she saw Teddy Vickers emerge from the breakfast room to put out a new plate of cheese nibbles. She ran over to him, grabbed him by the shoulder, and spun him halfway around. A few of the cheese nibbles fell on the floor.

"Theodosia?" Teddy said, looking a little unbalanced.

"Teddy, we need your help!" Theodosia said in a hoarse whisper.

Teddy glanced about the lobby. That's when he saw Detective Tidwell, Drayton, and four well-armed officers slinking in, trying to look unobtrusive but failing miserably. His face pulled into a look of deep concern.

"What's wrong?" Teddy asked. "It's not Harold, is it?" He licked his lips nervously. "Are you here to . . . ?"

"We need to ask you a few questions," Tidwell said, bulling his way to the front of the group.

"Just show Teddy the FBI photo," Theodosia prompted. "Then we'll know if we're on the right track or not."

Tidwell opened his laptop and showed Teddy the single photo that he'd downloaded.

Theodosia pointed to the photo. "Has this woman been staying here? Is she a guest?"

Teddy's face darkened as he squinted at the photo. "Um . . . maybe?"

At that moment, Angie walked in from the dining room. She saw Tidwell, Theodosia, Teddy, and the SWAT team, and took a step back. Her shoulders sagged and her face went slack. "You're here to arrest Harold?" she said in a frightened whisper.

"No," Theodosia said. "Come take a look at this photo. We think this might be our suspect and that she's possibly been staying here all along."

"What!" Angie said. She was so stunned she seemed rooted to the floor, unable to take a single step.

"What's going on?" Harold suddenly loomed in the doorway behind Angie.

"Mr. Affolter, we need you to look at this photo," Tidwell said. "Tell us if this woman has been a guest here."

"Why are you asking about one of our guests?" Harold sounded agitated, bordering on angry. "Haven't you people made us jump through enough hoops?"

"Please just calm down and take a look," Theodosia urged. "See if you can identify this person."

Angie managed to find her voice. "Wait, are you saying you might have found the killer? The one that took down the hot-air balloon?"

"It's a possibility," Tidwell hedged. "Obviously we're still investigating. But before we can do anything at all, we need to identify this woman and ascertain if she was a guest here."

Angie turned to Harold. "You look," she said. "I'm too frightened."

Harold came forward and took a look at Tidwell's photo. He blinked and stared at the screen. Then his jaw tightened as if he were grinding his teeth together. "Yes," he said. "She's staying here."

"You're absolutely sure?" Tidwell asked. "This is Brooklyn Vance?"

"That's the woman who's been staying in 5C," Harold said. "One of the small guesthouses across the courtyard. But she's not registered as Brooklyn Vance." Now he sounded more confident in his answer.

"What name is she registered under?" Theodosia asked.

Harold glanced over at Teddy Vickers. "Teddy? Can you . . . ?"

Teddy practically broke a leg running to the check-in desk. He slipped on a pair of reading glasses, and then his fingers clicked against computer keys. "You said room 5C?" He cleared his throat officiously. "That room is registered to a Gail Winter."

Tidwell made a sound somewhere between a trumpeting elephant and an angry rhino. "That's one of her aliases," he said.

Guests at the Featherbed House who were all dressed up and on their way out for dinner gasped in amazement when they saw Tidwell's SWAT contingent thunder through the lobby, slam through the double doors, and rush out onto a patio filled with damp tables and limp umbrellas. The group spun past a goldfish pond, hooked a left past a small greenhouse, ran down a cobblestone path, and then pulled up short at the path that peeled off to the guesthouses. From there they tiptoed up to the door of room 5C.

Tidwell gave a sharp jerk of his head. "Officers?"

In unison, the four SWAT team members un-holstered their weapons and stood at the ready.

Tidwell held out a hand. "Key."

Teddy handed over his passkey.

Tidwell stuck the key in the lock, turned it hard, and jumped back. The four officers stormed into the room, yelling, "Police! Hands up!"

The room was empty. Brooklyn Vance wasn't there.

"Gone," Tidwell declared as he stepped inside and looked around for himself. "We must have just missed her."

"Did she skip out on her bill?" Theodosia asked.

"We always take a credit card imprint," Harold said. "Of course, if she's registered under an alias, her card was probably fake, too."

Drayton poked his head in as the SWAT team continued to scout the room. "My goodness, it looks as if a knockdown, drag-out fight took place in here!"

5C had once been a cozy little cottage with a four-poster bed, lovely cream-colored armoire, and a pink paisley rug. Now it was a wreck! Sheets were tangled, damp towels were scattered all over, the down comforter was twisted up and lying on the floor, closet doors hung wide open, and hangers looked like they'd been pitched everywhere.

"Did anyone hear a fight going on?" Tidwell asked.

"No, no, this is fairly typical," Teddy hastened to explain. "Whenever we have a single woman staying with us, they wreak absolute havoc on our guest rooms. Pretty much trash them."

"Is that true?" Drayton asked Angie.

She nodded. "I'm afraid so."

"Are Brooklyn's clothes gone? Her luggage?" Theodosia asked. But as she looked around she could see for herself that Brooklyn, or whatever the woman's name was, had emptied the place out.

"Everything's gone but the towels," Angie said. "And sometimes they take those as a parting gift." She scrunched up her face and looked at Tidwell. "What now?"

"All we can do is put the word out to law enforcement," Tidwell said.

"Local law enforcement?" Theodosia asked.

"Local, state police, FBI, probably customs and border patrol," Tidwell said. "This is a woman who quite possibly masterminded a triple homicide. We want her bad."

"But why did she stick around for such a long time?" Drayton asked.

Tidwell shrugged. "Playing games. Taunting us and getting her jollies?"

"I think she stayed in Charleston so she could throw up a smoke screen and point her finger at other possible suspects," Theodosia said. "Brooklyn was smart. She kept her ear to the ground and gathered as much information as she possibly could."

"But after the hot-air balloon crash she could have just skipped town," Angie said.

"Think about it," Theodosia said. "Brooklyn couldn't leave town, it would have looked way too suspicious. So she stuck around for a while, stirring up trouble, following the investigation as close as she could, and dropping innuendos here and there. And then she played her hunch with Townsend and was right. He had the flag and she took it away from him at gunpoint. Or maybe she did a hot prowl on all the players—Tawney, Slawson, Earl Bullitt, even Harold here—and narrowed it down through process of elimination."

"Do you think she was the one who stole my drone?" Harold asked.

"Most likely," Tidwell said.

Theodosia and Drayton stepped outside and hovered at the edge of the patio, watching the SWAT team wrap it up. Tidwell was calling in the crime scene squad, one officer was stringing yellow tape across the guest room door, and the other officers were milling about quietly. They looked subdued and a little disappointed that they hadn't been involved in a major shoot-out.

"Face it," Drayton said to Theodosia. "You put some serious heat on Brooklyn. Toward the end she must have known you were on her tail."

"But I wasn't close enough," Theodosia said.

Drayton cast his eyes skyward. "Thank heaven for that."

33

❧

Theodosia arrived home feeling a bundle of mixed emotions. On the one hand, she felt completely disheartened that they hadn't been able to lay their hands on the very dangerous Brooklyn Vance. They'd come so darned close—had been hot on Brooklyn's pointy little designer heels—but now the woman had blown out of town like an ill wind.

On the other hand, Pete Riley's plane had touched down an hour ago. And right this minute he was probably turning on lights in his apartment and setting grocery bags on his kitchen counter. He'd be gearing up to cook a fabulous dinner for the two of them. And Theodosia knew that when she walked in, he'd greet her with open arms and tender kisses.

Feeling a little drained—it had been a strange and busy day—Theodosia let Earl Grey out into the backyard and went upstairs to change.

What to wear? she wondered. Go uptown casual with jeans and a sweater? Go downtown *chic* with a little black dress?

Wandering into her walk-in closet, Theodosia hunted

around, trying to shift her mind from being in hot pursuit of a murder suspect to business as usual. After a few minutes of shuffling through racks of clothes, she decided on a black sweater and slacks with a camel jacket tossed over her shoulders. She figured that outfit would project a welcome-home-kiss-me-feed-me message all wrapped up in one.

In the powder room, Theodosia had to face her hair. Due to the wind, lingering rain, and industrial strength humidity, her so-called "do" had taken on a life of its own. What most women longed for—tremendous body and fullness—Theodosia had spent her life trying to tame. She brushed her auburn hair until it crackled and then pinned it up in a messy, but hopefully cute, chignon. Theodosia touched up her mascara, put a pouf of tinted moisturizer on each cheek and rubbed it in, and added a nice lip gloss in a pinky-watermelon shade.

Okay, ready to go. Time to hit the road.

Humming to herself, thinking about how the FBI would probably take charge of the search for Brooklyn Vance—Tidwell had called it a barely controlled snake hunt—Theodosia grabbed Earl Grey's leash, a handful of his "good dog" treats, and headed out the back door.

She found Earl Grey with his entire head stuck in the lower branches of a palmetto tree.

"What are you looking at?" Theodosia asked him. She hoped he hadn't sniffed out a bird's nest. Last year, a pair of starlings had built their nest in the low hanging branches of one of her boxwoods, and Earl Grey had practically worried them to death. She'd had an image of the poor momma bird sitting on her nest and pleading with her eggs to hatch so they could all pick up and fly to a safer home.

Earl Grey pulled his head out of the shrubbery and wagged his tail at Theodosia. He was in a good mood; she should be, too.

Okay, Theodosia told herself. Time for a serious attitude adjustment on her part. She was heading over to Pete

Riley's apartment where he'd promised to cook her a fabulous dinner. The brown butter sea scallops would probably be delicious, but whatever he came up with, even if he just opened a can of tuna, would be better than eating dinner without him. She'd missed Riley this past week. More than she thought she would.

Theodosia was also bursting with things to tell him. She knew she could keep the conversation rolling for hours just by bringing him up to speed on the drone killings, the historic flag, the suspects, Townsend getting shot, and the genuine possibility that Brooklyn Vance was the mastermind and killer.

Only one thing worried Theodosia. Once Pete Riley joined the hunt for Brooklyn Vance, would he want her to step aside?

Probably.

Would she?

That remained to be seen.

Theodosia bent down and clipped Earl Grey's leash to his collar. Unfortunately, the rain had started up again. The warmth of the day had drained away and a cold drizzle was pattering down. Theodosia thought about ducking back inside to grab her rain hat, the one that made her look like Paddington Bear, and decided not to. The rain, along with the walk over to Riley's place, would do her good. Help clear her head.

Together, she and Earl Grey picked their way across the wet patio and followed the cobblestone path around the side of the house. Tendrils of fog, a product of the rapidly cooling air meeting the warmth of the day, swirled at her feet, and a dark mist made it difficult to see more than ten feet ahead of her. Overhead, trees drip-dripped with rainwater and wind stirred the air. Theodosia could almost smell a hint of saltiness carried in by the surging Atlantic.

And there was something else, too.

Theodosia felt the tiny hairs prickle at the back of her neck. Something stirred deep down in the limbic part, the reptile portion, of her brain.

Someone there? Someone watching me?

There was a faint rustle from deep inside the hedge that ran along her path, and then a rapid-fire *chi-chi-chi*. Almost like a bird's warning call.

Theodosia stopped dead in her tracks as a new sound, a high-pitched humming sound, filled her ears. Almost as if someone had turned a blender on high. As if the next-door neighbors were sitting on their back patio whipping up a pitcher of brandy alexanders.

In this rain? No, that noise sounds more like . . .

Theodosia took a step backward as a stiff breeze lifted her hair and a whirling, twirling drone missed cutting off the top of her head by a mere two inches. If she'd stayed where she was, if she hadn't felt a buzz of anxiety, the drone would have nailed her for sure!

Jerking hard on Earl Grey's leash, Theodosia pulled him tight against her hip. Then she ducked down, frightened, but fighting to keep her wits about her. Because keeping her wits meant . . . survival.

Like an enormous mechanized vulture, the drone circled back and swooped low over Theodosia's and Earl Grey's heads once again. Fighting to defend his turf, Earl Grey struggled against his leash. Growling, his muzzle pulled into an angry snarl, he stretched his head up to snap at the drone, to rip the object right out of the air!

"No!" Theodosia screamed.

She yanked his leash, pulling him back again. From a crouched position, she dropped to her knees and wrapped her arms tightly around Earl Grey's head and chest, shielding him as best she could.

But the drone wasn't about to quit. It came zipping at her again, bobbing and wobbling, as if the thing was taunting her.

"Stop it!" Theodosia screamed to her unseen adversary. But she pretty much suspected who it was.

It's Brooklyn. It has to be Brooklyn. But where is she?

Theodosia's eyes probed the pathway just ahead, as fog continued to spill in. Darkness was thick all around her. Trees and shrubs that flourished along the pathway, making it so hidden and charming, now served as a hiding spot for her attacker.

If she could just pull her phone out of her bag and call for help . . .

"You're not such a good little amateur detective now, are you?" Brooklyn's voice cackled from somewhere in the bushes. "Sweet little Theodosia, always getting in the way. Trying to pry into everyone's life. Well not anymore!"

Theodosia strained her eyes, trying to see.

Where is she?

"I know it's you, Brooklyn! Give it up! The police are looking for you," Theodosia shouted out.

"You want me to give up and miss all this fun?" Brooklyn called back.

Between the darkness and the drizzle and the fog, Theodosia could barely see more than a few steps in front of her. She blinked rain from her eyes and wiped frantically, wondering if she should retreat or try to crawl forward. She had Earl Grey to think of. Reaching the street might give her a chance to cry out for help. Retreating to her backyard could mean she'd end up a sitting duck. What to do?

"Get down," she whispered to Earl Grey. "Down, boy." Earl Grey scrunched down obediently. "Stay."

Without making a conscious decision, Theodosia began to crawl forward on her hands and knees, inching her way along the cobblestone path. Grit dug into the palms of her hands; the knees of her slacks were damp from soaking up standing water.

Theodosia had managed to crawl perhaps a foot and a

half when her right knee slammed into something rock-hard. Her face scrunched in pain and she wobbled wildly, almost losing her balance and falling face-first. Instinctively, her hands flew out to steady herself . . . and knocked against something standing in her way.

What is that?

Theodosia's fingers hastily explored. They touched wood that was splintered and worn.

This has to be . . .

It was the wooden ladder that Shep had left leaning against the side of her house. And next to it was some sort of rake. He'd cleaned *some* of the gutters, but obviously hadn't finished the job.

God bless you, Shep.

Making a split-second decision, Theodosia sprang to her feet. She grabbed hold of the ladder and muscled it around, putting it directly in front of her and shielding her from the drone. Maybe in the darkness, Brooklyn wouldn't see what she was doing.

Blips of adrenaline pulsed through Theodosia's veins as she vowed to end this standoff once and for all.

This time, when the drone came spinning toward her, Theodosia gave the ladder a powerful shove. It teetered for a sickening moment and then fell forward. She held her breath and prayed the ladder would hit its mark.

It did.

The wooden ladder toppled against the drone, cutting off its flight path. The wildly spinning drone clunked hard against the heavy ladder like a mosquito hitting a screen door. The motor revved loudly, then was immediately driven to an ungodly high-pitched scream. The drone whirled and wobbled, batting at the ladder frantically. Then it spun wildly off course.

"Stop that! What are you *doing*?" Brooklyn screamed.

As the crazed drone flew into the nearby bushes, Theodosia shoved the ladder away from her. Then, grabbing the rake that had been leaning against the house, Theodosia twirled it like a soldier with a lance and ran forward, jabbing the tines directly at Brooklyn. With a lucky thrust, she managed to hit Brooklyn right above her collarbone.

"Ouf!"

Brooklyn let out a surprised gasp and toppled over backward. Her arms flailed wildly as her fingertips fought to find feeble purchase on nearby branches. Didn't happen. Brooklyn landed flat on her back on the wet cobblestones. Her hands curled into claws as she fought to draw a shaky breath. When she finally gasped, it sounded like a death rattle.

Dear Lord, have I killed her?

But no. Brooklyn wasn't done for yet. Like the toughminded killer she was, she struggled to right herself, to get back on her feet.

That's when Earl Grey took over and lunged full bore at Brooklyn. Powerful hind legs propelled him upward as he sailed gracefully through the air. When his front paws hit squarely on Brooklyn's chest, his full weight took her down, like a linebacker swatting a broken field runner.

This time Brooklyn stayed down. But she found her voice and started to scream her head off.

"Get this miserable dog off me!" Brooklyn's eyes burned black and hard like a pit viper. "Don't let this hideous creature bite me!"

"Stay right where you are, Earl Grey," Theodosia commanded. She grabbed the wooden ladder and muscled it toward Brooklyn. "Until I shove this ladder . . ." Theodosia heard a grunt and another shocked scream. "That's it. Got her," Theodosia said with satisfaction.

The downed drone was still whirling wildly in the bushes, like some weird automated salad spinner. It shredded leaves, dug up chunks of turf, sent bits of greenery flying through the air.

Theodosia didn't mind. She calmly pulled out her phone and dialed 911.

34

A squad car with two officers showed up some three minutes later. Detective Tidwell arrived a minute behind
them.

Tidwell slid out from behind his steering wheel, cut
across the front yard, and picked his way carefully along
the slick cobblestones. When he reached Theodosia, he
stopped dead in his tracks. Brooklyn was sprawled beneath the wooden ladder, looking like a medieval torture
victim who'd been pilloried in place. Theodosia was sitting on top of the ladder. Earl Grey was standing next to
her munching one of his "good dog" treats.

The corners of Tidwell's mouth twitched, then curled
up ever so slightly. "Miss Browning, we have to stop
meeting like this."

"She came after me," Theodosia said. Her voice was
shaky and frayed around the edges. She looked drop-dead
tired, edging into sheer exhaustion. "Brooklyn tried to
kill me." Theodosia fought to hold back a sob. "She tried
to kill my dog."

Brooklyn had been lying there, flipped out and grunting unintelligible sounds. When she heard Theodosia and Tidwell talking to each other, her caterwauling started up again tenfold.

"Let me up!" Brooklyn shrieked in a scratchy voice that could probably wake the dead if not the entire neighborhood. "This crazy witch tried to *kill* me and now she's holding me prisoner! She just about broke my back and then her dog bit me! For all I know the mangy mutt is *rabid*."

Earl Grey glanced sideways at Theodosia, as if looking for some kind of permission. Theodosia shook her head. *No.*

Tidwell stepped closer and kicked the ladder hard, sending a violent shudder up and down its length. "You're the one who's rabid," he said in a steely voice. "Do you know what the law does to someone who's unable to control their impulses? When they murder three innocent people in cold blood? We lock them up."

"Get me out of here!" Brooklyn screamed again. She gripped the treads of the ladder with dirt-rimmed fingernails and shook it hard. "My ribs are fractured and I'm in pain! I'm soaked to the bone and freezing to death!"

"What you need is a ride in a nice warm police car," Theodosia said. "That should cheer you up."

As she said it, another car pulled up to the curb in front of her house. A car door slammed, and footsteps ran toward them.

"I heard it over my police scanner!" Bill Glass shouted as he emerged from the fog. He was breathless and eager as he danced about. "You caught the killer?"

"Did you seriously doubt that we wouldn't?" Tidwell asked.

"Holy bat guano!" Glass yelped as he caught sight of Brooklyn Vance trapped beneath the ladder. "That fancy pants PhD chick's the killer?" He looked at Tidwell, who nodded his confirmation. Then Glass squinted at Theodosia. "You're wearing lipstick," he said. "Looks good."

Theodosia gave a faint smile.

Bill Glass finally had the presence of mind to remember his camera. "Boy oh boy, this is some kind of crazy storybook ending," he said as he fiddled with his camera and held it up. "I gotta get a few shots of this!"

"Nooo!" Brooklyn wailed from her makeshift prison beneath the ladder. "Don't you dare!"

Glass glanced at Theodosia again. "That dog. He's yours? Could you move him into the shot? Tell him to look real fierce?"

Theodosia glanced at Tidwell, who gave a "who cares" shrug.

"Why not," Theodosia said. She led Earl Grey into the frame until he was practically standing on top of Brooklyn.

"Get that filthy mutt away from me!" Brooklyn screamed as Bill Glass happily clicked away. "He's drooling! I can feel his hot doggy breath!"

"Perfect," Glass said. He gazed at Theodosia. "I might even have the perfect caption for my pictures."

Theodosia lifted an eyebrow.

Glass grinned. "Ding dong, the witch is dead."

"One more shot," Tidwell told him. "And then get lost."

"No problemo," Glass said. His shutter whirred and clicked, and then, like the proverbial Shadow from the old radio show, he was gone.

Tidwell signaled to the two police officers who'd been standing there, both of them looking amused and curious. "You can haul her away now. Cuff her, check her for weapons and keys. Oh, and you might find time to read her her rights, too."

The officers lifted Brooklyn up and frisked her professionally. One of the officers gathered up her wallet and the keys to her rental car and turned them over to Tidwell.

"Thank you," Tidwell said.

"Who is she?" Theodosia asked. "Open her wallet and see what her ID says."

Tidwell flipped open the wallet and picked through it. "Which ID?"

"Seriously?"

"There are three IDs in here," Tidwell said. "Probably all phony."

"Car keys," Theodosia said. Tidwell handed over Brooklyn's car keys and watched as Theodosia hurried out to the street and punched a button on the key fob.

The headlights for a silver Buick flashed on.

"We have to check her car," Theodosia said. With one hand on the car door, about to pull it open, she paused. "Do we need a search warrant?"

Tidwell shook his head. "Under these circumstances, no."

Tidwell waited on the curb while Theodosia searched through the car. Front seat, glove box, back seat, underneath the seats. She found nothing.

Then Theodosia popped open the trunk and found a shiny stainless steel briefcase wedged in between two suitcases and a black nylon duffel bag. The briefcase was the kind international couriers carried chained to their wrists. But maybe that was only in the movies.

"Is it locked?" Tidwell asked her.

Theodosia laid the briefcase flat and popped both tabs. They opened right away. "Not locked," she said.

"Well?" Tidwell rocked back on his heels expectantly.

Theodosia opened the briefcase. And there, in all its red and white glory, was the stolen Navy Jack flag. The flag that had flown in countless battles and that thousands had died for. The flag that had inspired a nation.

And we can't forget the three men who died because of it just last week, Theodosia told herself.

"So it's there, is it?" Tidwell called to her.

Theodosia reached in and reverently held up the flag. But she kept it sheltered, under the trunk lid, so it wouldn't get wet. "This is it."

"That's *my* flag!" Brooklyn screamed from the back seat of a black-and-white police car. She was hammering at the side windows, pounding on the metal grate. Theodosia imagined she could see spit flying from Brooklyn's mouth. She figured that if Brooklyn strained any harder, she might give herself a stroke.

"Time to go see a man about a flag," Tidwell said.

Theodosia was about to close the trunk when tires screeched and a plethora of lights flashed behind her. She turned and squinted, not sure what was going on. Two vehicles had just arrived—a van and a car. More police? The FBI?

Dale Dickerson of TV8 jumped out of the lead vehicle. "Hey, cutie," he called to Theodosia. Then, arms open wide, he said, "Come here and give me some sugar, will you? And the inside scoop?"

Theodosia sprinted toward Dickerson, splashing through puddles, flying over wet grass. At the very last second, she streaked right past him, practically spinning him around in her slipstream. Not giving him the slightest of glances.

Then her toes left the ground as she leapt into the out-stretched arms of Pete Riley.

"There you are," Theodosia said as she snuggled against Riley's protective bulk. He planted multiple kisses on her lips, nose, and cheeks until she ducked her head shyly and said, "What took you so long?"

"I was busy grilling scallops," Riley said, looking as though he never wanted to let her go.

"But how did you . . . ? Oh." Theodosia turned her head and gazed back at Tidwell. He was standing there looking like the fat cat who'd swallowed the canary. Maybe a couple of them. "You called him," she said to Tidwell.

"No, I gave Detective Riley a direct *order* to come over here," Tidwell said. "I suspected you might be in dire need of personal police protection."

"Hey, what about me?" Dickerson asked. He looked glum, as if the playground bully had just stolen his cookies.

"Oh, you'll get your story," Tidwell said. "But I'm guessing that's all you'll get."

Theodosia remained snuggled securely in Pete Riley's

arms as they slowly walked back to confer with Detective Tidwell.

"What about the missing money?" Theodosia asked Tidwell. "The missing five million dollars from SyncSoft?"

"I received word from our financial forensics people," Tidwell said. "They dug through several bank accounts and traced the money." He reached down and patted Earl Grey on the head. "Donald Kingsley took it. Used some of the money to purchase the flag from a European dealer."

"What about the rest of the money?" Riley asked.

"I'm guessing some of it ended up with Tawney," Tidwell said.

"Uh oh," Theodosia said. "Sounds like there might be a serious clawback."

"So who actually *owns* the flag?" Riley asked.

Tidwell's burly brows lifted. "Well, it's on our soil now and will be placed for safekeeping in our police property room. After that . . . who knows? Could end up in a local museum."

Dickerson moved in to join them. "Say now," he said to Theodosia. "Since you pretty much captured that Vance woman all by yourself, do you think I could get a quick interview?"

Theodosia shook her head. "Right now I have a dinner date."

"And after that?" Dickerson asked.

"That, Mr. TV reporter, is none of your business," Theodosia said. She smiled then, her eyes firmly focused on Pete Riley and nobody else.

FAVORITE RECIPES FROM
The Indigo Tea Shop

Walnut and Cream Cheese Tea Sandwiches

12 oz. cream cheese, softened
1 Tbsp. cream
½ cup walnuts, finely chopped
1 Tbsp. finely chopped green pepper
1 Tbsp. finely chopped onion
1 tsp. lemon juice
Salt and pepper
20 slices white bread

IN small bowl, beat cream cheese, cream, walnuts, green pepper, onion, lemon juice, salt, and pepper until blended. Spread mixture on 10 slices of bread; top with the remaining 10 slices. Trim off crusts and cut each sandwich in half diagonally. Yields 20 tea sandwiches.

Super Easy Lemon Cake Mix Scones

1¾ cups lemon cake mix
¾ cup flour
1 stick soft butter
1 egg
3 Tbsp. milk
Juice from ½ lemon

PREHEAT oven to 325 degrees. Mix together cake mix and flour. Cut in butter until mixture is crumbly. Add in egg, milk, and lemon juice, and mix until dough begins to form. Roll out on floured surface until 1 inch thick. Using circular cookie cutter, cut scones and place on greased pan. Bake at 325 degrees for approximately 25 minutes or until golden brown. Yields 10 to 12 scones.

Cinnamon Vanilla Honey Butter

½ cup butter, softened
½ cup powdered sugar
½ cup honey
1 tsp. cinnamon
1 tsp. vanilla

COMBINE all ingredients in a mixing bowl. Beat on medium speed until well blended and somewhat fluffy. Refrigerate until ready to serve. Yields 1 cup.

Eggnog Scones

1½ cups all-purpose flour
½ cup sugar
¼ tsp. salt
2 tsp. baking powder
6 Tbsp. butter, cubed and softened
1 egg
¼ cup sour cream
¼ cup eggnog

PREHEAT oven to 350 degrees. Combine flour, sugar, salt, and baking powder in a large mixing bowl. Cut in butter until mixture is crumbly. Combine egg, sour cream, and eggnog in a separate dish, then add to dry mixture. Combine until mixture holds together. If needed, a splash more of eggnog can be added. Pat dough into a large circle, about ½ inch thick. Now cut dough into 10 to 12 triangles and place on well-greased baking sheet. Bake scones for approximately 25 minutes or until golden brown. Yields 10 to 12 scones. (Hint: For a sweet topping, combine ½ cup powdered sugar with 2 Tbsp. eggnog and drizzle over scones.)

Cheddar and Pimento Tea Sandwiches

8 oz. white Cheddar, finely shredded
2 Tbsp. mayonnaise
2 Tbsp. sour cream
3 Tbsp. chopped pimentos
¼ tsp. black pepper
14 slices sandwich bread

IN medium bowl, combine cheese, mayonnaise, sour cream, pimentos, and pepper. Stir well to blend. Spread pimento mixture on 7 slices of bread. Top with remaining bread slices. Trim off crusts and cut sandwiches diagonally in half. Yields 14 tea sandwiches.

Angel-Hair Pasta with Lemon and Herbs

1 pkg. (8 oz.) fresh angel-hair pasta
⅓ cup butter
3 Tbsp. lemon juice
2 Tbsp. chopped fresh parsley
¼ tsp. marjoram

COOK angel-hair pasta per package directions. While pasta is cooking, combine butter, lemon juice, parsley, and marjoram in a saucepan. Heat the butter sauce, but don't boil it. When pasta is cooked, drain well, and place in a large bowl. Pour in the sauce and mix well. Serves 4 as a side dish. Note: You can turn this into a main dish for 2 by adding cooked pieces of chicken.

Super Easy Banana Pudding Pie

1 pkg. (5 oz.) French vanilla pudding mix (instant, no-cook)
2 cups milk
1 can (14 oz.) sweetened condensed milk
1 pkg. (8 oz.) cream cheese, softened
1 tub (12 oz.) Cool Whip, thawed
7 ripe bananas, sliced
1 graham cracker crust

USING blender or electric mixer, combine pudding mix and milk. In a separate bowl, blend condensed milk with cream cheese until smooth. Then fold in Cool Whip. Combine both mixtures, stirring until smooth. Place sliced bananas in piecrust. Spread mixture over bananas and refrigerate until time to serve. Yields 1 regular-sized pie.

Grilled Cheese with Apples and Arugula

8 slices bread (apple, cinnamon raisin, or any type of fruit bread)
Soft butter
½ cup Granny Smith apple, thinly sliced
1 cup baby arugula
4 slices cheese (Cheddar, Swiss, etc.)

PREHEAT oven to 350 degrees and also heat an electric griddle to 350 degrees. (You can use a large medium-hot frying pan, but you'll have to do the sandwiches 2 at a time.) Butter one side of each slice of bread. Gently flip four slices over so butter side is down. Top each of these slices with sliced apple, cheese, and arugula. Add the remaining slices of bread, butter side up. Place sandwiches on grill or in pan, and heat for 5 minutes on each side. Transfer sandwiches to a parchment-lined baking sheet, place in oven, and bake for 5 minutes to allow cheese to melt. Slice sandwiches on the diagonal and serve warm. Yields 4 sandwiches.

Haley's Scone Sliders

8 Cheddar or savory scones (any type)
8 slices ham, warmed
8 slices Cheddar or Muenster cheese
Honey mustard, prepared

SLICE the scones in half as you would a hamburger bun. Add a slice of ham and cheese to each scone. Spread on honey mustard. Place tops on scones and serve two sliders to each guest. Yields 4 servings. (Hint: Add a green salad for a nice luncheon plate.)

Featherbed House Stuffed Mushrooms

12 whole, fresh, cleaned mushrooms
2 Tbsp. oil
¼ cup onion, finely chopped
1 pkg. (8 oz.) cream cheese
¼ cup Parmesan cheese, grated
¼ tsp. black pepper

PREHEAT oven to 350 degrees. Tear off mushroom stems and chop until fine. Heat oil in skillet and add stems and onions. When stems and onions are cooked, set aside to cool. Transfer to bowl and stir in cream cheese, Parmesan cheese, and black pepper. Mixture will be very thick. Using a spoon, mound each mushroom cap with stuffing. Place caps on greased baking sheet and bake for approximately 20 minutes. Yields 12 mushrooms.

Strawberry Butter

 1 stick butter, softened
 1 cup strawberries, chopped
 1 Tbsp. powdered sugar

COMBINE all ingredients and beat on high speed for
about 2 minutes until fluffy. Yields 1 cup.

Detective Riley's Sea Scallops with Brown Butter

 12 fresh sea scallops
 Sea salt
 Black pepper
 ¼ cup oil
 3 Tbsp. butter
 1 Tbsp. finely chopped shallot
 Juice of ½ lemon
 ⅓ cup flat-leaf parsley, finely chopped

PAT scallops dry with paper towels, then season lightly
with salt and pepper. Heat a large sauté pan over medium
heat and add oil. Sauté scallops on one side until well-
browned (about 2 minutes), then turn and cook the other
side. Transfer scallops to a platter and keep warm. Carefully wipe any remaining oil from pan, then add butter
and shallot. Cook for 1 minute, then add lemon juice and
chopped parsley. Place 3 scallops on each of 4 warm
plates. Spoon butter and shallot mixture over scallops.
Serves 4. (Hint: Serve with rice, salad, or your favorite
vegetable.)

Laura Childs

Gilded Age Tea

Celebrate what was known as the Gilded Age (1870s to 1900) with an elegant, upscale tea. Decorate your table with fancy china, linen napkins, lots of baroque candlesticks, and over-the-top floral arrangements. Mix in any kind of bronze statues (we're talking angels, dogs, people—the sky's the limit) or even miniature paintings on small easels. Start with rich buttermilk scones and Darjeeling tea. Tea sandwiches might be brie with fig jam, or cucumber and herbed cheese. Slices of coconut cake would be a perfect dessert.

Sip and See Tea

A "Sip and See" is a fun tradition that originated in the South, but has caught on all across the country. This tea party is a special venue for new moms to introduce their newborn baby to family and friends. It's generally a casual occasion, so a buffet tea works beautifully. Cream scones with jam, chicken salad and egg salad tea sandwiches, and lemon tea cakes can be spread out on a sideboard for guests to help themselves. Serve sweet tea if the weather is warm, a nice Earl Grey if it's cool.

Father's Day Tea

Dads love teatime, too, just as long as the food is skewed to their liking. In this case, think of blueberry or apple scones for starters. Entrées could include roast beef and Cheddar tea sandwiches, buttermilk biscuits with ham and black jam, or turkey-cranberry sliders. Serve an orange pekoe tea and finish with brownies and gingersnap cookies.

Kentucky Derby Tea

This is the next best thing to sitting in a private box at Churchill Downs on that first Saturday in May. Invite all your guests to wear a fancy hat and serve real mint juleps or mint tea in frosted glasses garnished with a wedge of lemon. Your menu might include brown sugar scones, a pecan and apple salad, BBQ pulled pork on cornbread, and a banana pudding trifle. Be sure to have racing programs printed up so everyone can pick their favorite horse!

Nancy Drew Tea

Theodosia's not the only one who can throw a Nancy Drew Tea. Pull out your old Nancy Drew books or borrow a few from the library. Add twisted candles, clocks, tolling bells, and anything that ties in with a Nancy Drew title. Start with lavender scones and then serve herbed cream cheese and cucumber sandwiches and chicken salad on brioche. Serve a "mystery" tea such as Harney & Sons Murder on the Orient Express or Adagio's The Mystery.

Honey Bee Tea

Set up a tea table in your garden, then add lots of greenery and some furry bees you find at the craft store. Serve cream scones with honey and Devonshire cream, a mixed green salad with sliced apples and candied pecans, and miniature grilled skewers of chicken and vegetables. Your tea could be spiced plum or an Egyptian chamomile. For dessert, serve pound cake with honey ice cream. Tiny jars of honey would make a lovely favor for your guests to take home.

Parisian Tea

Channel the Champs-Élysées or the Left Bank with a romantic Parisian tea. Serve Mariage Frères tea, French onion soup, sliced apples and Boursin cheese on walnut bread, and turkey and brie on a croissant. Dessert can be a puff pastry with berries and cream or that very Parisian cookie—the macaron!

TEA RESOURCES

TEA MAGAZINES AND PUBLICATIONS

TeaTime—A luscious magazine profiling tea and tea lore. Filled with glossy photos and wonderful recipes. (teatime magazine.com)

Southern Lady—From the publishers of *TeaTime*, with a focus on people and places in the South as well as wonderful teatime recipes. (southernladymagazine.com)

The Tea House Times—Go to theteahousetimes.com for subscription information and dozens of links to tea shops, purveyors of tea, gift shops, and tea events. Visit the Laura Childs guest blog!

Victoria—Articles and pictorials on homes, home design, gardens, and tea. (victoriamag.com)

Texas Tea & Travel—Highlighting Texas and other Southern tea rooms, tea events, and fun travel. (teaintexas.com)

Fresh Cup Magazine—For tea and coffee professionals. (fresh cup.com)

Tea & Coffee—Trade journal for the tea and coffee industry. (teaandcoffee.net)

Bruce Richardson—This author has written several definitive books on tea. (store.elmwoodinn.com/tea-books.aspx)

Jane Pettigrew—This author has written thirteen books on the varied aspects of tea and its history and culture. (janepetti grew.com/books)

A Tea Reader—by Katrina Avila Munichiello, an anthology of tea stories and reflections.

AMERICAN TEA PLANTATIONS

Charleston Tea Plantation—The oldest and largest tea plantation in the United States. Order their fine black tea or schedule a visit at bigelowtea.com.

Table Rock Tea Company—This Pickens, South Carolina, plantation is growing premium whole-leaf tea. Target production date is 2018. (tablerocktea.com)

The Great Mississippi Tea Company—Up-and-coming Mississippi tea farm about ready to go into production. (great msteacompany.com)

Sakuma Brothers Farm—This tea garden just outside Burlington, Washington, has been growing white and green tea for almost twenty years. (sakumabros.com/sakumabroswp/)

Big Island Tea—Organic artisan tea from Hawaii. (bigisland tea.com)

Mauna Kea Tea—Organic green and oolong tea from Hawaii's Big Island. (maunakeatea.com)

Onomea Tea—Nine-acre tea estate near Hilo, Hawaii. (onotea .com)

TEA WEBSITES AND INTERESTING BLOGS

Teamap.com—Directory of hundreds of tea shops in the United States and Canada.

Afternoontea.co.uk—Guide to tea rooms in the UK.

Cookingwithideas.typepad.com—Recipes and book reviews for the Bibliochef.

RTbookreviews.com—Wonderful romance and mystery book review site.

Adelightsomelife.com—Tea, gardening, and cottage crafts.

Jennybakes.com—Fabulous recipes from a real make-it-from-scratch baker.

Cozyupwithkathy.blogspot.com—Cozy mystery reviews.

Southernwritersmagazine.com—Inspiration, writing advice, and author interviews of Southern writers.

Thedailytea.com—Formerly *Tea Magazine*, this online publication is filled with tea news, recipes, inspiration, and tea travel.

Allteapots.com—Teapots from around the world.

Fireflyspirits.com—South Carolina purveyors of sweet tea vodka, raspberry tea vodka, peach tea vodka, and more. Just visiting this website is a trip in itself!

Teasquared.blogspot.com—Fun, well-written blog about tea, tea shops, and tea musings.

Blog.bernideens.com—Bernideen's teatime blog about tea, baking, decorating, and gardening.

Possibili-teas.net—Tea consultants with a terrific monthly newsletter.

Relevanttealeaf.blogspot.com—All about tea.

Stephcupoftea.blogspot.com—Blog on tea, food, and inspiration.

Teawithfriends.blogspot.com—Lovely blog on tea, friendship, and tea accoutrements.

Bellaonline.com/site/tea—Features and forums on tea.

Napkinfoldingguide.com—Photo illustrations of twenty-seven different (and sometimes elaborate) napkin folds.

Worldteaexpo.com—This premier business-to-business trade show features more than three hundred tea suppliers, vendors, and tea innovators.

Fatcatscones.com—Frozen, ready-to-bake scones.

Kingarthurflour.com—One of the best flours for baking. This is what many professional pastry chefs use.

Teagw.com—Visit this website and click on Products to find dreamy tea pillows filled with jasmine, rose, lavender, and green tea.

Californiateahouse.com—Order Machu's Blend, a special herbal tea for dogs that promotes healthy skin, lowers stress, and aids digestion.

Vintageteaworks.com—This company offers six unique wine-flavored tea blends that celebrate wine and respect the tea.

Downtonabbeycooks.com—A *Downton Abbey* blog with news and recipes. You can also order their book, *Abbey Cooks.*

Auntannie.com—Crafting site that will teach you how to make your own petal envelopes, pillow boxes, gift bags, etc.

Victorianhousescones.com—Scone, biscuit, and cookie mixes for both retail and wholesale orders. Plus baking and scone making tips.

Englishteastore.com—Buy a jar of English Double Devon
Cream here as well as British foods and candies.

Stickyfingersbakeries.com—Scone mixes and English curds.

Teasipperssociety.com—Join this international tea community
of tea sippers, growers, and educators. A terrific newsletter!

Teabox.com—Wonderful international webzine about all aspects of tea.

Serendipitea.com—They sell an organic tea named Plum
Crazy. Also check out their recipe for Plum Crazy Punch.

PURVEYORS OF FINE TEA
Adagio.com
Harney.com
Stashtea.com
Serendipitea.com
Bingleysteas.com
Marktwendell.com
Globalteamart.com
Republicoftea.com
Teazaanti.com
Bigelowtea.com
Celestialseasonings.com
Goldenmoontea.com
Uptontea.com
Svtea.com (Simpson & Vail)
Gracetea.com

VISITING CHARLESTON
Charleston.com—Travel and hotel guide.

Charlestoncvb.com—The official Charleston convention and
visitor bureau.

Charlestontour.wordpress.com—Private tours of homes and
gardens, some including lunch or tea.

Charlestonplace.com—Charleston Place Hotel serves an excellent afternoon tea, Thursday through Saturday, 1 to 3 PM.

Culinarytoursofcharleston.com—Sample specialties from Charleston's local eateries, markets, and bakeries.

Poogansporch.com—This restored Victorian house serves traditional low-country cuisine. Be sure to ask about Poogan!

Preservationsociety.org—Hosts Charleston's annual Fall Candlelight Tour.

Palmettocarriage.com—Horse-drawn carriage rides.

Charlestonharbortours.com—Boat tours and harbor cruises.

Ghostwalk.net—Stroll into Charleston's haunted history. Ask them about the "original" Theodosia!

Charlestontours.net—Ghost tours plus tours of plantations and historic homes.

Follybeach.com—Official guide to Folly Beach activities, hotels, rentals, restaurants, and events.

Keep reading for a preview of Laura Childs's
next New Orleans Scrapbooking Mystery . . .

MUMBO GUMBO
MURDER

Available now from Berkley Prime Crime!

Monsters were out tonight. As well as two girls who'd definitely come to party.

"Jeepers!" Ava cried. "That skull puppet is a spooky devil."

Malevolent dark eyes peered from the hollow sockets of a bleached white skull. Shrouded in purple velvet, the creature's jagged teeth protruded rudely while its spidery, skeletal fingers reached out to stroke the arms of unsuspecting visitors along the parade route.

"You've never been up close and personal with the Beastmaster Puppets before?" Carmela asked her friend. They were standing on a crowded sidewalk in front of Zebarz Cocktail and Cordial House in the French Quarter of New Orleans, watching the kickoff parade for Jazz Fest.

"I've seen these puppets at Mardi Gras, sure, but never like this." Ava took a step back as a scabrous wolf head leaned in and tried to nuzzle her ear. "Keep walking, big guy," she muttered.

"Take a look at the skeleton puppet," Carmela said as a brass band blared out raucous foot-stompin' music, a gigantic float glided past, and a dozen Beastmaster Puppets mingled with the crowd to thrill and chill.

"The skeleton does kind of bother me," Ava said.

"Interesting, since you have an entire retinue of skeletons dangling from the rafters of your voodoo shop," Carmela said. She was the proprietor of Memory Mine Scrapbooking Shop over on Governor Nicholls Street; Ava Gruiex owned Juju Voodoo a few blocks away on Conti Street.

"But those skeletons are under *my* control."

"The giant puppets remind me of the bulbous heads on some of the Mardi Gras floats," Carmela said. As a New Orleans native and diehard parade fanatic, she was loving this, taking it all in practically by osmosis. Fact is, you could toss a string of colored lights onto a goat cart, roll it down Bourbon Street, and Carmela would stand on the curb and cheer. She was addicted to New Orleans mirth and merriment that much.

Ava Gruiex, on the other hand, was a different type of party girl. Slightly loose in her ways, she was a free spirit open to trying just about anything. And while Carmela was a jeans and T-shirt gal, Ava favored tight leather pants, skanky tops, and peekaboo lingerie. Of course, they both adored hot music and cold beer.

"The thing that amazes me the most is that real people are working their buns off *inside* those puppet costumes," Carmela said.

The Beastmaster Puppets were indeed manned by a myriad of people who dressed head to toe in black ninja-style clothing with black gauze masking their faces. They were the beating heart of the puppets and controlled the bobbing and weaving as well as the puppets' arms. On the really large puppets, outlier puppeteers, also dressed in black, manipulated long sticks attached to the puppets' limbs and faces. Sticks, that when worked carefully, made the puppets look both ethereal and peculiarly animated.

"Check this one out," Carmela cried as a banshee puppet flitted past, its bug-eyed, witchy face poking forward as a trail of diaphanous garments fluttered behind it.

"Crazy," Ava said.

Carmela was smiling at the puppets, grooving with the mood and the music. In the flickering light from the antique streetlamps, her face fairly glowed with excitement, her nearly flawless complexion enhanced by the high humidity that seemed to hold the Crescent City in a perpetual cocoon-like embrace. Carmela's honey-blond hair was a tousled, choppy mop and her eyes an inscrutable blue-gray that often mirrored the flat shimmer of the Gulf of Mexico.

Ava shook back the long mane of dark hair that framed her exotic face. "Witches and banshees I can handle, no problem," she said. "It's when the puppets become this . . . active, when they take on human dimensions, then I get creeped out."

"I guess that's what makes these giant puppets so popular," Carmela said. She took a quick sip of red wine from her geaux-cup and said, "Uh oh, take a look at what's coming next."

A hush fell over the crowd as the final parade unit appeared. It was a contingent of black-caped, chalk-faced vampires that seemed to crawl stealthily out of the darkness.

"The Vampire Society," someone behind them said in quiet, almost reverent tones.

Four masked riders sat astride coal-black horses, the horses' coats glistening like an oil slick and reflecting the purple-and-red neon signs from the nearby bars.

The vampires marched behind the riders in precise formation. Most of the men (and women) were tall and thin, and appeared to glide almost soundlessly.

Ava wrinkled her nose. "With that funky white makeup they look like a doomsday cult."

Carmela studied the vampires, whose faces were painted a ghostly white. Their eyes were kohl-rimmed orbs, their mouths a glistening bloodred that sported glowing white fangs. It was a look that definitely gave her pause.

Not so nice. Not that friendly.

"I guess it's just playacting," Carmela said finally, lifting her shoulders as if to shrug off any sort of malevolent vibe that might hover in the night air. "Perfectly harmless." Then, "Come on, let's follow along behind. We'll head over to Royal Street and check out the food booths."

Ava fluttered a hand. "You just uttered the magic words—food booths. You think they'll have barbecued shrimp, andouille gumbo, and fried crawfish?"

"Gotta go find out."

New Orleans was, of course, a foodie paradise. New restaurants, food halls, cocktail lounges, delis, and bakeries were opening at a dizzying rate. Here's where those uninitiated to the dining delights of the Big Easy routinely lost their minds over gumbo, beignets, po'boys, red beans and rice, plump Gulf oysters, muffulettas, and bread pudding. To say nothing of creamy, rich crawfish étouffée, which was practically a New Orleans obsession.

Linking arms, Carmela and Ava trailed along behind the Vampire Society.

They turned the corner at Dumaine Street, walked past the Praline Factory and Toups's Italian Bakeshop, and then turned again onto Royal Street.

"Will ya look at this!" Ava cried. "Royal Street's been turned into a gigantic street fair."

And she was right. All up and down Royal Street, for a good half dozen blocks, were food booths, food trucks, fortune-tellers, musicians, booths selling beads and T-shirts, and street artists. Revelers were cheek to jowl everywhere you looked—a mob of eating, drinking, dancing, good-time folks that formed a bobbling, jostling sea.

"This is what I need right here," Ava said, diving toward a frozen daiquiri stand. "We need two in . . . what flavors do you have?" She scanned the rainbow-hued liquors lined up on the counter.

"Piña colada, amaretto, pineapple, blueberry, mudslide, and strawberry shortcake," the bartender said, rubbing his hands on his red and white striped apron.

"What's a mudslide?" Ava asked.

The bartender shrugged. "Chocolaty rum?"

Ava turned to Carmela. "*Cher*?"

"Amaretto," Carmela said.

"Two amaretto daiquiris, please," Ava said.

The bartender nodded, tipped a bottle into a slurry of ice, and sent it whirring through his daiquiri machine.

Once they'd grabbed their frozen concoctions, Carmela and Ava strolled along the sidewalk past several antiques shops. Royal Street was where the absolute primo shops and galleries were located, where even the locals shopped for that perfect crackle-glazed oil painting, mantel clock, or piece of antique silver to grace their dining table.

"What a perfect night," Carmela said, as they allowed themselves to be swept along by the surging crowd. "Nice and warm . . ." She tilted her head back and smiled at the view over the Mississippi. "With a crescent moon dangling in an indigo-blue sky."

"A fitting salute to our Crescent City," Ava said. "Plus everything you want to eat and drink. It really is a fabulous . . ."

BANG! CRASH!

Like a clap of thunder, the noise rolled down Royal Street, crackling and booming out. Revelers paused, heads turned, and a woman gave a high-pitched scream.

There was a pregnant pause. And then it came again . . .

CRASH! SMASH!

. . . jolting everyone out of their musical-sugary-deep-fat-fried reverie.

"Somebody's shop window was just stove in," Ava said.

"When this many people are boogying together, something crazy's bound to happen." She sounded a little shaky, a little philosophical.

But Carmela was instantly on alert. "That wasn't just any window." She raised up on tiptoes and gazed down the street, not unlike a prairie dog who'd just sensed impending danger. "I think it was the front window at Dulcimer Antiques! At Devon Dowling's shop!" She peered down the street again, deeply concerned for her friend. "Yes, that's where the crowd's starting to gather. Come on!"

Together, Carmela and Ava weaved and dodged their way along the crowded sidewalk, angling toward Dulcimer Antiques. "'Scuse me, 'scuse me," Carmela said breathlessly as she stepped on toes and caused several revelers to spill their drinks as she flew past, practically towing Ava along after her.

When they finally got to Dulcimer Antiques, the street in front was a madhouse. People milled about, screaming and pointing. The large plate glass window that fronted the store had been completely shattered. Glass lay everywhere.

"Was it terrorists?" one woman shrieked.

Another woman had blood trickling down her face and was starting to weep. She'd obviously been hit by a shard of flying glass.

"Something got tossed hard against Devon's shop window," Carmela said, making a hurried assessment. "Maybe from inside?" There was a gigantic hole in the center of the window, surrounded by jagged pieces of glass, as sharp and dangerous as shark's teeth.

"This is terrible!" Ava cried. "People are hurt!"

"Where's Devon?" Carmela wondered out loud. Worry engulfed her as she shoved her way to the front door. She put a hand on the brass knob, twisted it forcefully, and . . . got nowhere.

"Locked," Carmela said. She knew Devon had to be

inside because she could hear his pug, Mimi, barking frantically.

"Devon!" Ava cried out. Now she looked even more frightened.

More gawkers gathered as Carmela pushed her way back to the broken window. She peered through the break into the dark interior of Devon's shop, trying to fathom what had gone on here. Sterling silver teapots, priceless Chinese vases, and antique clocks lay smashed in pieces. Lamps had been toppled. But it was difficult to see . . . very far back in the shadows.

"Devon?" Carmela called out in a strangled voice. Was he in there? Could he hear her?

She looked about frantically, saw a man wearing a giant foam baseball mitt on one arm, and snatched it from him.

"Hey!" he cried.

Carmela didn't stop to apologize or explain. She pulled the foam mitt onto her own arm and batted aside shards of glass as she lifted a leg and stuck it through the shattered window. She had to find Devon, she had to see if he was okay. Had he possibly sustained some sort of cardiac incident and collapsed against the front window? Was someone in there with him? Had there been a knockdown, drag-out fight? Was Devon in dire trouble?

Carmela swatted another nasty shard aside and stepped all the way through the window, her shoes immediately crunching hard upon broken glass.

"Devon?" Carmela called out, louder this time. "Mimi, sweetheart?" The little pug danced toward her, eyes rolling in fear, still barking frantically.

Crunching her way forward, Carmela stepped carefully into the darkened shop. Two steps in, then three. She stopped and drew a shaky breath. The place carried the scent of old canvases, dusty furniture, and something else . . .

Carmela shook off the mitt and reached around blindly, finally touching a lamp. She fumbled with the switch, feeling grateful when it came on with a tiny click, spilling its warm yellow glow.

"Devon?" Carmela said again.

Then her eyes were drawn downward by Mimi's terrified bark. And there, sprawled on a Persian carpet, eyes drooped shut, head in a puddle of dark crimson blood, was Devon Dowling!

WATCH FOR LAURA CHILDS'S
NEXT TEA SHOP MYSTERY

Lavender Blue Murder

A British-themed hunt ends in a blast of buckshot and
sends Theodosia scrambling for answers.

AND ALSO THE NEXT
CACKLEBERRY CLUB MYSTERY
FROM LAURA CHILDS

Battered Eggs

Between a truck heist, missing person, and gruesome killing, Suzanne hopes the "something borrowed, something
blue" at her wedding doesn't turn out to be bloody blue
murder.

Find out more about the author and her mysteries
at laurachilds.com or become a Facebook friend
@LauraChildsAuthor.

NEW YORK TIMES BESTSELLING AUTHOR

LAURA
CHILDS

"Murder suits [Laura Childs] to a tea."

—*St. Paul (MN) Pioneer Press*

For a complete list of titles,
please visit prh.com/laurachilds